The Jekyll Island Club

Patricia M. Clark

Writers Club Press
San Jose New York Lincoln Shanghai

The Jekyll Island Club

Published by Writers Club Press
an imprint of iUniverse.com, Inc.

For information address:
iUniverse.com, Inc.
620 North 48th Street
Suite 201
Lincoln, NE 68504-3467
www.iuniverse.com

ISBN: 0-595-09525-9

Printed in the United States of America

Acknowledgements

For Lou and my best creations—Christopher, Michael, and Kelly. And Jo Ann Jasper, friend and agent, who believed in my dream in those dark moments when I couldn't.

Prologue

August 18, 1919. Jekyll Island, Georgia

Jenny Morgan paused near the steps of the wide veranda, unsure if the distant thunder was the sole reason she felt so thoroughly surrounded by menace. If she had realized it was the last night she would spend on the island, perhaps she wouldn't have taken the next step. A sudden breeze propelled her forward, up the stairs into the eye of the approaching storm. Despite the thick, sultry air, Jenny felt a chill when she entered the kitchen, and she resolved never again to cater for this famous millionaire member of the Jekyll Island Club.

Although she was tense and jumpy while she set the drinks and plates of food on the table, she froze when she felt the Arctic blue eyes following her movements. She whirled around and almost caught his naked expression before he put the mask back in place. In that brief moment of exposure, she saw arrogance and contempt.

Embarrassed, Jenny blushed and retreated to the safety of the kitchen. As the others arrived, cigar smoke filled the small, screened porch, as thick and dense as the stifling air outside. Jenny refilled glasses and plates, nauseated by the smoke and tension that heightened the atmosphere already charged by frequent flashes of lightning. Deals at the table started with cards but quickly spilled over into business.

The hours passed and the storms abated. Ultimately, fatigue diminished her concern. Stale smells of cigar smoke, shellfish, and whiskey assaulted her while she cleaned the deserted porch. She sensed his presence, and the hair on the back of her neck stood up. Desperately trying to conceal her panic, she turned and realized the old man was amused by her terror. Powerful arms roughly pushed her, forcing her down on the hard wicker couch. Jenny was small for fourteen, certainly no match for the huge man.

Remotely aware of the pressure of his body and the tearing of her clothes, Jenny keenly recognized the smell of his fetid, sour breath and the searing pain when he entered her with no caveat. The old man's intermittent groans rang in her ears until, finally, he moaned, plunged into her for the last time, and collapsed beside her.

Battered, her back showing every mark from the weave of the wicker, Jenny was unsure what to expect next. Then, hearing his penetrating snorting sounds, she realized he was asleep. In a moment of crystal clarity, she understood this event would alter her life forever. As she gathered her clothes, rage replaced terror, and she rifled through his pockets to find the cash the other members of the Jekyll Island Club had left to cover their gambling losses.

Overwhelmed by the pain and reality of her rape, she stuffed the bills into the folds of her apron. Consequences! An inner voice screamed that word relentlessly as Jenny disappeared into the shadows of the black night.

Chapter One

Present Day

Senator Ted Drew, primed to exploit the optimistic energy palpable in the chamber of the United States Senate, approached the podium to deliver his address on health care. Born into a powerful political family, he was famous before winning the Senate seat. This impassioned speech would guarantee Drew's party would nominate him as their presidential candidate. Major wire services, tipped off by Drew's executive assistant and political guru Chandler Cole, were amply represented.

Tall, with striking hazel eyes, Drew had avoided becoming fodder for the Washington rumor mill. In spite of the microscopic scrutiny his personal life had been subjected to, not a hint of impropriety had ever been associated with his name. Drew was faithful and very devoted to his lovely wife, Claire.

The birth of their son, Adam, seemed like a miracle. After four years of trying to conceive a child, Ted and Claire had consulted a prominent specialist. They discussed their options, which included diagnostic testing, multiple injections, and in vitro fertilization. The Drews were still considering their alternatives when Claire realized she was pregnant.

Chandler Cole, black hair slicked back, removed a minuscule piece of lint from his perfectly tailored suit. He was ecstatic about the birth of Drew's son, but he was motivated solely by his fervent belief the baby would increase Drew's electability. The press was already calling the possibility of a Drew Presidency the "new Camelot" describing his age, his attractive blond wife, and now, his infant son.

"Ladies and gentlemen, this morning I am pleased to announce the birth of my son, Adam Michael," Ted Drew began. "His birth serves as a reminder that we must deal with the issue of health care for the sake of all our children."

Partisan applause inundated the chamber.

"I stand before you today to introduce a bill that will revolutionize the delivery of health care. The changes I propose will bring meaningful reform and create a health care system that will provide for every citizen of this country. I further pledge not to bring five hundred lawyers to Washington to accomplish this task. Under my plan, only health care professionals will be involved in the framing and execution of the provisions of this system."

Drew's evocative voice echoed throughout the recesses of the chamber, music to Chandler Cole's ears. No one could deliver a speech like Ted Drew, and Cole listened intently until an anxious page handed him a note. He frowned but accepted the slip of paper and read the message. Chandler Cole waited until Drew finished his speech before approaching the podium.

Jack Carter, eager rookie with an earnest face, watched as applause rippled through the chamber. Carter had the job of covering Ted Drew for his paper through the November election. Convinced Drew would be elected, Carter embraced the task enthusiastically. The speech ended and thunderous applause accompanied the standing ovation. Jack Carter felt a rush of emotions as he stood in the hallowed chambers. Haunted by ghosts of eloquent speakers from simpler times, Carter suddenly realized he hadn't felt similar patriotic sentiments since he was a small boy.

Ted Drew covered the microphone with his hand, leaning over to hear what Chandler Cole whispered. Drew quickly masked his look of extreme concern; but Jack Carter caught his reaction, and it forced his instincts into full alert mode.

The applause continued while Drew smiled and waved at the cameras so they could capture the charming visage of the next President of the United States. Finally, Drew and Cole ambled toward the exit. There was something about that brief expression on Drew's face that made Jack trust his instincts, so he followed them at a discreet distance. Drew's distinctive limo was easy to follow in the light mid-morning traffic, at least until the rain began to fall.

The heavy rain distracted Mark Breaugh as he guided the Blazer along the tortuous road. The old dog appeared in the headlights as Mark's wife, Emily, screamed.

"Look out, Mark," Emily said and grabbed her enormous belly as if that would somehow protect her soon to be born child.

"Sorry, babe," Mark said as he swerved to avoid the ancient combination of several indistinguishable breeds.

"Slow down, Mark," Emily said as she laughed softly. "The first goal is for all of us to reach the hospital alive."

"Yeah, I'm sorry I scared you," Mark said as he ran his hand over the black stubble on his troubled face.

"I can't believe it's finally going to happen," Emily said as she reached for Mark's hand.

An hour later, Emily Breaugh breathed a sigh of relief when Mark pulled the Blazer into the D.C. General emergency room parking area. The beefy security guard didn't buy Mark's protests about their emergency justifying parking the Blazer in the reserved lot. Mark went out to move it while Emily was escorted up to 2 West.

Three hours later, the delivery room was crowded with the anesthesiologist, the obstetrician who was also Mark's brother, and several nurses.

Mark, who watched the scene nervously, tried to focus the video camera he had borrowed from his parents.

"One more good push ought to do it, Emily," Dr. David Breaugh said. "Then I'll finally get to see my niece."

"Good job, Emily," David said a few minutes later. "Let's see. Lots of curly, dark hair. If I've guessed correctly, that hair should be on her head. If not, your kid has a really hairy butt, Mark."

"Mark, I don't think I want your brother in here next time," Emily said as she grabbed the gown that covered her husband's scrubs.

"That's good," David Breaugh said as he guided the baby's shoulders out. Her feeble cries quickly escalated into a series of loud wails. After her cord was cut, the nurse took Melissa to the warming bed to clear her airway and complete an assessment. Then Melissa Breaugh was handed to her proud, emotional parents for an introduction.

"How's she doing?" David Breaugh asked the nurse when she walked by.

"Her Apgar's 8," the nurse whispered. "Her respirations are depressed and her color is off a little."

Dr. Kelly Marlowe waited just outside the doors of the neonatal intensive care unit at D.C. General. Senator Ted Drew was due to arrive momentarily, so she was again reviewing his son's chart. Director of the unit for three years, Marlowe was seriously considering resigning. There was too much death to deal with and no time for a life of her own. Nearing forty, she dreamt about the children she still wanted to have, and she no longer found jokes about biological clocks humorous.

The entourage got off the elevator, looked in Kelly Marlowe's direction, and approached her tentatively. She recognized Senator Ted Drew immediately and extended her slender hand.

"Senator Drew, I'm Dr. Kelly Marlowe," she said.

"What's wrong with my son?" Ted Drew asked nervously.

"He's developed pneumonia, Senator," Marlowe said.

"That's not so bad," Drew said. "You can treat that, right?"

"We've obtained cultures and started him on antibiotics," Marlowe said. "He has a high fever and his lungs are full of fluid. I've called in an infectious disease specialist."

"He's going to be OK, isn't he?" Ted Drew asked weakly.

"The next twenty-four hours will be critical," Marlowe said. "We'll do everything we can for your son, Senator. Would you like to see him?"

Concealed behind a post, Jack watched the Drew party get on an elevator and then charged up the stairs to the sixth floor. Breathless upon his arrival, he stepped into the corridor and spotted Drew talking to an attractive blond woman. Close enough to catch the bulk of the conversation, he listened intently.

When Drew went through the doors to the unit, Carter walked to a pay phone in the waiting room. He drummed his fingers on the stand, impatient for his editor to answer the call.

"This is Dobson," the bored voice said.

"Murray, I've got a hot lead," Jack Carter said urgently. "I'm down here at D.C. General with Senator Drew. His kid is sick."

"Are you sure this isn't another wild goose chase?" Murray Dobson asked skeptically.

"Yes, I'm positive," Jack Carter said as he crossed his fingers.

"I heard the doctor tell Drew the next twenty-four hours would be critical," Carter said. "That's a big story even if nothing else is going on. But something else is going on, Murray. I can feel it."

"You reporters and your feelings," Murray said wearily. "I remember the last time you had a feeling. Remember that hot story in LA you begged me to let you cover? That feeling turned out to be salmonella. You got sick and I got nothing except your inflated expense account."

"This is different, Murray," Jack Carter said.

"It better be, Jack," Murray Dobson said.

The stars twinkled brightly and provided the only disruption in the endless curtain of black night until Kelly Marlowe spotted the red, blue, and white blinking lights of the chopper. Marlowe felt the haunting phenomenon again and shuddered. She loathed her sixth sense, her unsolicited ability to predict death was about to claim a victim.

The craft carrying death approached, and the explosion of sound from the rotation of the blades replaced the low whir of the engine. Marlowe searched the eyes of the nurse standing next to her for some sign she sensed death coming, but all Marlowe saw was fatigue and stress. Cool, crisp, spring air provided enough of a temperature difference to make their tense, rapid expirations rise like smoke.

When the row of white lights on the pad began to blink in a continuous pattern, the chopper began its descent. The huge words, D.C. General, printed on the middle of the pad became the primary target for the pilot's landing. When the runners made contact, the pilot eased the craft gently onto the pad.

A tall EMT opened the door and spit out the details in short, half sentences. "Seventy-two hour old female," he said as they lowered the cart to the ground. "Acute respiratory distress. Her lungs are full. Can't suck it out fast enough. Her vitals are going to hell."

The tiny infant's body was lost in the full sized cart surrounded by medical paraphernalia. Marlowe noticed the infant's color was dusky and each breath required maximum effort. The EMT continued his status report as they pushed the cart into Trauma Room One.

"I need blood gasses, a chest film, a SMAC, and get respiratory down here STAT," Marlowe said as she put her stethoscope on the tiny, heaving chest.

The nurse handed Marlowe the pediatric endotracheal tube as Marlowe moved into position behind the infant's head.

"OK, it's in," Marlowe said after she guided the tube gently into place.

"She's got a left pnuemo," Marlowe said. "We'll have to put a chest tube in."

The monitor behind them launched a loud protest indicating the absence of a traceable heart rhythm. Ancillary staff charged in the room to lend their support as a cacophony of anxious voices joined the resuscitation effort.

Chapter Two

Jaimie Carpenter walked along the beach behind her father's house in San Diego, watching the waves move gently back and forth, flirting with the sand like an old lover trying to charm his way back into a lost relationship. In her youth, the sea had cast a magic spell over Jaimie and now felt like a friend, constant and dependable.

Farther down the same stretch of beach, laughter echoed out of the open windows of the weathered cedar house. The laughter seemed intimate, vaguely sexual in nature. Jaimie reached the back door of the house at the exact moment the deeply tanned, elderly man with paint streaked across his face came out the door. He greeted Jaimie absently, climbed in the red convertible, and drove away.

Jaimie entered the house occupied by her maternal aunts, Samantha and Grace Collier. She wandered through the huge, deserted kitchen into the studio where the glaring sunlight momentarily blinded her. Floor to ceiling glass windows occupied the wall that faced the ocean, providing abundant light and a magnificent view. Samantha was humming while she dabbed the brush in the paint and moved it swiftly across the canvas. She was short like Jaimie with the same brown eyes and auburn hair. While

Jaimie's hair was straight and fell naturally, Aunt Sam's was naturally curly, as wild and untamed as many parts of her personality.

"Who was that?" Jaimie asked as Grace Collier joined them.

"That's Sam's latest flame," Grace said mischievously. With her blue eyes, short gray hair, and regal height, Grace looked like she must belong to some other family.

"Now be nice, Grace," Sam said. "Just because you're between boyfriends at the moment, that's no reason to be mean."

"I think we're too old to call them boyfriends," Grace said. "When you hit sixty, shouldn't you call them gentlemen callers or something?"

"Calling them something like that takes all the romance out of it," Sam said.

"That's your problem," Grace said. "Too romantic."

"Grace, I'm an artist," Sam said. "That's just the way we are."

"Well, I've got to get to work," Grace said.

"Good-bye, Aunt Grace," Jaimie said as she walked over and hugged her.

"Good-bye, dear," Grace said, returning Jaimie's gesture. "I'll see you tomorrow. I'm glad you got to piggy back some vacation onto the medical conference. We don't get to see enough of you since you moved to Atlanta."

Sam began to paint again as Jaimie moved closer to get a better view of her latest creation.

"Is there going to be just one person walking along the beach?" Jaimie asked.

"I think so," Sam said. "I never know for sure until I get farther along. I guess that's the creative thing."

"Do you ever get tired of painting the ocean?" Jaimie asked.

"I guess not," Sam said. "It's the one constant in everything I paint. My obsession, I suppose."

Jack Carter waited in the lobby of D.C. General, reading his byline while he sipped a cafe mocha. His front-page article hinted that Drew's son was in critical condition. A strange, new illness was the culprit though the story lacked specific details.

A maintenance man wearing a light gray uniform walked by carrying a bucket of tools and a small stepladder. Carter watched as he got on the crowded elevator. Jack chuckled as he tossed the paper and the empty coffee cup in a trash can and headed for the elevators.

Thirty minutes later, Carter was dressed in the gray uniform of a maintenance man. He wore a tool belt and carried a large bucket containing a variety of light bulbs. A folded work order was sticking out of the breast pocket of his shirt.

Carter paused by the doors of the neonatal unit and took a deep breath, trying to calculate the odds of pulling off his ruse without getting caught. Summoning another burst of courage, he moved forward and the doors exploded open. The blinking lights and alarms that sounded at frequent intervals created a chaotic atmosphere, and Carter just stood there, feeling lost. He was seriously considering fleeing when a nurse walked up to him.

"You look a little green around the gills," she said, laughing.

"I'm new here," Carter said, blushing profusely. "I have a work order to change some light bulbs."

"I can't believe you're here," she said. "I just sent that order down yesterday. It usually takes you guys a week to get up here. I'll show you where to start."

An hour later, Senator Ted Drew entered the unit wearing jeans, a sweater, and a terrified expression. Carter picked up his bucket and began working near the small isolation room where a nurse cared for the Drew baby. A tall, thin doctor with a beard and kind brown eyes approached Ted Drew.

"Good morning, Senator," he said.

"How's he doing, Dr. Sampson?" Ted Drew asked.

"He isn't responding to the antibiotics," Sampson said.

"I thought he had pneumonia," Drew said. "Why aren't the antibiotics working?"

"I don't know for sure," Ben Sampson said. "We've admitted several babies with this same infection in the last couple of days. It seems to be a very virulent form of strep. We've tried all the antibiotics currently available, but none of them seem to control the infection."

"How many babies have you had with this strep infection?" Drew asked.

"Your son is the third," Ben Sampson said.

"What happened to the other babies?" Drew asked.

"They didn't make it," Sampson said. "I've contacted the CDC."

"Are you a specialist?" Ted Drew asked.

"I'm an infectious disease specialist," Ben Sampson said patiently. "I can give you the names of other specialists if you'd like, Senator."

"I'm sorry, I wasn't trying to insult you," Drew said. "My wife and I have waited a long time for this baby."

"I understand," Ben Sampson said. "We'll do everything possible for your son, Senator."

"Is this contagious?" Drew asked.

"No one who has been near these babies is sick," Sampson said. "I don't think it's spread by casual contact. Until I'm sure, we're using the strictest isolation procedures."

"I appreciate your efforts," Drew said. "I don't know what will happen to my wife if Mark dies. She's very fragile emotionally."

A series of beeps from Sampson's pager interrupted their conversation. "Excuse me, Senator," Sampson said. "I've got an urgent call. Why don't you get ready to see your son?"

Sampson walked to the desk, picked up the phone, and dialed the number to the emergency room. While he waited, Sampson watched a nurse help Ted Drew put on a gown, a mask, and gloves. Jack Carter moved across the room to catch Sampson's conversation.

"Hi Ben, this is Kelly," Marlowe said.

"What's going on?" Sampson asked when he heard Marlowe's greeting.

"I have another baby down here with the same symptoms," Marlowe said. "Can you come down for a consult?"

"I'll be right there," Sampson said. "Any news from the lab?"

"They think this bug is probably strep," Marlowe said. "If it is, it's a new strain."

"The symptoms all fit a toxic shock-like syndrome," Sampson said. "Are they sure it isn't strep-A?"

"That's the first thing they looked for," Marlowe said. "It's close, but it's not like anything they've ever seen before."

"These babies look fairly normal when they're born," Sampson said. "Thirty-six hours later their lungs turn to mush."

"I worked at the CDC for a year," Marlowe said. "I still have contacts there. I'll call and get them on this."

"That's a good idea," Sampson said. "I called them last night. If you know someone, maybe we can bump this up the chain of command. This bug scares the hell out of me."

"Dr. Sampson," an excited nurse shouted. "Tell Dr. Marlowe the Abbott baby is crashing."

Marlowe raced to the elevators, fished the master key out of her pocket, and inserted it into the lock. The car arrived quickly and Marlowe's warning look to a visitor who wanted to hitch a ride deterred his movement toward her. She inserted the key into the emergency slot on the interior panel and the car sped to the sixth floor. When Marlowe entered the unit, a nurse threw her a gown and mask.

"His heart rate jumped to one fifty," the nurse said.

"How are his gasses?" Marlowe asked as they entered the isolation room where multiple monitors displayed blinking lights. Several alarms sounded simultaneously, announcing some new crisis.

"Bad and getting worse," the nurse said as they looked at the screen. Multiple leads from monitors measuring his vital statistics obscured most of the infant's body.

"OK, let's get started," Marlowe barked.

Outside the windows of the room, Robert Abbott's helpless parents witnessed the scene. They couldn't hear anything Marlowe shouted, but when they saw her lips move, a member of the staff performed the assigned task. The monitors blinked and alarmed in response as the process continued.

Eventually, one of the nurses walked over and closed the curtains. Grant Abbott waved frantically, trying to get her attention, but she didn't see him. Feeling powerless, Grant took his distraught wife back to her room to wait for someone to come and tell them if they still had a future.

"I'm calling it," Marlowe finally said wearily. "The time of death is 10:06 a.m."

Marlowe sat in the small, dark call room at the back of the unit. After the Abbott baby died, she spent an hour trying to comfort his distraught parents. Finally, she watched them leave clutching a teddy bear that would be the only tangible reminder they once had a son.

Usually, after death had claimed its latest victim, she felt a reprieve until the next time. Marlowe realized that ever since the Drew baby had been admitted, the unrelenting feeling of being surrounded by an army of death had gripped her. Though she wore a long sleeved shirt, scrubs and a lab coat, she continued to shiver.

A shaft of light from the doorway blinded and distracted Marlowe until the door closed.

"Is someone in here?" Ben Sampson asked tentatively.

"Yes, it's me," Marlowe said.

"Is it OK if I turn on the light?" Sampson asked.

"Yeah, sure," Marlowe said.

"I can't identify the pathogen," Sampson said. "I've never seen anything like it before."

"What do you think it is?" Marlowe asked.

"I don't know for sure," Sampson said. "It starts in the lungs. They disintegrate, fill up with pus, and then the infection spreads quickly. This is the third baby, isn't it?"

"Yes, and I have a terrible feeling this is only the beginning," Marlowe said.

The ambulance raced along the coast highway in Destin, Florida. Its rapid pace was at odds with the laid back way of life demanded by the local tourist industry. The driver was blinded by the huge yellow sun that appeared to be falling off the edge of the earth into the glistening waters of the Gulf. In the back, EMT Jeff Price worked feverishly on the small infant.

At Destin Community Hospital, Dr. Riley Kane had his feet propped up on the desk near the CB unit. Kane was forty-two and wore scrubs most of the time. Kane possessed a dark complexion coupled with thick, coarse, black hair that grew out of control over his entire body. It was a source of constant amazement, numerous jokes, and several hairy nicknames.

"Base, this is unit 41," Price said.

"Go ahead 41," Kane replied.

"I have a newborn," Price said. "He's approximately forty-eight hours old in acute respiratory distress. He was born at home."

"Any fetal distress at birth?" Kane asked.

"The mother denies it," Jeff Price said. "I'm not so sure. This kid's lungs are full."

"Maintain his airway and start an IV," Kane said. "What's your ETA 41?"

"My ETA is ten minutes," Jeff Price said.

"I'll be waiting for you," Kane said.

"Hang in there, kid," Jeff Price said to his small patient. "You'll have to try not to freak out too much when you see all that hair. He may be the world's hairiest human but he's also a good doc."

Chapter Three

The San Diego Civic Center was packed with medical professionals attending the symposium dubbed "Pathogens of the Next Millennium." Simultaneous presentations were occurring in all ten conference rooms. In number four, the distinguished looking speaker approached the podium to announce the presenter.

"Our first speaker is Dr. Jaimie Carpenter from the CDC in Atlanta," he said. "Dr. Carpenter graduated from Johns Hopkins Medical School and completed an internship and residency in internal medicine at Johns Hopkins Hospital. She has been with the CDC for seven years. Dr. Carpenter's address is entitled, 'One Antibiotic Away From Disaster'. Please welcome Dr. Jaimie Carpenter."

"Thank you, Dr. Terry," Jaimie began after the applause ceased. "I always like being the opening speaker at a conference. Everyone is still excited about being out of town and you're awake."

Laughter filled the room as Jaimie darkened the lights from the control panel on the podium and the first slide appeared on the huge screen behind her.

"As we head into the 21st century, our attention seems to be focused on AIDS and other viral agents," Jaimie said as brightly colored pictures of various viruses filled the screen. "The real threat may come from common bacteria we identified long ago. Staph and strep are household names, so familiar no one seems concerned about them. Everyone assumes we have a vast army of antibiotics to use against them. It may just be that the frequent use of that army of antibiotics has caused our tenacious enemy to find a way to fight back.

"Antibiotics developed in this century controlled the spread of bacterial infections," Jaimie said. "Our enemy can be elusive. The bacteria we arrogantly assumed we had conquered only went into hiding. They mutated and suddenly reappeared with a startling virulence."

A slide appeared on the screen showing a large hotel. "At a Legionnaire's convention in Philadelphia in 1976, 182 people became ill and 29 died. We completed what we at the CDC call a quick and dirty survey. In these cases, we can rush in, identify the cause of the illness, and recommend a remedy. The epidemiologists identified that those who were ill belonged to a distinct group of American Legion conventioneers who all stayed at a single hotel in Philadelphia. A formerly unidentified bacterium was found growing in the hotel's water storage unit and spreading to rooms via the air-conditioning units. The infecting agent was eliminated and that was the end of the mini epidemic."

"In the early eighties, toxic shock syndrome caused a panic and resulted in many lawsuits," Jaimie said as the slide showed a woman on a respirator. "Women of child bearing age were affected by this quickly spreading, deadly infection. Bacteria usually cause illness when their numbers reach critical mass or by releasing a toxin. In this case, both characteristics were present. The culprit this time was the familiar staphylococcus bacterium. When staph is allowed to grow in large numbers, an environment provided by the high absorbency tampons in use at the time, it secretes a poisonous toxin. Once we realized the tampons were the problem, the manufacturers stopped making the high absorbency type. Within several months, the reported numbers of menstrual cases dropped to the same levels as those reported in non menstrual cases."

The smiling face of Jim Henson surrounded by the Muppets filled the screen. "In May of 1990, Jim Henson died as a result of exposure to a new strain of strep-A," Jaimie said. "The infection seemed to be accompanied by a toxic shock-like syndrome. The syndrome was characterized by infection, shock, acute respiratory distress, and renal failure."

Jaimie flipped through a series of slides showing celebrities attending Henson's funeral. "During his three week fight for life, Henson was given antibiotics to attempt to control this highly resistant strain," Jaimie said. "None of those available at the time were able to stop the infection."

The next series of slides showed the lower extremities of several patients. The raw, graphic shots revealed large areas where the flesh seemed to have been eaten away which caused excited exclamations that rippled through the audience. "Great Britain, spring of 1994," Jaimie said as newspaper headlines filled the screen. "Informing the public not to panic as bacterium death toll rises to 12 and nicknaming the bug the galloping gangrene certainly did cause panic, but I suppose they also sold newspapers.

"The culprit in these cases was once again strep-A," Jaimie said. "This condition is known as necrotizing fasciitis. It closely resembles the toxic shock-like syndrome previously described and may be identical.

"Austin, Texas. May 1998. An outbreak of strep-A caused twenty-six deaths. That brings us to our most recent occurrence. Since January, we have been investigating a cluster of strep-A illnesses in Chicago. To date, we have 248 confirmed cases. They involve both toxic shock pneumonia and necrotizing fasciitis.

"The virulence of these new strains is frightening," Jaimie said as the next series of slides showed various color-coated capsules rolling down an assembly line. "Resistance to antibiotics is now a major concern. These infections and toxic shock-like sequelae spread rapidly, often leaving us with no effective weapons with which to fight back. Drug research cannot keep up the emergence of these new strains."

Enlarged, colored photos of the various identified strains of staph and strep bacteria filled the screen. "So these are our current foes," Jaimie said as she flipped through the slides. "The incidence of these infections has been relatively small to date. But what if these common bacteria were able to unite with some other pathogen?

"Thucydides described in great detail a plague that struck in ancient Athens," Jaimie said as the slide changed to reveal an army of small, angry bacteria dressed in ancient garb and carrying spears.

"That epidemic raged for three years," Jaimie continued. "It fits all the criteria, epidemiologically and clinically, for influenza complicated by a bacterial infection.

"The 1918 pandemic is widely believed to have been a combination of influenza and some other pathogen," Jaimie said as a slide showing masses of people wearing masks appeared on the screen. "One school of thought is that the other pathogen was a strain of strep or staph. Suppose we have a similar outbreak of influenza coupled with a new strain of bacterium or just a highly communicable strain of staph or strep. And then suppose that new strain is so resistant to antibiotics we are left defenseless?"

Mark, Emily, and David Breaugh stood in a corridor just inside the first set of doors that led to the neonatal intensive care unit at D.C. General. It seemed like a kind of no man's land with a set of automatic doors on either side. Through the doors to their left, Melissa was fighting for life. Melissa had only been a patient for forty-eight hours, but Mark had a feeling this was one of the places they brought you when they delivered bad news. They didn't notice Jack Carter, who was kneeling on the floor, using a screwdriver to remove the screws from a panel on the wall.

"What happened, David?" Mark Breaugh asked his brother tentatively as he held his wife's hand. "Last night you said she was going to be OK."

"I know," David Breaugh said wearily as he looked into the tear filled eyes of his brother and sister-in-law. "We thought at first it was just a simple case of pneumonia," David said timidly as Ben Sampson joined them.

"What do you think it is now?" Mark asked.

"I still think it's pneumonia," Ben Sampson said. "I just haven't ever seen a form of it that progresses this rapidly. It's as if her lungs are disintegrating."

"That's why every breath is such a struggle?" Emily asked.

"Yes," Sampson said.

"There's something else you haven't told us," Mark said as he stared intently into Sampson's earnest brown eyes.

Sampson stared back, hesitated, and then looked down at the floor. "This might be a new form of strep that's infecting newborns. None of the antibiotics we've tried so far are working. Her kidneys are shutting down."

"She's going to die, isn't she?" Emily asked as she reached for David Breaugh's hand while Sampson looked away.

"I don't have the results of the lab tests," Sampson said. "If it is this new form of strep, her prognosis is very guarded."

"Excuse me, Dr. Sampson," the nurse said as she peeked through the doors. "There's a phone call for you."

"I'll be right back," Sampson said as he patted Emily's hand and went into the unit.

"He seemed grateful for the interruption," Mark Breaugh said sarcastically.

"It's not his fault," Emily said. "He doesn't know how to tell us."

"I don't care that it isn't his fault," Mark said. "I can't believe we're going to lose her. We waited so long for her and now this."

"Mark, I can't make it through this if you don't hold me," Emily said as she walked over to him and put her arms around him. "I need for you to hold me, Mark."

In a small room down the hall from where the Breaughs contemplated their possible loss, Chandler Cole waited with Ted Drew. Poll results raced through Cole's mind as he tried to compute the ramifications of the death of Drew's son. Cole finally decided the sympathy the death would evoke could be enormous and might actually enhance Drew's chances.

The bold headline dominated the front page of the newspaper Cole was reading. Carter's article insinuated an epidemic was infecting newborns at D.C. General and declared Ted Drew's son was barely clinging to life. As a result of the story, D.C. General was inundated with phone calls from anxious parents. The same scenario was occurring at pediatrician's offices around the area, where frantic parents waited for hours to have their babies examined.

Ted Drew could think of nothing but the loss of his son and the effect that loss might have on his wife, Claire. Drew loved his wife and worried about her emotional and physical fragility.

A few minutes later, Ben Sampson and Kelly Marlowe entered the room. The sad, compassionate look on their faces left no doubt in either man's mind about the fate of Adam Michael Drew.

The Gardens, a popular restaurant in San Diego, was crowded. Tropical plants, frequently spaced torches, and soft music added to the ambiance. Logan Carpenter looked at his daughter, Jaimie, with a mixture of pride and concern. She had grown into her beauty in her late twenties, but she either hadn't noticed or didn't care.

After his wife, Candace, left them when Jaimie was five, Logan Carpenter raised her alone. Logan knew Jaimie had never understood or forgiven Candace for her abandonment. Though Candace saw Jaimie frequently after she left, Jaimie made it clear in thousands of little ways that Candace would suffer a life sentence for her choice.

When Candace left, Logan enlisted the aid of Candace's sisters, Samantha and Grace, to provide a feminine influence for Jaimie. Their eccentric, earthy approach to life had helped his shy daughter become more outgoing.

Tonight, while they waited for their drinks, Logan could see the smile playing at the corner of Jaimie's lips.

"What's the smile for?" Logan asked.

"I'm trying to decide whether we should play out the usual scenario," Jaimie said.

"Which scenario are you talking about?" Logan asked.

"You know which one," Jaimie said, laughing. "The one where you ask me how I am. I say fine, how are you? Then you ask me if there's anything new, and I say no. Then you get frustrated because that's not really what you want to know, so you try to ask the question another way. I innocently pretend I still don't get it."

"Then you could take pity on your poor father and just tell me," Logan Carpenter said as he smiled at his daughter.

"I think that would take all the fun out of it," Jaimie said mischievously.

"Only for you, Jaimie Carpenter," Logan said.

Jaimie chuckled loudly as the waiter served drinks and took their dinner orders. When the waiter left, Jaimie pretended she didn't remember their conversation. Logan looked at her with an expression that was a cross between amusement and annoyance.

"Where were we?" Jaimie asked as Logan growled audibly.

"You can be so infuriating sometimes," Logan said as Jaimie laughed.

"OK, I'll make an exception," Jaimie said. "Everything at work is going fine. No, I haven't been dating anyone. I'm not serious about anyone and there don't seem to be any likely candidates on the horizon. Are you satisfied?"

"No, I'm not," Logan said. "Are you happy, Jaimie?"

"I don't know," Jaimie admitted. "I'm not sure I know how to answer that. You have to quit worrying so much, Dad. I think you did a great job with me."

"I had a lot of help from your aunts," Logan said. "Sometimes I think we may have succeeded too well."

"What do you mean?" Jaimie asked.

"We wanted you to be strong and independent," Logan Carpenter said. "I get the feeling you won't allow yourself to even consider the possibility of a relationship. You really believe you won't ever get married, don't you?"

Before Jaimie could say anything, her pager began to emit a series of urgent noises. Jaimie looked at it and noted the number.

"It's Sara from the CDC," Jaimie said.

"I thought you were on vacation," Logan said.

"I am," Jaimie said. "It must be some kind of emergency. That's the only reason Sara would call."

Logan Carpenter watched his daughter walk across the crowded dining room and thought about her mother. Candace had been his only real love, and he was never the same after he met her. Logan was sure Jaimie had never met anyone like that, and he feared what would happen when she did.

Jaimie found a phone and dialed Sara McCartland's number at the CDC.

"Sara," Jaimie said when she heard the familiar voice.

"Jaimie, I'm sorry to bother you while you're on vacation," Sara said. "We've got a crisis brewing."

"What's going on?" Jaimie asked.

"We've been getting reports from the D.C. area about an illness that's hitting newborns," Sara said. "Within seventy-two hours of birth, the infected babies are dead."

"How many cases have been reported?" Jaimie asked.

"Twelve so far," Sara said. "Until tonight, I thought the illness was isolated to the D.C. area."

"What happened tonight?" Jaimie asked.

"I got a report late this afternoon from Florida about a case down there," Sara said. "I finally reached the treating doc a little while ago. His description of the infection matches the reports we've been getting from D.C. I've booked you on the first flight out in the morning bound for D.C."

"That's fine," Jaimie said.

"You know that off the wall theory of yours?" Sara asked.

"Which one?" Jaimie asked.

"The one about another pandemic like the one in 1918," Sara said.

"Yes," Jaimie said uncertainly.

"It might not be so off the wall," Sara said.

Chapter Four

Sara McCartland, Chief of Research at the CDC in Atlanta, opened the Fed Ex package and placed the first slide under the lens of the high powered microscope. At fifty-five, Sara had never totally lost her Scottish accent or her blond hair, though time had added gray streaks to the latter. The microscope was connected to the computer, and when Sara pressed enter, the organism came to life on the screen.

"So, there you are," she said out loud.

The organism changed shape and color when Sara entered more commands. She stared at the microbe in disbelief. The first time Sara felt this way was in 1976 when she saw the Legionella bacterium through the microscope and realized she had never seen anything like it before. That assignment was Sara's first quick and dirty survey.

The pathogen moved, and Sara watched the familiar shape squirm as if it wanted to escape. It was definitely a bacterium but with important differences. Sara's stomach, her compass for measuring her reaction to stress, began to burn as she removed the slide from the microscope.

Sara headed for the Director's office. Martin Bennet had been resisting retirement for five years, more afraid of boredom than his wife's threats about taking solo trips. The CNN news report captured his attention, so he didn't notice Sara standing in his office.

"The newborn epidemic continues in the Washington, D.C. area," the announcer said. "There are unconfirmed reports thirty newborns have either died or been admitted to local hospitals in the last week. There are speculations a previously unidentified form of strep-A is causing these infections.

"In other news," the announcer continued as Bennet hit the off button on the remote control.

"They seem to have well informed sources," Sara said.

"Yes, they do," Bennet said as he looked up at Sara.

"We really do have an epidemic on our hands, Martin," Sara said. "I just finished looking at the slides from Florida and confirmed a match. It's newborn pneumonia just like the cases in D.C."

Before Bennet could respond, his phone rang. "Martin Bennet," he said. "Sara's right here. I'll put her on. It's Barry Grieg from the FDA."

"Hi, Barry," Sara said. "Do you have anything for us?"

"I hope so," he said. "After we talked, I asked the research group to put together any information they had on drug treatments for strep-A. This bug is so ominous I decided to book a flight to Atlanta this afternoon. We can talk about what we've got when I get in."

Jaimie was relieved that she got the last seat on the plane for the first leg of a journey that would eventually take her back to Atlanta. This flight was headed for Washington, D.C., where Jaimie was to meet with Dr. Kelly Marlowe to collect blood and tissue samples to take back to the CDC.

After the plane landed, Jaimie retrieved her suitcase and flagged a cab. Marlowe was in an isolation room examining a small patient when Jaimie arrived in the neonatal intensive care unit. A nurse showed Jaimie where she could put on a mask and gown. After they were in place, she snapped on a pair of latex gloves and entered the small room set apart from the others.

"Dr. Marlowe, I'm Dr. Jaimie Carpenter from the CDC," Jaimie said as she looked at the blinking monitors.

"I'm glad you're here," Marlowe said. "There's a stethoscope hanging on the end of the isolette."

Jaimie walked over and reached for the stethoscope.

"Listen to her lungs," Marlowe said as Jaimie complied and placed the instrument on the barely visible heaving chest. No matter where Jaimie placed it, she could hear the sounds indicative of a severe build up of fluid.

"The course is always the same," Marlowe said when Jaimie finished. "They are born with near normal Apgar scores, and there is nothing to indicate a problem. Within twenty-four hours, their lungs begin to fill up and their temp rises. It looks like pneumonia, so we do cultures and zap them with antibiotics. Nothing touches the infection. The clinical course is rapid; respiratory distress, renal shutdown and finally, respiratory or cardiac arrest."

"How many cases have you had?" Jaimie asked.

"This is the twentieth one in six days," Marlowe said.

"Any contact among the cases?" Jaimie asked.

"No," Marlowe said.

"Any common denominator at all?" Jaimie asked. "Same delivery room, same doctor, same nurse?"

"No, and no one else has been infected," Marlowe said. "I've had an infectious disease doc, Ben Sampson, in on this from the beginning. We don't think it's airborne. The only thing they all had in common was the fact they died within seventy-two hours of birth."

"Can I get blood samples from the parents?" Jaimie asked.

"Sampson already has that in the works," Marlowe said. "Let's go to my office. I'll call and find out if they've all been collected."

Medical journals were spread out over every available surface in Marlowe's office.

"Just throw those on the floor," Marlowe said as she sat down in the chair behind the desk. "I've been trying to read everything I can get my hands on to see if there's anything out there like this."

"There isn't," Jaimie said quietly.

"I was afraid that might be the case," Kelly Marlowe said.

"Dr. Marlowe, I need tissue samples from the victims," Jaimie said.

"I anticipated that," Marlowe said. "The pathologist should have them ready."

"You've anticipated everything I need," Jaimie said. "I appreciate your thoroughness and your help."

"We've got to figure out what this is," Marlowe said. "You've got to find an answer before…."

"Before what?" Jaimie finally asked when she realized Marlowe's train of thought had derailed.

"Before it's too late for all of us," Marlowe said.

Dr. David Breaugh sat in the waiting room at D.C. General with Mark and Emily, watching the rain fall as another storm front barreled through the area. They watched the huge raindrops splatter the sides of the glass until David Breaugh broke the silence.

"I wish I could think of something to say to you that would help," David said quietly.

"Tell us Melissa isn't going to die," Emily Breaugh said as she held her husband's hand.

"I'm so sorry," David said. "I always try to search for the right words to tell a patient's family their loved one is going to die. Maybe that's the problem. The words don't matter. There isn't anything you can say that can take the pain away."

"Mr. and Mrs. Breaugh," Ben Sampson said as they all turned around to look at him. Sampson stood there and the expression on his face conveyed the message before he spoke.

"We did everything we could think of," Sampson said uncertainly. "The infection just overwhelmed her."

"Can we see her one last time?" Emily asked.

"Sure, I'll take you back there," Sampson said.

Thirty minutes later, when Mark and Emily Breaugh left the unit, they saw Senator Ted Drew talking to Ben Sampson.

Jack Carter hovered inside the neonatal unit, pretending to be working on the cold air return duct. His latest front-page article chronicled the death of Ted Drew's son and included the fact other states were reporting cases.

Ted Drew had reluctantly agreed to an autopsy, hoping it would provide information that might help determine the cause of his son's death. He was back at D.C. General visiting his wife, Claire, who had developed a severe post op infection. When Drew learned Jaimie was there, he asked to speak with her. He waited in the same room where he had been informed of his child's death.

"Thank you for seeing me," Ted Drew said after Jaimie entered the room. The Senator looked pale, drained, and totally unlike the handsome, smiling persona frequently seen on t.v.

"I'm sorry about your loss, Senator," Jaimie said as she shook his hand.

A resigned nod was Drew's only response. The long pause that followed caused Jaimie to consider whether she should say something or wait for a cue from Drew.

"I understand this infection has killed babies in other states," Drew finally said.

"Yes, we received a report from Florida yesterday and one from St. Louis this morning," Jaimie said.

"I want to make sure you do everything possible to stop this infection," Drew said as he stared into Jaimie's eyes.

"I assure you we'll do everything possible to find the source, Senator," Jaimie said quietly.

"I hope so," Ted Drew said. "I want you to see the pain in my eyes so you understand how important this is. I don't want you to forget this meeting."

The D.C. medical examiner, Dr. Alfred Gruenloh, waited impatiently for Jaimie to join him for the Drew post. Gruenloh's eyebrows, his only distinguishing physical characteristic, grew out of control over his small blue eyes and captured the immediate attention of anyone who saw him.

Jaimie remembered Gruenloh, or Dr. Death, as everyone referred to him. Jaimie had attended medical school at Johns Hopkins when Gruenloh was a professor. All the medical students were required to attend twenty-five autopsies conducted by Gruenloh, whose post mortem antics made him a legend. The first post Jaimie attended was on an eighty-year-old man who had died of lung cancer. Gruenloh removed the cancerous organ and walked over to the group of nervous students, thrusting the black mass into each of their faces.

"After this, you'll know what to say when some idiot tries to tell you smoking doesn't cause cancer," Gruenloh proclaimed. "You can tell them about the black lung I stuck in your face."

The student next to Jaimie leaned over and hurled, causing a long diatribe from Gruenloh. Jaimie felt apprehensive as she walked down the corridor to the morgue to meet Gruenloh again.

"It's about time," Gruenloh said irritably when Jaimie entered the morgue. "We're going to do this in the isolation room."

Jaimie put a gown, mask and gloves on without comment and followed Gruenloh into the room where the Drew baby waited.

Gruenloh readied the microphone, turned the tape on, and began dictating without preamble. Jaimie watched as he droned the vital statistics of Adam Michael Drew. Gruenloh proceeded quickly while Jaimie thought about her meeting with Ted Drew. His teary, pain-filled eyes haunted her, and she had a difficult time looking at the tiny corpse.

"I guess you think I don't remember you," Gruenloh said a few minutes later as a startled Jaimie looked at him.

"Excuse me," Jaimie said uncertainly.

"You were standing right next to that med student who vomited," Gruenloh said. "I could always tell the ones who weren't going to make it. I could look into their eyes and see it. I challenged them so the ones who couldn't cut it would get out and stop wasting everyone's valuable time. I could tell you'd make it."

"We were all terrified of you," Jaimie said.

"That was the idea," Gruenloh said.

"Look at these lungs," Gruenloh said as Jaimie moved closer. "The tissue has just disintegrated. That's where the infection begins. The baby is born, expels the fluid from its lungs and takes its first breath. Isn't it ironic that the breath of life starts the chain reaction? The colonies of bacteria multiply and begin to attack. The bacteria just eat all the healthy tissue and the lungs fill up with pus. Then it spreads rapidly."

"Have you ever seen anything like this before?" Jaimie asked.

"No, this is the most virulent bacteria I've ever seen," Gruenloh said. "This is going to kill a lot of babies."

Jaimie's flight back to Atlanta had been announced, but there was a delay in the boarding process. Jaimie looked at the t.v. mounted overhead while she waited. The familiar face of Tom Brokaw appeared on the screen.

"The NBC nightly News with Tom Brokaw," the announcer said.

"Good evening," Tom Brokaw said. "Tonight, there are frightening reports from Washington, D.C. about an infection that kills babies within three days of birth. The CDC is involved but, as of now, there is no word on what may be causing these deadly infections.

"And in other news," Brokaw continued as Jaimie got up to board her flight.

The cab rounded the main drive leading to the CDC, and Jaimie was surprised she saw so many lights burning at such a late hour. After he stopped the vehicle, the amiable cab driver got Jaimie's suitcase out of the trunk. Jaimie was afraid something might disturb the contents of the cooler filled with tissue and blood samples, and she had held it securely during the drive from the airport.

"There must be something mighty important in there," the small black man said kindly. "You've been clutching that all the way here."

"There is," Jaimie said as she smiled and handed him a generous tip.

"Why thank you, ma'am," the man said as he tipped his hat and got back in his cab.

Jaimie approached the entrance to the CDC with the cooler in one hand and her suitcase in the other, wondering when she crossed the line from young lady to ma'am. Another rite of passage, Jaimie concluded as she slid her ID through the slot and pushed the door open.

Sara McCartland was talking to a tall, thin man with curly red hair when Jaimie appeared in her doorway after dropping the tissue samples in the lab. When Sara noticed Jaimie standing in her doorway, she greeted her warmly.

"Jaimie, it's good to see you," Sara said as Barry stood up. "This is Dr. Barry Grieg. He's head of research at the FDA. He flew down so we could talk about what antibiotics might be available to treat this bug."

"Nice to meet you," Jaimie said as she walked over and extended her hand.

"The pleasure is mine," Barry Grieg said as both his mouth and his expressive green eyes smiled at Jaimie.

"There have been more cases reported since I talked to you this morning, Jaimie," Sara said.

"How many?" Jaimie asked.

"Eight," Sara said. "Two in Denver, one in New Jersey, and five in New York. I've kept a lot of people here late so we might as well go to the conference room."

On the elevator ride to the fifth floor, Barry Grieg watched Jaimie unobtrusively. The conference room was noisy and crowded when they entered. Sara went to the front and began speaking.

"I'm sorry about keeping all of you here so late," Sara said. "I'd like to introduce Dr. Barry Grieg of the FDA. I invited him here to help us figure out if there are any antibiotics we could suggest when we send out the next bulletin.

"Jaimie stopped in D.C. on her way here from San Diego," Sara said. "I asked her to return early from vacation, so no more whining about late hours."

Laughter erupted from the back of the room in response to Sara's remark.

"We're calling this strain of strep-A newborn pneumonia," Sara said. "So far, we have confirmed reports from six states. This is a vicious strain that strikes newborns, causing illness and death within seventy-two hours.

"That's right," Sara said as exclamations of surprise filled the room. "Near normal Apgars at birth, rapid onset, and death within seventy-two hours. Jaimie brought back tissue samples from D.C. I've asked Dave's team to put a rush on the studies to identify the mode of transmission."

"I spoke with the treating doctors in St. Louis, D.C., and Florida," Jaimie said. "There doesn't seem to be a common denominator. I don't think it's airborne."

"I need six teams," Sara said. "We need to do a quick and dirty survey in each of the cities where cases have been reported. The rest of you are on stand by. All days off and vacations are canceled until we get a handle on this."

"What about antibiotics, Dr. Grieg?" Jaimie asked.

"There are three currently approved," Barry said. "We can recommend their use in your bulletin."

"OK, I'm going to recommend the strictest isolation procedures for now," Sara said. "I think that's it."

The phone on a desk in the front of the room began to ring. Sara walked over and picked it up.

"Sara McCartland," she said.

Jaimie watched Sara's face as the conversation unfolded. Sara had been Jaimie's mentor and surrogate mother since Jaimie came to Atlanta, so she knew the solemn expression on Sara's face meant trouble.

"Thank you for calling, Dr. Bruce," Sara said as she hung up. "That was Dr. Nigel Bruce calling from London. A baby died there this morning. It looks like our new bug. Ladies and gentlemen, we have a pandemic on our hands."

CHAPTER FIVE

The morning twilight flooded in the wide terrace doors to the bedroom of the CEO of Sayer Pharmaceuticals, Wendel Garrett. He looked to see if his wife, Margo, was still asleep next to him in the huge, raised bed. Her steady, even breathing indicated he hadn't awakened her.

Wendel decided to get up and take a morning run, a daily ritual for most of his fifty-four years. It was cool in Atlanta, and Wendel wore long sweats as he began his stretching exercises on the front porch. Distinguished looking rather than overtly handsome, Wendel was tall and lanky. He finally began jogging down the mile long drive that led to his estate.

Later, Wendel broke his blueberry muffin in half, poured himself a cup of coffee, and unfolded the Atlanta Constitution. The bold headlines proclaimed there was a pandemic involving newborns. After he finished the article, he poured another cup of coffee and picked up the remote control.

"The Today Show," the announcer proclaimed as Wendel put the contents of a packet of Equal into his coffee.

"Good morning," Katie Couric announced. "It has been fourteen days since the world first became aware of a form of strep-A called newborn pneumonia. The death toll rises daily. This morning we have an exclusive interview with Senator Ted Drew, who lost his son to this deadly disease.

"Senator Drew, I'd like to offer my condolences for your loss," Katie said.

"Thank you, Katie," Ted Drew said.

"I understand that you want to make a public statement," Katie said.

"My wife and I want to express our thanks for the cards and letters that have been flooding in since Adam died," Drew said.

"I'm sure everyone can understand how difficult this has been for you," Katie said.

"Yes, it has," Ted Drew said. "That's why I want to publicly demand that the CDC spare no expense and suspend other activities in order to pursue their investigation of strep-A."

A week later, Jaimie Carpenter pulled her car into the heavily guarded CDC parking lot. She looked at the protesters who stared back, waving their signs to attract her attention. Ten minutes later, she was sitting in the chair by Sara McCartland's desk, scanning the stacks of data gathered by the CDC staff.

Sara was attempting to use chopsticks to eat her broccoli beef without much success.

"Please tell me there's a plastic fork in that bag," Sara said.

"They always put one in there for rookies," Jaimie said as she reached into the bag.

"Do you think we'll ever eat a meal that we don't have to pull out of a bag again?" Sara asked.

"I don't know," Jaimie admitted. "I never thought I'd see a bunch of protesters outside this building."

"They're frustrated," Sara said. "Seventy-five per cent of the babies born in this country in the last two weeks are dead. They need to have someone to blame."

"We're as frustrated as they are," Jaimie said. "There's one guy out there who really gives me the creeps. He carries a sign that says 'The End Is Near'."

"Do you think he's right?" Sara asked.

"I hope not," Jaimie said. "When you think about the death toll and the fact so many women are getting abortions, you begin to speculate."

"The preliminary data indicate the mothers were exposed to the strep, but they have no active infection," Sara said. "The samples from the fathers show no sign of it at all."

"The mothers have to be carriers," Jaimie said.

"That's how it looks," Sara said. "They are exposed and pass it on to the fetus."

"Nine months is quite a window of opportunity," Jaimie said. "All we have to do is figure out what single exposure might have occurred over that period of time."

"Do we have the final culture and sensitivity report?" Sara asked.

"Yes, I called the lab right before I came up here," Jaimie said. "The bug is resistant to all three of the antibiotics currently available."

"Then we have to hope the surveys give us our common denominator," Sara said.

Sara took a hefty bite out of an egg roll about the same time her phone rang. She waved at Jaimie, who reached over and picked up the receiver.

"Sara McCartland's office," Jaimie said. "OK, I'll turn it on."

Jaimie got up and walked over to turn the t.v. on.

"That was your boss," Jaimie said. "He said we should watch the special report and call him back."

The solemn face of President Andrew Moore filled the screen. "Good evening, America," he said without the slightest hint of the charismatic smile that was his hallmark.

"First, I want to offer my condolences to those of you who have lost children to newborn pneumonia," he said solemnly. "The entire nation feels your pain. This morning, I directed that emergency funding be allocated to the CDC to hire more researchers and provide for travel and overtime expenses to determine the cause of this terrible illness.

"I also want to urge everyone not to panic," President Moore continued. "This tragedy need not divide us. Let us try to find a common ground so we can help each other get through this crisis."

"Now the circus really begins," Jaimie said as she got up to turn off the t.v.

"Now we spend all our time explaining why we can't find a solution instead of looking for one," Sara said.

Barry Grieg was tired and the second cup of coffee he sipped in his office at the FDA did nothing to alter that fatigue. The Director's early morning flight to D.C. had arrived late, so his boss was moody and recalcitrant. Barry was tired of bureaucrats who were more worried about containing damage than finding solutions.

If the CDC couldn't come up with a common source of contamination, Barry knew the only other viable option would be some type of antibiotic treatment. There were several promising antibiotics currently being tested, but they all had side effects.

"The CDC doesn't know what's causing this?" Gilbert Drake asked.

"They know it's a form of strep," Barry said patiently.

"They don't have any idea how the mothers got it?" Drake asked.

"That's right," Barry said. "They have survey teams out to see if they can identify a common source."

"What happens if they can't do that?" Drake asked.

"Then antibiotics are the only hope," Barry said. "The three antibiotics currently in use don't work. There are four more in the testing stages, but they all have side effects."

"We're going to have to approve their use, aren't we?" Drake asked.

"Yes, we are," Barry said. "I talked to Grayson at the White House. I explained the drugs haven't been tested but they don't care. They want the public to think we're doing something."

"Go ahead and approve them," Drake said. "Make sure everyone understands these drugs haven't been tested. Have the legal department draw up some kind of consent form for the parents to sign. Is there anything else we can do?"

"I think we should call an emergency meeting of all the pharmaceutical companies," Barry said. "We could give them samples of the bug and see if anyone has an experimental drug that might work."

"Set it up," Drake said.

"The public wants action," Barry said. "What they don't want to look at is the fact that sometimes the side effects of these drugs can be as bad as the cure. For us, it's a no win situation. If we recommend the treating doctors use them, we get blamed for the side effects. If we don't recommend their use, we are withholding treatment. I worry about another kind of disaster farther down the road. Remember Thalidomide?"

Oprah Winfrey moved down the aisle as applause rippled through the studio. Her audience was attentive and enthusiastic.

"There is an epidemic sweeping this country," Oprah said solemnly. "The panic this has caused is immeasurable. The number of abortions has risen dramatically, and most women of child bearing age are choosing not to get pregnant until there is a cure or some explanation for these infections.

"Today, we have grieving parents with us," Oprah said. "Their babies died within several days of birth. They have come to share their stories with us."

After the commercial break, the sad faces of four sets of parents filled the screen.

"One of the first babies to die was Melissa Breaugh," Oprah said. "Her parents, Mark and Emily, are here to talk about their daughter. Can you tell us about Melissa?"

"She was our first child," Emily Breaugh said as a picture of Melissa filled the screen. "We had difficulty conceiving for a long time. The day Melissa was born was the happiest day of my life."

"The day Melissa died was the saddest day of my life," Mark Breaugh said.

The weekly news conference was held in the largest meeting room at the CDC. Representatives of every imaginable news service from all over the world deluged the CDC with requests to attend. A lottery system was initiated, and the winners were setting up their equipment for the live broadcast.

Officially, cases of newborn pneumonia had been reported in all fifty states and the developed countries. Field survey teams had worked feverishly to identify a common source but had been totally frustrated with the results. Jaimie, Barry Grieg, and Sara joined Martin Bennet at the table in front of the room.

"If I could have your attention ladies and gentlemen," Bennet said. "We would like to assure everyone we are doing everything possible to identify how newborn pneumonia spreads. The mothers are exposed to this bacterium sometime during their pregnancy and pass it on to their babies. Within twenty-four hours of birth, the infected babies become symptomatic. We have recommended that all newborns be kept in the hospital for at least forty-eight hours. We are continuing to recommend the same isolation precautions we recommend for AIDS. At this point, I would like to turn this over to our Chief Epidemiologist, Dr. Sara McCartland."

"We have multiple teams in every state completing surveys," Sara said. "Their goal is to determine some common source, some common denominator that will tell us how these mothers were infected. All of this information is then entered into our database. I want to reassure the public we have been tracking all newborns since this began. No newborn who has been infection free for forty-eight hours has subsequently become ill.

"I wish I could tell you more," Sara said. "At this point, we would welcome questions."

"You have no idea how the mothers got it," a reporter asked.

"That's true," Sara said.

"Is this contagious?" a newswoman asked.

"It is not spread by casual contact," Sara said. "I'd like to address another issue. We are developing an amniocentesis test to check for strep-A. I want to urge pregnant women to wait until that test is available before making the decision to have an abortion."

"Is there any treatment for this infection?" a reporter asked.

"This bacterium is resistant to all three of the drugs approved by the FDA," Sara said. "We asked Barry Grieg from the FDA to come, so I would like him to discuss those issues."

"We have released four experimental drugs for use against strep-A," Barry said. "The preliminary tests indicate this form of strep is also resistant to them."

"Then there's no treatment at all for this?" a reporter asked as the room exploded in dialogue from all quarters.

"If I can have your attention for a moment," Barry shouted as the uproar died down. "There may be drugs in development we don't even know about. That's why I'd like to invite representatives of all the major pharmaceutical companies to come to the CDC."

Sara and Jaimie were watching the evening news in Sara's office while they ate another cold meal. The opening scenes showed the protesters picketing outside the CDC, and then the video showed several abortion clinics where the same scenario was occurring.

"The bombing at this abortion clinic in Philadelphia this morning was apparently the last straw for the Moore Administration," the announcer said. "Late this afternoon, President Moore ordered federal troops to begin guarding abortion clinics around the country until the crisis ends."

"Every time I think it can't get any worse, it does," Jaimie said after Sara turned the t.v. off.

"When you take away hope, anything can happen," Sara said. "Most people would say that the next generation represents hope."

"If there's no next generation, there's no hope?" Jaimie asked.

"A lot of people look at it that way," Sara said. "If the pandemic continues, think about the effect it will have on the economy."

"All those industries geared toward providing services to children will go under," Jaimie said.

"Have you thought about what it would be like to live in a world with no future?" Sara asked.

Wendel Garrett looked out the tinted windows of his limousine as his driver fought the Atlanta traffic to get him to the CDC. Garrett's gaze moved from the heavy traffic to the blinking light on the car phone. Keeping the caller on hold was a power tactic he used frequently.

"Sorry," Garrett said several minutes later when he picked up the receiver. "As I told you, we will discuss it when I get back from this meeting. Right now, we have to figure out a way to contain this mess. Just give me a little more time."

Fifteen minutes later, Garrett was sitting in the crowded conference room at the CDC. He was furious he wasn't seated at the first table, a place of honor and recognition he expected.

"Good morning, ladies and gentlemen," Barry Grieg said. "I asked you to come to this meeting today to ask for your help. We need to work together to find an antibiotic to treat newborn pneumonia.

"I realize many of you may have reservations about sharing data that could then be stolen from you," Barry continued. "The director and I have discussed with the Patent Office granting emergency patents to protect you. We hoped you would share any information you have regarding antibiotics to treat strep-A. We have also discussed suspending other rules in order to expedite making any possible treatment available immediately."

Dialogue erupted around the room.

"Just how far are you willing to bend the rules?" Wendel Garrett asked.

"We are very aware babies are dying," Barry replied. "We will consider suspending all the rules."

"Then you'll let us put it out on the market right away?" Garrett asked.

"After we have a chance to confirm that the strep isn't resistant to the proposed drug," Barry said.

"What happens if the antibiotic I develop ends up having unexpected side effects?" Garrett asked. "I won't have time to do proper testing. What protection do I have I won't get sued?"

"What are you proposing?" Barry asked.

"We're going to have to have some kind of guarantee," Garrett said. "We need some government protection so that if we come up with an antibiotic, we won't lose our shirts if we find out there are side effects farther down the road."

"I can't give you that kind of guarantee," Barry said. "What we propose is a warning from the FDA that indicates the drug has not been tested. We also recommend having the parents sign an experimental drug consent form. If the bug isn't resistant to the new drug, we will approve emergency human trials."

"That doesn't give us much incentive," Garrett said.

"On the contrary, you'll still have your profit margin," Barry said. "In addition, think about how grateful the public will be."

"Can we get samples of the bacteria?" another drug rep asked.

"The CDC staff has prepared samples for all of you," Barry said. "I would be very interested in speaking with anyone who might be developing an antibiotic. Please contact me."

"I don't think you've adequately addressed my concerns," Wendel Garrett said.

"I can't provide you with absolute guarantees," Barry Grieg said.

"Can't or won't?" Garrett asked.

Sara McCartland dimmed the lights as the video of the brilliantly colored organism squirmed across the wide screen behind her desk casting an eerie glow throughout her office. Barry Grieg, fresh from his dissection by Wendel Garrett, joined Sara and Jaimie in the office.

"Did Garrett seem cooperative?" Jaimie asked.

"No, he's more interested in profit then anything else," Barry said. "I don't trust him at all. I've had problems with Sayer before. Now I understand why."

"Did anyone have a drug that might work?" Sara asked.

"Several reps told me they were developing antibiotics that have possibilities," Barry said. "They took samples of our friend up there to do sensitivity testing. They're supposed to let me know."

"I'm not sure I'd call this bug a friend," Sara said as the video of the pathogen changed color and shape. "Although it's hard not to admire the complexity of this one."

"What do you mean?" Barry asked.

"Technically, it's a bacterium," Jaimie said as the picture changed. "It increases in number as you can see, but it also releases a toxin that causes the shock-like symptoms."

"It also has properties that make it seem like a virus," Sara said.

"What are they?" Barry asked.

"It invades at the cell level and then hides," Jaimie said as the image changed to show the bacteria entering the cells. "When the baby is born and expels the fluid from its lungs, the bacteria immediately invades and attacks the lung tissue."

The video showed the spread of the bacteria throughout the lungs. "That process causes the lungs to fill up with pus," Sara said. "As you can see, the lung tissue here is just eaten away with bacteria. Simultaneously, the bacteria enters the blood stream."

"That causes the shock-like symptoms that cause death so rapidly," Jaimie said. "You couldn't design a more efficient killing machine."

"What did you say?" Barry asked as he looked at the screen.

"If you sat down and designed a bacterium, you couldn't engineer a better bug for its sheer killing efficiency," Jaimie said.

Chapter Six

FBI agent Alex Tanner stared at the pictures he had tacked onto the bulletin board in the Atlanta field office. Two eight-year-old girls with wide toothless grins, long blond hair, and innocent faces stared back. Alex Tanner had been in Atlanta for three months trying to solve their murders. Tanner, thirty-eight, had short black wavy hair and deep-set brown eyes. He always looked as if he needed a shave and could grow a full beard within a week.

His long, thin legs were sprawled on his desk. Tanner sipped coffee from a large mug as he studied the board, convinced the answer was right in front of him. That elusive missing piece was a source of constant frustration.

When the phone rang, Tanner was still distracted, so he didn't answer it immediately.

"Tanner," he said absently when he finally picked up the receiver.

"Hello," Tanner said when there was no response.

"I want to talk to an FBI agent," the voice said tentatively.

"I'm an FBI agent," Tanner said. "What did you want to talk about?"

"I know why those babies are dying," the voice said nervously.

"What babies?" Tanner asked impatiently, unwilling to deal with whatever kind of crank was calling this time.

"You know, those babies dying of newborn pneumonia," the voice said.

"What about them?" Tanner asked.

"They are dying because of an accidental contamination," the voice said.

"What kind of contamination?" Tanner asked.

"I've got to go," the voice said. "It was a terrible accident, but I think they might try to cover it up."

"Who?" Tanner demanded as the line went dead.

Jaimie Carpenter gazed out her large office window at the huge group of protesters and members of the press corps. She pressed her hand into her aching back, the result of a few hours of restless sleep on the small, uncomfortable couch by her desk. The rays from the sun spotlighted the blossoms on the cherry trees that lined the front drive, sparkling from a remaining coat of dew.

She got another cup of coffee and reviewed the mountain of computer notes that had been gathered since the pandemic began. The surveys completed by the various teams were extremely detailed. Jaimie couldn't find a single question or issue they had failed to address. Despite their best efforts, the source of this infection remained a mystery.

Sara walked into Jaimie's office, handed her the latest print outs, and immediately dropped into the chair in front of the desk.

"I'm so far past tired I can't think straight," Sara said.

"I know what you mean," Jaimie said.

"I caught part of a news conference on t.v. before I came up here," Sara said. "The right to lifers and the abortion rights activists are urging women to wait to get abortions."

"It's about time both sides realized there was a common ground in this," Jaimie said. "I wish we could figure out how strep-A infected these women."

"There's only one theory that makes sense," Sara said.

"You mean some novel combination of an environmental contamination coupled with the flu?" Jaimie asked.

"It's the only explanation I can think of," Sara said.

Though it was late, the Atlanta restaurant was crowded, a tribute to the good food it served twenty-four hours a day. Barry Grieg thought Alex Tanner looked weary as the waitress served them coffee, eggs over easy, waffles, and bacon.

"It's been a long time, Alex," Barry Grieg said.

"You haven't been out of D.C. much," Alex said.

"I know," Barry said as he poured strawberry syrup over everything.

"You still do that?" Alex asked.

"What?" Barry asked.

"Drown everything in syrup," Alex said, laughing.

"Yes, I do," Barry said defensively. "I did quit smoking and drinking. What did you want to talk to me about?"

"I've been getting phone calls from this guy," Alex said. "He says he knows how the babies who are dying from newborn pneumonia got infected."

"How do you know he isn't some crackpot?" Barry asked.

"He might be," Alex said. "I have this feeling he's telling the truth. He says the whole thing was an accidental contamination someone is covering up."

"Who?" Barry said as he ate a slice of bacon.

"He won't say," Alex said. "I figured since you were a doctor you could tell me if something like that could happen."

"I guess it's possible," Barry said. "There are a couple of doctors at the CDC I think you should talk to."

"Why?" Alex asked.

"They've been tracking these infections from the very beginning," Barry said. "If anyone would know the answer to your question it would be them. They've told me some things about this bug."

"Like what?" Alex asked.

"They said you couldn't design a more efficient killing machine if you tried,"

"Did they tell you someone designed it?"

"No, but they can't figure out how this bacteria infected these mothers. Maybe there's a connection. And Alex, there's a doctor named Jaimie Carpenter who will interest you. I've been wanting to see more of her myself, but she's been working around the clock since this began."

"You're not here that much, remember?" Alex reminded him.

"For her I'd make a special trip," Barry said. "I like her a lot. She's kind of unusual in a way."

"What do you mean?" Alex asked.

"She's very honest," Luke said. "She's a beautiful woman but I don't think she realizes it. She doesn't play any games. There's no attempt to keep you guessing. She's the only woman I ever met who is exactly what she appears to be."

The sheets of steady, cold rain struck the windows of the neonatal intensive care unit at D.C. General so hard it seemed like the rain was falling sideways. Marlowe could hear it while she checked the struggling infant's lungs. For the first time in forty days, no baby had been admitted with newborn pneumonia, but the terrified parents of several infants were camped out in the intensive care waiting room anyway.

Marlowe had interviewed this child's parents on admission, and their first anxious question had been about newborn pneumonia. Their joy at their daughter's birth had been tempered by the reality they could lose her. They seemed reluctant to embrace her as if any expression of pleasure might seal their fate.

Since the crisis began, brief naps were her only respite, so Marlowe was beyond exhausted. She sat down in the chair by the window with the infant's chart, aware of the headache only sleep would relieve. As she entered her notes into the infant's record, she doubted if anything would ever seem normal again.

The overhead lights in the unit were dimmed, but Marlowe could see the multi colored lights on the monitors blinking continuously as she fought the fatigue that engulfed her. She finally closed her eyes.

The surreal landscape was barren and the rain had stopped, replaced by a thick, dense fog that made identifying anything difficult. Eventually, Marlowe saw the troops moving away from her in a slow, measured retreat. She watched in fascination until one of them turned around to look at her.

Fascination turned to horror when Marlowe realized he had no face, only rotting flesh, with barely visible facial bones. The thing began laughing and was joined by the others as maniacal laughter surrounded her. Unable to block out the hideous cacophony, she closed her eyes until the unpleasant clamor became background noise. She looked again and realized the army of death had disappeared. When the metal chart hit the floor, Kelly Marlowe's eyes shot open.

The tall man with dark, wavy hair caught Jaimie's attention immediately; his long, muscular body filled her entire doorway. Jaimie noticed the dimple on his chin and the intense, dark brown eyes that were more guarded than unfriendly.

"Can I help you?" Jaimie asked as she smiled at him.

"I'm looking for Dr. McCartland and Dr. Carpenter," he said as he returned Jaimie's smile.

"You've found them," Sara said as she rose. "What can we do for you?"

"My name is Alex Tanner. I'm an FBI agent."

"Barry called and told us about you," Sara said as she motioned for Alex to sit. "He said you were getting phone calls about some kind of contamination."

"Yes, I've gotten four of them."

"Why don't you believe these are crank calls?" Jaimie asked.

"I did at first. There's just something about the desperation and remorse I can hear in his voice. I brought the tapes so you could listen to them," Alex said as he pulled the small tape recorder out of his pocket and pressed play. Though the recorder was small, the caller's nervous voice filled the room.

The best and brightest medicine had to offer were assembled in the large conference room at the CDC. Researchers from all over the country had been invited to attend to brainstorm about newborn pneumonia. Sara and Jaimie spent the hour before the session began greeting the participants. Finally, Sara called the jam session to order.

"Ladies and gentlemen, we'd like to begin by welcoming you to the CDC," Sara said. "This meeting is unprecedented, but I hope it might represent a beginning that will lead to establishing better communication links which will continue after this meeting ends.

"I'd like to introduce Jaimie Carpenter," Sara said as she motioned to Jaimie, who was sitting beside her. "She has worked on this from the beginning with me.

"Now that we have the preliminaries taken care of," Sara said. "There are some statistics I'd like to share with you, and then we'll open this up for discussion. At that point, let your imaginations go wild. We haven't been able to identify a common source of contamination, but it's possible we just haven't looked in the right place."

Sara dimmed the overhead lights and continued. "These first graphs show the cases reported to date as well as the geographic locations. As you can see, the higher population areas have a higher concentration of cases. The only areas in the world not reporting cases are in the underdeveloped countries. Our computer hasn't identified any large clusters so the reported cases are roughly proportionate to the population density.

"The first reported cases were in the Washington, D.C. area," Sara said. "On day five, a case was reported in Florida. By day six, reports began to come in from around the country."

The graphs changed as Sara continued. "The next series of graphs depict the reported cases from day one to the present. As you can see, the curve started out slow for ten days and then rose dramatically as the days passed. The stats remained the same until day forty when the curve began to drop. The number of reported case continues to drop.

"The next graph shows the percentage of newborns actually infected," Sara said. "That statistic has remained fairly steady since the onset at roughly seventy-five percent. I wish we could tell you the reasons for these statistics but I can't. I'd like Jaimie to discuss what we've looked at so far."

Jaimie stood up and took Sara's place. "When the first cases were reported, we sent out teams to all the cities to do quick and dirty surveys. The teams looked at possible hospital exposures first but couldn't find a common denominator. We obtained blood and tissue samples and identified the pathogen.

"After that we began to expand the surveys," Jaimie said. "We looked at every possible exposure from the time of conception on but found no common source. We have begun testing anything these mothers might have been exposed to including food, drugs, condoms, tampons, literally anything we could think of. We have also collected blood samples from all the mothers, babies, and fathers to try to identify some common characteristics. At this point, we are considering the possibility there are multiple exposures involved here. Perhaps some environmental contamination and a flu exposure. We have asked you to come here to help us figure out if there is something we have overlooked."

The overhead picture changed to show strep-A bacteria swarming on screen.

"That is our common enemy," Jaimie said as she looked behind her. "Where it came from and how it infected these mothers and babies remains a mystery. Our job is to solve that mystery."

Alex Tanner had been out of his office for most of the day, investigating a series of dead end leads pertaining to the murder of the two girls. The beautiful spring weather was a frustrating reminder winter had come and gone without a solution. Tanner had to run to reach the phone in his office before it stopped ringing.

"Hello, this Tanner," he said breathlessly.

"I had to talk to you again," the familiar voice said.

"If you really want to feel better about this you need to tell me more," Alex said. "You don't have to tell me your name. Just tell me the name of the place where you work or what was accidentally contaminated."

"If they find out I told you they might fire me or worse."

"What do you mean by worse?"

"I'm not sure," the voice said. "They keep telling me they're going to report this, but I'm not sure anymore."

"I can tell the guilt is tearing you apart. You need to think about doing the right thing for these babies so it can't happen again."

"They promised me it won't happen again."

"Do you believe them? Have they done anything else they said they would do?"

"No, they haven't."

"Start by telling me what your company produces," Alex said.

"I work for a pharmaceutical company. The largest one in the area."

"What was contaminated?" Alex asked, trying to hide his excitement.

"I've said too much already," the voice said nervously. "I think they're following me. I think they might kill me."

"Then meet with me," Alex said. "I can protect you."

"I don't know," the voice said uncertainly.

"Think about it," Alex said. "Think about the possibility it might happen again. You've got to help me stop them."

"I'll think about it. Oh, God, I've thought about this enough. You know where the Five Points Intersection is?"

"Yes," Alex said.

"I'll meet you tomorrow night at eight on the third level of the A-1 Parking Garage on Peachtree Street. I'll be waiting near the elevators," the voice said as the line went dead.

Chapter Seven

The man exited the downtown Atlanta phone booth and looked around carefully but didn't spot anyone. Charley McGrath was nervous; clandestine activities were not his area of scientific expertise. If Charley followed through with his plan to meet Tanner, he would have to select a route that would make it difficult for anyone to follow him.

Paranoia! Charley McGrath prayed he was afflicted with that mental illness. He wanted the recurring feeling that caused the hair on the back of his neck to stand up to be from a guilty conscience. Ever since he had discovered the contamination, Charley McGrath sensed someone was following him.

Adding to his burden was the severe case of insomnia that plagued him. To him, sleep seemed rather like an unwelcome stranger. When Charley did manage to fall asleep, his dreams included the screams of thousands of helpless, sick babies. Fatigue, guilt, despair, and the overriding realization it was time to end the pain summarized his feelings.

Unlike Charley, his pursuer had extensive training in covert activities. The man walked leisurely, just another face in the busy downtown crowd. There were no quick movements, no obvious stares, nothing to indicate the man had any particular interest in McGrath. Charley's fear would have been exacerbated if he had known the man considered Charley a weak link, one he might have to eliminate.

It had been forty-five days since Jaimie Carpenter last slept in her own bed. Most nights, she grabbed a few hours of restless sleep on the couch in her office. Instead of surrendering to exhaustion, Jaimie saw the events of the preceding weeks float through her consciousness like scenes from a long movie.

The late afternoon meeting held at the CDC was attended by a weary, cranky group of staff members. Sara informed them the number of reported cases of newborn pneumonia continued to drop. As she listened to Sara report the latest data, Jaimie sensed that although the immediate crisis seemed to be resolving, their reprieve might be short lived.

Sara instructed all her staff to leave the building, telling them rest and fresh minds were what was needed at this point. Jaimie went home but lapsed into an uneasy, dream filled slumber punctuated by the faces of Ted Drew, Dr. Gruenloh, and a very handsome Alex Tanner reminding her she was looking for some kind of contamination.

The next morning, a dull headache assaulted Jaimie's sinus passages, so she swallowed two extra strength Tylenol with her second cup of coffee. She felt disoriented, her underlying fatigue still affecting her. Before she read the latest computer projections, Jaimie turned on the t.v. in her office to catch Sara's live interview.

"This morning, we are privileged to have Dr. Sara McCartland with us," Matt Lauer said. "Dr. McCartland is from the Center for Disease Control in Atlanta, and we asked her to join us to discuss newborn pneumonia. It's good to have you with us, Dr. McCartland."

"Thank you, Matt," Sara McCartland said.

"What can you tell us about the spread of newborn pneumonia, Dr. McCartland?" Matt asked.

"The latest data indicate the number of reported cases continues to drop," Sara said. "That statistic has remained constant for the last eight days."

"Does that mean the crisis is over?" Matt asked.

"I wouldn't say it's over," Sara said. "It gives us at the CDC some hope that perhaps this was a limited exposure."

"Do you know what caused these infections?" he asked.

"No, I guess you could say we know more about what didn't cause it at this point," Sara admitted.

"Do you think it's safe for women to consider getting pregnant?" he asked.

"I can't tell them they aren't at risk," Sara said. "We now have an amniocentesis test available so we can identify the babies who are at risk."

"Do you have any idea when you might know how this illness is spread?" he asked.

Jaimie flipped the t.v. off before Sara could respond. She already knew the answer to that question, and it was a source of constant frustration.

As usual, Charley McGrath worked late. His employer had given up trying to convince Charley to work from nine to five. Any concerns about a lack of productivity on Charley's part had been quickly eliminated the first year; and his employer accepted that Charley was not a morning person, but his work exceeded that of other employees.

One of the reasons Charley McGrath was a night person was the fact he had no life other than his work. Whether this was by choice or circumstance even Charley wasn't sure. Charley was in his mid-fifties and combed his gray hair from one side of his head to the other in an unsuccessful attempt to create the illusion he wasn't bald. In addition, Charley was at least a hundred pounds overweight.

Dinner consisted of a candy bar, a Coke, and a bag of Cheez It that Charley ate while he finished entering data into the computer. He had to leave early to meet Alex Tanner, and he felt nervous but relieved. Charley logged off the computer and picked up another candy bar to munch on the short ride to Five Points.

Alex Tanner also worked late but instead of eating his dinner from a machine, he ate at a deli near Five Points where he could get his favorite foot long sub. Tanner savored the first bite of his sandwich and thought about the man he was about to meet. Alex could feel the man's tension, fear, and remorse in every phone conversation.

The man said he worked for a pharmaceutical company; and if they were the source of contamination, it could be anything. He smiled when he considered talking to Jaimie Carpenter might be necessary to clarify the medical ramifications of any information he received. Tanner thought about Jaimie and certainly wasn't upset about the prospect of seeing her again. Barry Grieg was right when he said she was a beautiful woman. She also seemed friendly but slightly shy as if she guarded some of her feelings very carefully. Alex checked his watch and left the deli to meet his informant.

Charley McGrath pulled his red Jeep into a space far away from the elevators on the third level of the A-1 Parking Garage. He wanted to leave if something didn't feel right, and he was afraid he wouldn't be able to exercise that option if he parked too close to the elevators. Charley felt relieved as if a great burden was about to be lifted from his shoulders.

When got out of the Jeep, he felt fine as he began walking toward the elevators. Halfway there, he suddenly sensed malice and fate reaching out for him. Frozen by fear, Charley considered getting back in the Jeep and driving away. More afraid of living with his secret than the danger, Charley began walking forward again.

A noise from behind startled him. Before Charley could turn around to look, he felt searing pain as strong arms grabbed him from behind. Charley was confused, and when he tried to speak, he had such difficulty breathing that the words never reached his lips. Suddenly, Charley felt free as if he were floating. The man holding him from behind cursed as he dragged Charley's heavy body toward the red Jeep.

Five Points is one of the busiest intersections in Atlanta, and it took Alex a long time to negotiate his way through the busy traffic. The garage attendant seemed bored when Alex took his stub from the machine and drove up the ramp. The third level had many empty spots, and Alex pulled into one near the elevators.

After he turned off the ignition, Alex stayed in the car for a few minutes, but no one approached the elevators. Alex was always bothered by these kinds of meetings. The intentions of informants remained as hidden as their agendas, and Alex had the experience to know this scenario could be a set up for some other purpose.

Alex decided he had put off the inevitable long enough, so he got out of the vehicle, locked the door, and walked slowly toward the elevators. When he reached them, he stood near the single, exposed overhead light, feeling very vulnerable. A young couple got off the elevator. They stared at him curiously when they realized he wasn't getting on. Their pace picked up noticeably and they glanced back frequently to make sure he wasn't following.

Minutes seemed like hours, and Alex did some stretching exercises to relieve the stress. He could hear someone start a car but wasn't alarmed until he heard the tires squeal as the vehicle rounded the corner. Then the headlights appeared and Alex could tell the driver had floored the vehicle. As the car screamed down the lane toward where Alex was standing, he realized he could either press himself close to the elevators or dive into a space between parked cars on the other side.

Alex drew his weapon and extinguished the glaring overhead light. Then bright, blinding headlights approached at a high rate of speed as Alex finally made his choice.

Jack Connelly, Deputy Director of the FBI in Washington, reviewed the report. Connelly's thick, gray hair was cut short and his lined, weathered face showed signs of fatigue and concern.

"So you think McGrath was your informant?" Connelly asked.

"Yes, I do," Alex said. "The last time I talked to the informant, he told me he worked for a pharmaceutical company. I called the local police after the red Jeep almost hit me. They called back yesterday to tell me the Jeep belonged to Charley McGrath. He worked for Sayer Pharmaceuticals."

"Where did they find McGrath's body?" Jack asked.

"A couple of miles from the parking garage," Alex said. "All they found in his pocket was a parking stub from the A-1 Garage. They think it was a car jacking and murder, because the driver just barreled through the exit without paying."

"Maybe it was just a car jacking," Jack said.

"I talked with this guy enough to believe what he was telling me. We were able to trace all his calls to the local Atlanta area. Sayer is the only drug company of any significant size located in Atlanta."

"Wendel Garrett has some big political connections," Jack said.

"That doesn't mean he's innocent," Alex Tanner said.

"That's true, but we better be damn sure we're right before we start accusing him of anything."

"What do we know about Garrett?" Alex asked.

"When Garrett got out of medical school he did some research on new drugs. There were some problems with that research."

"What kind of problems?"

"Officially, there was never enough evidence to charge him with anything," Jack said. "The FDA received complaints that Garrett had enhanced the results of his research regarding the efficacy of two of the drugs he worked on. The company he worked for asked him to resign and he did. Two months later, he met Margo Sayer and they were married three months after that. Then he went to work for Garth Sayer, Margo's father."

"How long has he been with Sayer?" Alex asked.

"Twenty-five years," Jack said. "There have been whispers off and on about his research practices, but Garth Sayer always found a way to quiet those voices. Three years ago, Garth died and Garrett took over. Their stock prices soared two years ago when they introduced a new pregnancy test. The whole company's been torn apart. Garrett brought in a lot of new employees, and their security is among the tightest anywhere. They are supposedly doing all kinds of top secret research. The word on the Hill is that Garrett bought Congressman Holt. Supposedly Holt sponsored a bill that allowed Garrett to build an estate on Jekyll Island in exchange for a huge block of Sayer stock."

"Is that why you don't want to investigate this?" Alex asked.

"Of course we're going to investigate," Jack said. "We just have to be careful how we go about it. We need to figure out if Garrett or someone else at Sayer knew about the contamination and covered it up."

"There's Charley McGrath's murder to consider," Alex said.

"That's right," Jack said. "If someone at Sayer murdered Charley, they'd obviously do anything to cover it up."

"What do you propose?" Alex asked.

"This has to be done very quietly," Connelly said. "A public investigation would tip Garrett off and he might destroy all the evidence. We have to figure out a way to balance the public outcry for a cure with the need to find the cause. I think the only solution is to send someone into Sayer undercover."

"It would have to be someone with a lot of medical training," Alex said.

"That's what I was thinking," Connelly said. "Is there someone you know who might be qualified? Someone who would have enough knowledge to know what to look for. Can you think of anyone like that?"

"There's a doctor at the CDC who would be qualified," Alex said hesitantly.

"What's his name?" Connelly asked.

Alex Tanner's lunch invitation was unexpected but not unwelcome, and Jaimie had taken more care with her appearance than usual. The cool breeze tossed her auburn hair in several directions, but Alex Tanner thought it made her look more attractive as he watched her cross the busy street.

Jaimie entered the restaurant, spotted Alex, and headed for the table. He stood and greeted her when she reached it.

"Hi, Dr. Carpenter," Alex said awkwardly.

"Wow, such a formal greeting. Why don't you call me Jaimie?"

"OK," Alex said as he laughed softly.

Jaimie accepted the menu from the waiter and scanned it nervously when she realized Alex was staring at her. When she looked up and met Alex Tanner's stare, she felt as if his dark brown eyes were boring holes into her. Jaimie flushed, first from embarrassment then anger. Tanner was obviously sizing her up, but Jaimie wasn't sure why. The only thing she was sure of was that she didn't like it.

"Did I pass the test?" Jaimie asked irritably.

"I'm sorry, I didn't think this would be so uncomfortable."

The waiter arrived and took their drink orders.

"How have you been?" Alex asked after he left.

"Better since the number of reported cases of newborn pneumonia has dropped," Jaimie admitted, considering what Tanner meant by his 'uncomfortable' remark. "We still have to find an answer, but at least there aren't reports flooding in anymore."

"Suppose I told you I know how these babies might have been infected."

"How?" Jaimie asked with a shocked expression on her face.

"Remember that informant I told you and Sara about? He finally told me he worked for a drug company. The next night he was murdered in a parking garage. He worked for Sayer Pharmaceuticals."

"You think something at Sayer was contaminated?"

"Yes, and then someone covered it up and killed Charley McGrath."

"Who?" Jaimie demanded.

"We're not sure. The CEO of Sayer, Wendel Garrett, is a prime suspect. If Charley McGrath found out about contamination, he would take that information to someone high up in Sayer."

"Someone like Wendel Garrett," Jaimie said, finishing the thought.

"What does this have to do with me?" Jaimie asked after the waiter returned, took their entree orders, and left again.

"My boss has authorized an undercover investigation," Alex said as he looked at Jaimie. "We need someone to go into Sayer. It has to be someone with enough medical knowledge to know what they're looking for."

"What exactly would they be looking for?" Jaimie asked.

"Evidence that Garrett knew about the contamination that caused newborn pneumonia. Proof he covered it up and murdered Charley McGrath."

"God, do you realize what you're saying?" Jaimie asked.

"Yes," Alex said.

"That would make Garrett a monster," Jaimie said.

"Yes, it would," Alex agreed. "It also makes this a dangerous assignment for whoever goes in there."

"You want me to do this?" Jaimie asked as she looked at Alex with a stunned expression on her face.

Chapter Eight

The intense color display, its surreal characteristics enhanced by the flashing amber lights, became the backdrop for the scenes that followed. A procession of young men and women passed by Jaimie slowly, absolutely reeking of sorrow. The women clutched their stomachs, and when they looked at Jaimie, their eyes searched hers for some sign she understood their pain.

In the background a chorus of babies, mostly hidden by the dense smoke, howled continuously while they struggled for every breath. By the time their cries turned to hideous laughter, Jaimie could see Kelly Marlowe, Alfred Gruenloh, and Alex Tanner pointing their collective fingers at her, wanting to know why she wouldn't help the babies. From behind them, Senator Ted Drew emerged and approached Jaimie with a curious, sad expression on his face.

"More babies will die because you won't help," Drew said.

Jaimie sat up in bed, keenly aware of the cold sweat rolling down her face and trunk, overwhelmed by feelings of terror and guilt. The images from her dream rolled through her consciousness in rapid succession. She got up and looked at the first fingers of light that were just beginning to claw their way up the horizon.

As her respirations decreased to near normal, she realized her dream was a natural consequence of her lunch meeting with Alex Tanner. Jaimie had been astonished when she realized the implications of what Tanner suggested.

"You want me to do this?" she had asked incredulously.

"We need someone with medical knowledge to go in there. You would understand the medical issues. No agent could possibly fake that knowledge."

"I don't know anything about investigating crime," Jaimie protested.

"So, you won't do this?" Alex asked, the disappointment flooding his face.

"I'm just surprised. This is a lot to digest in a small amount of time."

"If the contamination happened once it might happen again," Alex said. "I thought you said you wanted to know the answer."

"I do, but I'm a doctor, not a detective."

"You're more of a detective than you know," Alex said. "You just hunt bugs instead of people. How are you going to feel if this happens again?"

"I refuse to let you bully me into doing this, Alex Tanner," Jaimie said as she stood up to leave. "I want a little time to think about it, and I don't think that's an unreasonable request."

Alex was stepping out of the shower when he heard his phone ring. Briefly, he considered letting the answering machine pick up, but some instinct told him he should answer it instead. With water dripping all over the carpet, he grabbed the towel and ran to pick up the receiver. The first part of his message began to play as Alex yelled over it so the caller wouldn't hang up.

When the message finally stopped, Alex could hear someone breathing, and he was about to make a comment when the caller began to speak.

"Alex, I've thought about it," Jaimie said. "I still have reservations but I have to know the answer."

"I'll talk to the Assistant Director and get back to you with the details."

"OK," Jaimie said.

"Jaimie," Alex said quickly.

"Yes," she said.

"Thank you," Alex said.

While he finished drying off, Alex thought about his lunch meeting with Jaimie. After she stormed out, he realized she had every right to be angry. Using guilt and any other lure he could think of, he had tried to bully her into participating. When he recalled the conversation, he was relieved Jaimie hadn't allowed him to do it without protesting. It was a side of his character he felt ambivalent about. Although it got results, he understood it indicated a lack of sensitivity.

Jaimie had no real reason to help them other than concern that the contamination would occur again. There was also an element of risk that Alex couldn't discount. Someone at Sayer had already killed once to protect their secret, and Alex didn't think they would hesitate to do it again if they were threatened. Alex dialed Connelly's number, considering what kind of plan he would come up with.

Two days later, Jack Connelly walked through the enclosed ramp that led to Hartsfield Airport in Atlanta. Flight 467 had just arrived from D.C. Connelly didn't spot Alex Tanner standing there in the crowd. Tanner grinned when Connelly finally picked him out and waved.

"How was your flight?" Tanner asked.

"The usual," Jack said. "You arrive two hours early and then the flight takes off late."

"Do you have another bag?" Tanner asked.

"No, this is it," Jack said as he held up his carry on.

"How did you intimidate Dr. Carpenter into doing this?" Jack asked as they started walking toward the parking area.

"What makes you think I tried to intimidate her?" Alex asked defensively.

"I know you pretty well, Alex," Jack said.

"Intimidation didn't work," Alex said. "I think it was guilt that got to her."

The early morning rush hour was beginning to wane as Alex drove to the Atlanta field office. Peach trees were in full bloom and everything seemed green and lush. Ten minutes later, Alex offered Jack Connelly a cup of coffee.

"Thanks," Jack Connelly said as the phone on Alex's desk began to ring. Alex picked up the receiver.

"Show her in," Alex said.

"Hi, Jaimie," Alex said when Jaimie appeared in his doorway.

"Hi, Alex," Jaimie said as she blushed slightly.

Alex liked Jaimie's shy response and the way the light from the window caught the dark auburn highlights in her hair. Her eyes and expression betrayed a genuine sincerity, and Alex found himself staring at her until he realized he should break the silence.

"Jaimie, this is the Deputy Director, Jack Connelly," Alex said.

"I'm pleased to meet you, Mr. Connelly," Jaimie said as she reached out to shake his hand.

"The pleasure is mine," Jack Connelly said as he stood up.

"Please sit down, Jaimie," Alex said. "Would you like some coffee?"

"No, thank you," Jaimie said.

"I was pleased when Alex called and said you would help us," Jack said as he studied Jaimie.

"Did he tell you I had reservations?" Jaimie asked.

"Yes, and I don't blame you," Jack said. "I've thought about those reservations, and I've made some basic decisions about how this should go. I think they'll address your concerns. You need to have an agent close by to help you. Someone who is also part of your cover."

"Who did you have in mind?" Alex asked.

"You, Alex," Connelly said as he stared at Alex.

"I'm already working on a case," Ales said, trying to hide his displeasure.

"A case you need some time away from," Jack said. "You've been in on this plan from the very beginning, and I'm not sure it will work if it isn't handled in a certain way."

"What do you mean?" Jaimie asked.

"I have concerns about getting you into Sayer," Jack Connelly said. "My sources tell me that when Wendel Garrett took over, he beefed up security. They only hire people who are married. Something about them being more stable employees or something. And don't even get into the discrimination issues. Somehow, that's what they've managed to do."

"What exactly are you suggesting?" Alex asked.

"I'm suggesting that Jaimie stage a very public argument with her boss at the CDC," Jack said. "One that enough people overhear so Garrett also finds out about it. Then Jaimie goes to Hawaii for a vacation. While she's there, she gets swept off her feet by one 'Alex Martin' and they get married."

Wendel Garrett and Rudy Fletcher, Chief of Security at Sayer Pharmaceuticals, were discussing damage control and finding a replacement for Charley McGrath in Garrett's plush downtown Atlanta office.

"I guess we should consider Charley's untimely death a blessing," Garrett said.

"I do," Rudy Fletcher said. "I could tell he was going to spill his guts. It was only a matter of time."

"Thank God the crime rate is out of control," Wendel said. "It seems like such a coincidence, doesn't it, Rudy?"

"Yes, it does," Rudy said as he stared at Garrett, trying to measure the sincerity of his response.

"Unfortunately, it leaves us hurting badly," Garrett said. "One of the projects Charley was working on is at a very delicate stage. Strangely enough, he was working on Maxicillin, a new antibiotic to treat strep-A. We're going to have to find somebody to finish it in a hurry. We have a window of opportunity here, and we have to beat the rest of the pack to the market with an antibiotic."

"You're going to have him start without the usual security checks?" Rudy asked.

"Definitely," Garrett said. "You'll just have to do a cursory check at first and then a more thorough security check after they start working here. It's going to be hard to find somebody qualified enough to do the research. I can't worry about the rest of it."

The stunned silence that filled Alex's office quickly evaporated when Jaimie and Alex realized the significance of Connelly's words.

"You've got to be joking," Jaimie said, her sentiments quickly echoed by Alex.

"I don't think this is a good idea," Alex said.

"It satisfies everyone's concerns," Jack said. "It's the only way we can be sure Alex will be close by to advise and protect you."

"We'd have to live together," Jaimie said with a horrified look on her face.

"That's what married people do," Jack said, laughing.

"I don't want to marry anyone," Jaimie said with distaste.

"Look, Jaimie, I want to do everything possible to protect you while you're inside Sayer," Jack Connelly said as he leaned over and looked earnestly into her eyes. "I know it'll be hard, but you'll just have to try to put up with Alex."

"Don't encourage her, Jack," Alex warned as Connelly laughed.

"This just keeps getting more complicated," Jaimie said.

"When this is over, we'll get the marriage annulled," Jack said gently.

"They'll need someone because McGrath is dead," Jaimie said. "Since they have a project to finish they might suspend some of their security rules."

"That's what I'm hoping," Jack said. "The first priority here is your security, and I think this plan is the safest way to accomplish all of our goals."

His code name was Dr. Jekyll, and he was having the same nightmare that had haunted him since he was a small child. It always began the same, this recurring dream that made him dread twilight and the black, empty night that followed. Bathed in the warmth of the sunshine, he would be walking barefoot along the beach on Jekyll Island, watching the waves. He could feel the wet sand between his toes, smell the sea, and hear the surf pounding on the shore.

Suddenly, the skies would darken ominously, and he felt fear and an awareness he was being chased by some unidentified terror. Flight seemed like the only viable option, so he would begin running to escape the unknown menace. He would turn around to get a look at his pursuer, but just about the time the face came into focus, he would wake up.

There was a time when he believed if he could understand what the dream meant, he would stop having it. His grandmother, Jenny Morgan, held the key to the mystery, and he had tried to pry the information out of her for as long as he could remember. But Jenny stubbornly held onto her secret, closing the door to her heart every time he broached the subject.

Jenny Morgan was his maternal grandmother, and she raised him after his mother unceremoniously dumped him on her doorstep when he was an infant. He would characterize his upbringing as reluctant but resigned. He always felt there was some obstacle that kept Jenny from really loving him.

Memories of a happy childhood formed the basis of Jenny's descriptions of Jekyll Island, but he sensed that she stopped living the day she left there. She told him how prominent East Coast millionaires, including Charles Goodyear, Jay Gould, J.P. Morgan, Joseph Pulitzer, John D. Rockefeller, and others bought up the island. After their purchase, they promptly named themselves the Jekyll Island Club and used it as a getaway and family retreat.

Jenny's father was a gardener for one of those prominent families and when Jenny was older, she would occasionally work for some of the members, cooking and cleaning up at their frequent parties. Jenny spoke glowingly of the activities and excitement that permeated the atmosphere on the island and changed world events. In 1910, the first draft of the Federal Reserve Act, the foundation of the nation's monetary system, was drawn up on Jekyll Island. And in 1915, the president of AT&T made the first transcontinental telephone call from Jekyll Island, speaking with Woodrow Wilson in Washington, D.C., and with Alexander Graham Bell in New York.

All those glorious, exciting details Jenny provided freely and proudly with a gleam in her eye. Every time he asked Jenny why she left the island, her whole manner and demeanor changed. At that moment, he always felt guilty as if he had committed some terrible wrong that caused Jenny to withdraw. He knew Jenny Morgan both loved and hated him, but he never understood the reason for her ambivalence.

On one occasion when he was very young, Jenny recalled her last night on the island, and he could see the physical change as her body tensed. Before she could tell him the whole story, she got up and left the room, unwilling to complete the rest of the narration. Eventually, Jenny Morgan was confined to the Gulf Shores Sanitarium with schizophrenia, and he doubted he would ever know what catastrophic event haunted his grandmother. On those intermittent occasions when he visited her, Jenny rarely recognized him.

All that changed one stormy night six years ago. Drenched from a continuous downpour, he had entered Jenny's room and she began to recite the details of the rape that took place on Jekyll Island. She stood near the window, a ghost of her former self. Her long, dirty fingernails and wild hair were testimony to the fear the staff felt about trying to approach her to address basic hygiene.

"It stormed that day," she began. "I knew something was going to happen, but I guess I was too young to understand. I shouldn't have gone to his estate that night. I sensed he was an evil man, but I never thought he was capable of anything like that. For a long time, I thought I would get over the way he smelled, the strange noises he made and the pain when he pushed me down and did that to me. But every time I tried to focus on anything else, the events of that day just came flooding back. I'm not strong enough to fight those demons."

Jekyll went to her side. For the first time, he held her close and she didn't push him away. The moment passed and her voices returned to engage her in a conversation that excluded him. While he stood on the steps of Gulf Shores, he allowed the rain to pour over his body as if it could somehow wash away all the accumulated pain.

Understanding what happened to his grandmother brought an end to Jekyll's confusion, but the rage and bitterness that replaced it were not healthy substitutes. The wound festered until he sought a way to channel his rage into activities that would even the score.

Dr. Jekyll was upset when he realized Charley McGrath had discovered the contamination. Charley's timely demise protected the bigger picture. Now that Charley was dead and they believed it was just an innocent contamination, he could continue to pursue his real agenda.

CHAPTER NINE

The group was restless. It was almost noon, and the meeting at the CDC had started at 7:00 a.m. Jaimie was excited about some of the interesting causation theories they'd discussed until she realized she wouldn't be part of the CDC's investigation. She would just have to hope her undercover assignment at Sayer made their search unnecessary.

Jaimie was about to stage a very public argument with someone she considered a close friend. She silently drummed her fingers on the table. Sara McCartland had hired Jaimie, and as the relationship grew, Sara became Jaimie's mentor. In many ways, Jaimie considered Sara a surrogate mother. She wasn't entirely sure she could pull this off despite the fact they had rehearsed the main elements of the quarrel.

While the soft overhead spots highlighted Sara's blond hair, Jaimie catalogued the qualities that made Sara such a trusted friend. She was distracted, thinking of those characteristics when Sara concluded the meeting.

"I think we've covered everything," Sara said as some of the staff members began to rise. "I do have an announcement I'd like to make. Effective immediately, Dr. Philip Richman will head up the newborn pneumonia team."

Restrained applause and the ripple of hushed whispers replaced the stunned silence as the group slowly filed out. Everyone knew that Jaimie wanted and deserved that job. Jaimie took a deep breath and approached Sara, who had a look of intransigence and resignation on her face.

"I can't believe you'd give Philip my project," Jaimie said in a voice loud enough to attract everyone's attention.

"It's not your project," Sara said. "I've made my decision, Jaimie."

"It's the wrong decision."

"I'm sorry you feel that way."

"Is that all you have to say?" Jaimie asked.

"When we talked the other day I told you this might happen," Sara said. "I hoped you'd be mature enough to understand."

"Mature enough? What has maturity got to do with this? I've been here a long time, and I've had my share of projects and assignments I didn't like. I asked for this because I really wanted to be involved with the solution. How could you do this to me?"

"It's my decision, and I'm sticking by it," Sara said.

"Fine, then you can find somebody else to do the administrative job," Jaimie said. "I quit."

"If that's how you feel, then that's probably the best solution for both of us."

The tears Jaimie brushed off her cheeks as she left the auditorium were genuine. She had always avoided altercations in which naked emotions were hurled around. At the moment, she was absolutely sure she never wanted to have a real fight with Sara.

While she packed the contents of her office into boxes, she felt nervous and agitated about the FBI investigation. So far, her relationship with Alex Tanner had been anything but pleasant, and she couldn't imagine how they would get through this charade without arguing frequently. Members of the CDC staff kept coming by her office to offer support, but the hardest conversation by far was the one she had with Philip Richman.

"Jaimie, I feel terrible," he said tentatively after he walked into her office. "I'll talk to Sara. I had no idea she was going to do this. I don't want you to go. We can work this out. Don't leave."

"It's OK, Philip," Jaimie said. "It may not seem like it, but it really is the best thing for now. I'll be fine."

"I'm still going to talk to Sara," he said kindly. "Let me see if I can change her mind."

Their first night on the island of Kauai, Jaimie arranged to meet Alex at a luau sponsored by the hotel where they were both staying. A very talkative attorney latched onto Jaimie, telling her all about his busy personal injury law practice. Jaimie tried to break free but he didn't stop talking long enough for her to move away. It was only after audience participation was demanded by the host and Jaimie's attorney had been dressed in a grass skirt and paraded to the front to sing that Alex could think about approaching.

"I didn't think he was ever going to leave," Alex said as the attorney began to belt out the chords of a familiar tune.

"I know," Jaimie said. "He'll be back soon. Do you want to go?"

"Good idea," Alex said. "How about a walk on the beach?

"How do you feel about being involved in this?" Alex asked as they walked along the deserted stretch of beach.

"I'm scared," Jaimie admitted.

"I think you'll do fine," Alex said.

"I was thinking we could start over," Alex said. "We're going to have to spend a lot of time together, and it would be a lot more pleasant if we called a truce. Maybe we could try to be friends."

"Friends, huh," Jaimie said. "What kind of friends?"

"What do you mean?"

"Well, there are different levels of friendship," Jaimie said. "There are casual friendships where you just kind of tolerate each other and exchange pleasantries. Then there is another level where there is some basis for trust. You kind of flirt around the edges of sharing your true feelings, but you're not sure you want to give away too much so you're still kind of careful. And, of course, there's always the third level. That's the one where you tell the absolute truth and share your deepest fears, your deepest secrets."

"Jaimie Carpenter, do you have to make everything complicated?" Alex asked as he stopped and stared into her eyes.

"It simplifies things for me. If I know the parameters, I won't say anything inappropriate."

"OK, fair enough," Alex said as they started walking again. "How about we try for the last one? It'll be a new experience for me. That's the one I always avoid like the plague."

Sara McCartland was fit to kill in a long black dress. Her hair had been professionally styled for the occasion, an annual Atlanta fund raiser. The live band struck up its rendition of "So Far Away" while Sara's escort went to get them drinks. Sara didn't notice Wendel Garrett approach or realize he was sitting next to her until he spoke.

"Well, Sara McCartland. It's been awhile, hasn't it?"

"Yes, it has, Wendel. How have you been?"

"Very well, thank you," Garrett said. "I guess you've really been swamped since the newborn pneumonia outbreak?"

"Yes, it's been a busy couple of months," Sara said.

"Any idea how it was spread?" Garrett asked.

"We've got lots of ideas," Sara said. "None of them have panned out so far."

"Things are starting to calm down, right?" he asked.

"Pretty much," Sara said tentatively.

"That seems like a tempered response," Garrett said.

"I guess it is," Sara said. "I think all the pressure finally got to me. I made a really dumb decision and my best doc quit. I don't know how I'm going to replace her."

"Who quit?" Garrett asked, trying to hide his enthusiasm.

"I don't know if you remember her or not. Her name's Jaimie Carpenter."

Jaimie's phone was ringing when she reached the door of her hotel room. All thumbs, she finally inserted the card, pushed the door open, and ran to pick up the phone.

"Hello," Jaimie said breathlessly.

"I guess you're out of breath because you've already been swept off your feet," Sara said, laughing. "That boy is a fast worker."

"Maybe it wasn't a good idea to let you in on this," Jaimie said.

"I couldn't resist," Sara said.

"I miss you already."

"You're the one who quit."

"I don't ever want to have a real argument like that," Jaimie said.

"I know, I thought you were going to crack for a minute."

"Just to satisfy my curiosity. What did you mean by that remark about maturity?"

"I could tell that one really got to you," Sara said, laughing. "I was afraid you were going to fold, so I tried to say something I thought would piss you off."

"It worked."

"I wanted to let you know I saw Garrett tonight," Sara said. "He was at the fund raiser like we thought he would be. I told him you left the CDC. He tried to pretend he wasn't interested but I could tell he was. Now that Charley McGrath is dead, he's going to need somebody to help with research and development. I think he'll contact you."

"I hope so. I can't call you for a while."

"Be careful, Jaimie," Sara said.

"I will," Jaimie promised.

The waves moved back and forth on Barking Sands beach, repeating their endless pattern as Jaimie and Alex sat on their grass mats. Someone at their hotel mentioned this stretch of beach was gorgeous, and this was the third day they had returned. Jack Connelly had sent profiles on all the major players at Sayer Pharmaceuticals, and they were trying to digest all the information.

"I didn't realize Luke Harper worked at Sayer," Jaimie said.

"Do you know him?" Alex said as he turned over and looked at Jaimie.

"I met him once," Jaimie said. "He's supposed to be brilliant. He developed the pregnancy test that made millions for Sayer."

"Was he nuts back then?"

"He was quiet," Jaimie said. "I met him at a conference when I first went to work at the CDC. That would have been about seven years ago. He was doing research at Stanford then, I think. According to this report, he's a paranoid schizophrenic but received treatment. Garrett promised to build him a private lab in a remote location, so he agreed to go to work for Sayer."

"How about Rudy Fletcher? Former CIA connections, former military intelligence. Now head of security for Sayer Industries. He'd be my choice for bumping off McGrath."

"Wendel Garrett seems fairly benign," Jaimie said. "Not much family. A close relative raised him. Married to Margo Sayer, heir to the Sayer fortune. He doubled that fortune in the three years since Garth Sayer died."

"We need to head back," Alex said. "I'm getting fried and very hungry."

Two hours later they watched the red-orange sunset as they sat at a table on an open porch sipping white zinfandel. The ocean glistened like a million stars until the sun fell into the water.

"Wow, the sunsets are amazing here," Alex said.

"Yes, they are," Jaimie said.

"I can't remember the last time I took a vacation," Alex said.

"Does this count?"

"Knowing Jack, it probably will," Alex said. "We need to talk about some things."

"OK," Jaimie said.

"We need to talk about our families," Alex said. "You know, the things a husband and wife would know about each other."

"Should I go first?" Jaimie asked as the waiter took their entree orders.

"Good idea," Alex said.

"I was born and raised in San Diego," Jaimie said. "I'm going to guess you already know that from Jack's report as well as my educational background and the fact I've never been married."

"How do you know there's a report on you?"

"A logical assumption," Jaimie said. "Am I wrong?"

"Well," Alex hedged.

"Third level friendship, remember?" Jaimie asked.

"OK, we did a check on you before we ever approached you."

"Maybe it would be easier if you just asked the questions between the lines," Jaimie said. "The ones the naked facts never explain."

"Why did your mother leave?" Alex asked.

"The women in my family aren't good at relationships," Jaimie said. "I think she loved us, but she couldn't stand being tied down so she ran away."

"It must have been hard for you," Alex said.

"I got even with her," Jaimie said. "I guess it started when she left. I decided to punish her by rejecting every overture she tried to make since the day she left. Things are awkward between us.

"I became my father's world after that, I guess," Jaimie said. "He was the proverbial room father and softball coach. I know he thinks the reason I avoid relationships is that my mother left, and I would never tell him the truth. But I think the real reason is that I don't think he ever stopped loving her. There's this kind of resigned sadness he wears like an old, favorite sweater. I'm not sure I want to feel that kind of pain."

Alex truly didn't know what to say and was extremely relieved when the waiter served them their lobsters. He glanced across the table and was caught off guard by how stunning Jaimie looked in the candlelight. He imagined himself walking around the table, pulling her up from the chair, and kissing her.

"What about your aunts?" Alex asked, trying to shake off the spell.

"I think their roles were to provide comic relief," Jaimie said. "That's going to be the hardest part. Not being able to tell them the truth."

"Fletcher might talk to them as part of his background check," Alex said. "They might give something away."

"I know," Jaimie said. "Neither one of my aunts ever married. Aunt Grace always picks men she knows will leave her, and Aunt Sam picks men who pretend to share her artistic flair."

"What will they think about our marriage?" Alex asked.

"My father will be relieved," Jaimie said. "Aunt Grace will be horrified."

"She hasn't even met me yet," Alex protested.

"She'll think she failed," Jaimie said. "She taught me to be practical, to give all my major life decisions a lot of thought. Aunt Sam, on the other hand, will think it's romantic. She always tells me I have this wild, free person inside me that's just waiting to find expression."

"They sound wonderful," Alex said.

"Different in some ways but I think they all kind of balanced each other out. What about you, Alex Tanner?"

"I was born and raised near Denver," Alex said. "I'm the oldest of four boys. My parents own a ranch. They've been married for forty years and as far as I can tell they seem happy. I went to the University of Colorado and joined the FBI. My job involves hunting serial killers and it requires a lot of travel. Of course, as Alex Martin, I own a computer software company."

"Have you or Alex Martin ever been married?" Jaimie asked.

"Nether one of us has," Alex said, laughing. "I've been engaged twice but didn't go through with it."

"Your idea or theirs?" Jaimie asked.

"Truth, right?" Alex asked as he took a deep breath and frowned. "OK, I think it was my fault the relationships didn't work out. At first, everything seemed great. They would tell me they understood about all the traveling. That worked for a while but when you miss birthdays, weekends, and holidays it gets old, and eventually they stopped trying to understand. It was only the last year or two that I accepted the fact I could have asked for a transfer so that I'd be assigned to one office. I think I used the traveling as an excuse because I didn't want to commit."

The garden at the LeLani Plantation looked gorgeous in the early evening light as Alex and Jaimie approached Judge Margaret Krettek, who was a personal friend of Jack Connelly. Flowers of every description and color were planted in little areas between the stone paths. Margaret had helped Alex and Jaimie make arrangements for their wedding the first day they arrived. Jack had even provided rings for the ceremony, eliciting several nasty comments from Alex. Two assistants from Krettek's office served as witnesses.

Margaret Krettek recited the familiar vows which Alex and Jaimie repeated. Jaimie was extremely nervous, experiencing difficulty saying the words. By the time Alex placed the plain, gold band on her finger, she thought she might be having an anxiety attack.

"You may kiss the bride," Margaret Krettek said as Alex smiled, put his arms around a surprised Jaimie, and kissed her tenderly but thoroughly.

Chapter Ten

Alex heard only the waves breaking against the shore and the softer sound of Jaimie's steady, even breathing. He was sitting next to her, watching the sun fall into the blood red horizon, mesmerized by her nearness and the scene.

Alex leaned over in time to catch Jaimie's smile and kissed her, gently at first and then with more urgency. She pressed her body against his chest and ran her fingers through his hair. Alex interrupted his kiss long enough to pull the cotton shirt over her head. Her nipples were already hard as he began to knead them, the low moan that escaped her lips providing incentive. Alex traced soft kisses under her chin and down her chest as she arched her back, calling his name softly. His mouth had barely reached her breast when he heard the phone ring the first time.

Jaimie begged him not to answer it, kissing him ardently to reinforce her request. The next strident ring ended Alex's trance, and his arousal was the only remnant of the dream after Jaimie and the beach disappeared. Alex almost fell off the couch when he reached for the phone.

"Hello," he said nastily.

"How was your wedding night?" Jack Connelly asked.

"I slept on the couch," Alex said.

"Not the way you dreamed it would be, huh?" Jack asked.

"I don't want to talk about dreams," Alex said.

"You're in a rotten mood," Jack said.

"Sorry," Alex said, tempering his response a little.

"You're coming back today, right?" Jack asked.

"Yes, we should get in about eight tonight," Alex said.

"I wanted to let you know what some sources told me. Wendel Garrett is very interested in Jaimie. Sara McCartland told me a drug rep from Sayer called one of the doctors at the CDC to get her phone number."

"Good, it's better that he pursue her," Alex said. "It makes it all seem more innocent that way."

The two-story house with dark green shutters sat back on the lot and had a covered porch that wrapped around the entire front and both sides. A white picket fence enclosed the yard and added considerable charm to the overall effect. The cab driver pulled the car into Jaimie's driveway. Alex laughed when he saw the house and the surroundings.

"What?" Jaimie asked.

"I wouldn't have figured you for the picket fence type," Alex said as he helped the driver take the bags out of the trunk.

"You thought modern with lots of marble and glass?" Jaimie asked.

"Something like that," Alex said.

"I might surprise you, husband," Jaimie said as she smiled at him, picked up her suitcase, and turned to walk up the driveway.

Alex handed the driver a tip, picked up the other bags, and followed her up the driveway. He felt warm, almost tingling, at hearing her call him husband.

The porch light was on by the time he reached the doorway. He put down the bags just inside and immediately felt the comfort of the house. Warm shades, gentle patterns and plaids had been mixed together carefully to create a snug, cozy effect.

"The bedrooms are upstairs," Jaimie said as she headed up.

When they reached the second floor landing, Jaimie turned to the right and entered a bedroom. She flipped the light on as Alex entered and put his bags down. The double bed was covered with a hand made quilt and another one rested on the rack over the bed. A cherry desk and a comfortable chair completed the furnishings.

"It's kind of small," Jaimie said.

"As long as I don't have to sleep on a couch I can handle it," Alex said. "Last night was kind of brutal."

"Do you want to see the rest of the upstairs?" Jaimie asked.

"Yes," Alex said.

Jaimie went in the hall, entered the room next to Alex's, and turned on the light. The entire room was paneled in dark cherry and bookshelves lined three walls with most of the fourth wall taken up by a stone fireplace. There was a small couch with two very inviting chairs on either side of the fireplace.

"This would be my favorite spot," Alex said.

"I know, I spend a lot of time in here," Jaimie said.

"Where does that go?" Alex asked as he walked over to a wrought iron circular staircase.

"There's a small room up there," Jaimie said.

Alex began climbing the staircase and Jaimie followed. When he reached the small landing, he saw the telescope that was pointed out the large skylight.

"Wow, what a neat toy," Alex said. "Show me how it works."

"It's hooked into a computer," Jaimie said as she turned on the terminal. "You enter what star or planet you want look at and it automatically points the scope in the right direction."

"I like it," Alex said as he looked through the lens. A few minutes later, he entered a new set of commands and resumed gazing at the stars.

"Alex," Jaimie said but she could tell he wasn't really listening.

"Alex," Jaimie said a little louder.

"Uh, yeah," Alex said.

"I've got to go get Jake," Jaimie said. "I'll be right back."

Alex turned from the lens, looked around the room and noticed for the first time that Jaimie had left. He returned to the study and opened a door that led into another bedroom. It was very large room decorated in shades of navy and tan. The fireplace from the study was a see through so any fire could be seen from both the study and the bedroom. Another quilt covered the massive four poster bed and large picture windows looked out onto the woods behind the house.

Alex heard a noise on the first floor and started down the stairs to find Jaimie. When he reached the bottom, the largest golden retriever he had ever seen was sitting six feet away, watching his every move. The dog turned his head slightly, studying Alex. Alex started to move but stopped immediately when he heard the low growl that began deep in the dog's throat.

"Hi there, big guy," Alex said, but his words only caused the dog to growl louder.

"I guess it's not going to help to tell you I didn't break in," Alex said.

"Jake, where are you?" Jaimie called as Alex heard the back door slam.

"He's in here," Alex called. "You should have told him about me. He's looking at me like I'm lunch."

"Jake, is that any way to greet a guest?" Jaimie asked.

Alex stood there as Jaimie came up behind the dog and roughed up his ears. The dog allowed her to pet him but still kept his eyes fixed on Alex.

"He's not usually this bad with strangers," Jaimie said.

"Hate is not too strong a word," Alex said.

Jaimie walked down the hall with the dog right behind. When she reached Alex, she held his hand so the dog could see her.

"Come on, Jake, he's not that bad," she said gently. "He kind of grows on you after a while."

"Thanks for the endorsement," Alex said.

The dog grudgingly allowed Alex to pet him but he was still jumpy and guarded.

"It's going to take him awhile," Jaimie said.

"Do you have any other pets you want to tell me about?" Alex asked.

"No, technically he's not my dog," Jaimie said, laughing. "My neighbor's son gave him to her, but she's sixty-five and he's a lot of dog for her. He stays over there while I'm working or when I'm out of town. Otherwise, he lives here. Actually, our shared custody works out very well. We both get to have a dog. Ellen gets the break she needs. I take him with me when I run so he gets some exercise."

"I guess I'll check my machine for messages," Jaimie said as she walked over to the phone. The dog followed Jaimie and sat down beside her, still watching Alex.

There were four hang ups, a message from Jaimie's father, and a message from Wendel Garrett, asking Jaimie to phone him regarding a job at Sayer.

Ms. Peterson, Wendel Garrett's secretary, was a tall, thin woman with short gray hair and a practiced, fixed expression. She stood so erect Jaimie checked her own posture as Ms. Peterson led her into Garrett's office. On three sides, huge windows looked out onto the perfectly manicured campus of Sayer Pharmaceuticals. A modern, massive oak desk occupied a space in the middle of the room. Garrett's desk look like a control panel at NASA, with enough screens and keyboards to convince anyone this office belonged to the person who manned the helm.

Jaimie sat down across from Garrett, and Ms. Peterson returned promptly with a tray of assorted pastries and hot coffee. Jaimie accepted the coffee but resisted the pastries.

"If there's nothing else," Ms. Peterson said and left the room.

"I was thrilled when you called me back," Garrett said as he smiled at Jaimie. "You mentioned on the phone you just got back from your honeymoon. Congratulations on your marriage."

"Thank you, Mr. Garrett," Jaimie said as she smiled back.

"I want you to call me Wendel," he said. "I saw Sara McCartland at a fund raiser. I want you to come work for me, Jaimie. I know what you were making at the CDC. If I doubled your salary, would you be interested?"

"That's very generous," Jaimie said. "I wasn't sure what I was going to do next."

"I can throw in some stock options in addition to the salary," Wendel said as he flashed her a charming smile.

"I wasn't trying to ask for more money," Jaimie said as she blushed slightly.

"Well, that's a first," Wendel said, laughing. "Come on, Jaimie. I need someone to finish the work on a new drug called Maxicillin. It will be used to treat strep-A. You've seen how devastating that illness is. Please help us find a treatment."

All Jaimie could think about was the fact she was being handed the dubious gift of yet another guilt trip. The only difference between Alex's and Garrett's was the fact Garrett probably knew how the babies got infected. Jaimie looked into Wendel Garrett's cold blue eyes and thought, "Did he murder the man whose job I'm taking?"

Dismissing the thought, Jaimie said, "I'd like to be part of that."

"I'm probably rushing you, but I need you to start right away," Wendel said. "By the way, I'm having a party Friday night at my estate. I'd like you and your new husband to come."

Jaimie met Alex for lunch after her interview with Wendel Garrett. Alex was sitting at a table in the front and waved to Jaimie as she walked through the door. The restaurant was crowded, noisy, and the waitress took forever to get to their table.

"How did it go?" Alex asked.

"Great," Jaimie said as she sat down across from him in the booth.

"I'll buy lunch," Jaimie said. "Garrett just doubled my salary with stock options thrown in for good measure."

"Wow, he really was anxious to get you," Alex said.

"Yes, he was," Jaimie said. "He wants me to start right away. If we had realized he would be this eager to hire me, we probably could have avoided getting married."

"There was no way to predict how many candidates he was considering for this position," Alex said. "Besides, maybe the fact you were married tipped the scales in your favor."

"I always knew there was more money in the private sector," Jaimie said. "Maybe I should think about a job change when this is over."

"I think you'd better avoid Sayer," Alex said. "If this goes the way we think it will, Sayer might not be a good place to work if Garrett's in jail. What do you think of Garrett?"

"Charming enough when he has to be," Jaimie said. "He used guilt just like you did. I guess that's a guy thing, huh?"

"Maybe," Alex said. "Did you meet Fletcher?"

"He wasn't there," Jaimie said. "I'm supposed to meet with him in the morning. Garrett downplayed the security check. He said it was just a formality."

"That might be a tough interview," Alex said.

"It won't be as bad as the phone call I have to make tonight," Jaimie said.

"What do you mean?" Alex asked.

"I've put it off as long as I can," Jaimie said. "I have to call my father and my aunts and tell them we're married."

Jaimie spent most of the next morning at Sayer filling out the usual paperwork. Fletcher's security questionnaire was extremely thorough, and it took Jaimie over an hour to answer all the questions. When she was finished, Jaimie was ushered into Fletcher's office, which apparently also served as his interrogation room.

The room was comfortably furnished, although considerably smaller than Wendel Garrett's office. Classical music was playing through an elaborate stereo system, and Fletcher rose as she entered. He looked the part of an ex CIA agent, tall and beefy with short, gray hair and a nose that had been rearranged on more than one occasion. But the eyes were guarded, not cold, and he smiled freely as if he knew that surprised people when they met him. Fletcher was careful and asked clever questions, designed to judge veracity; and Jaimie realized immediately he was intelligent.

"Everything in your resume screams caution," he said as he smiled at her. "I hope you don't mind my asking, but your marriage seems totally out of character. Wasn't it kind of sudden?"

"You already called my father?" Jaimie asked as she laughed.

Her answer caught Fletcher off guard for a minute, and then he laughed.

"I'm sorry, I just had this same conversation with him," Jaimie said. "Yes, it was very sudden. Maybe it was the ocean or the sunsets or maybe I'm just having an early mid life crisis. All I know is that when I met Alex it seemed so perfect. I guess time will tell."

After Jaimie finished her interview with Fletcher, he took her on a tour of the entire campus. Even Fletcher's casual dialogue seemed to Jaimie to be an attempt to ask duplicitous questions. Since the only part of her resume that was inaccurate was her marriage to Alex, she decided to answer all his questions spontaneously. Jaimie was tired after her first full day at Sayer, mostly from sparring with Fletcher.

Jake greeted her at her door and she could hear soft music playing while the smell of something wonderful wafted through the house.

"Honey, I'm home," Jaimie called as she walked into the kitchen.

"Hi, I felt like cooking," Alex said as he stopped chopping.

"It smells fabulous," Jaimie said. "You didn't tell me you could cook."

"I might have some surprises for you too, wife," Alex said as he threw a piece of steak to Jake.

"Are you two getting along better?" Jaimie asked.

"He's decided he'd rather eat steak than me," Alex said. "At least for now."

After they finished dinner, they went out on Jaimie's porch and sat on her wide swing. Jake accompanied them, sprawling his huge body on the floor in front of them.

"That was great," Jaimie said. "You're a good cook."

"I have a pretty limited repertoire," Alex said. "How did it go today?"

"Fletcher is very intelligent," Jaimie said. "He asks very carefully worded questions."

"CIA training," Alex said with a worried look on his face.

"Don't worry, Alex," Jaimie said. "I did OK. I knew what was coming."

"It's his job to be suspicious," Alex said. "He's going to be watching you like a hawk."

In a nondescript car parked down the street, Dr. Jekyll watched the couple as they sat on the porch swing talking. They looked innocent enough from a distance, but Dr. Jekyll didn't like additions to the equation. Sudden change always meant trouble, and he would have to watch the newlyweds very carefully.

The huge dog sat up, trying to get his share of attention, and Dr. Jekyll noted the dog's existence. He had a photographic memory, and this was just the sort of detail he would have to remember. If these two turned out to be a problem, he would have to take care of the dog before he could get to them.

Chapter Eleven

Molly Balky was thirty with long brown hair and striking gray eyes. She was standing in her new boss's office at Sayer thinking about beginnings and endings. Her husband's advice from the previous evening flashed through her mind, and she made a resolution to follow it this time. When Molly got nervous, she talked too much. She was determined to chart a different course in the relationship with her new boss.

Dr. McGrath monopolized Molly's thoughts while she straightened up the desk. He had been a difficult supervisor, and if Molly hadn't desperately needed the medical benefits Sayer offered, she would have quit.

One more visual pass and Molly closed the door, hoping Dr. Jaimie Martin would be an improvement. Molly began typing correspondence until an attractive woman with auburn hair and friendly brown eyes approached.

"Hi, I'm Jaimie Carpenter, I mean Jaimie Martin," she said as she extended her hand.

"I'm Molly Balky," she said as she stood up. "I'm your assistant."

"The job from hell," Jaimie said, laughing. "Just kidding."

"I'll show you around," Molly said as she opened Jaimie's door and walked in.

"Wow, this is nice," Jaimie said as she walked into the spacious office. "I came from the CDC. We didn't have offices like this."

"Is there anything I can do for you?" Molly asked as she looked around uncomfortably, determined not to break her resolution.

"Just show me where the coffee is," Jaimie said.

By the end of the day, Molly was grateful for the simple gift fate had handed her. Jaimie was pleasant and had a sense of humor, so Molly decided this one was a keeper.

Jaimie felt comfortable having Molly as her assistant though Molly seemed quiet and reserved. For the first several days, Jaimie reviewed the mountain of research material relating to Maxicillin. She tried to balance the reason she was there with her fascination about the possibility of finding a treatment for newborn pneumonia.

The Sayer computer system was cumbersome, and there were areas Jaimie couldn't access. She decided the first order of business was to understand what Sayer produced so she could come up with a list of possible products that could have been contaminated.

When Jaimie read the research data on Maxicillin she found references to alternate proposals that had been authored by Dr. Terry White. She asked Molly to get them for her. Three days later, Molly brought in a stack of printouts. Molly was frowning when she handed them to Jaimie and was about to do her usual quick retreat.

"Molly, why are you frowning?" Jaimie asked.

"Dr. White wasn't very happy about giving me these," Molly said.

"Why?" Jaimie asked.

"I don't know," Molly said as she turned to leave.

"Molly, sit down," Jaimie commanded as Molly complied. "Now, why do you think she didn't want to give them to you?"

"I'd be guessing," Molly said.

"Then guess, Molly," Jaimie said with exasperation. "I'm new here. I don't want to step on anybody's toes, so I need your help to understand things. Talk to me, Molly."

"Are you sure?" Molly asked.

"Yes," Jaimie said.

"Dr. McGrath didn't like any of Dr. White's ideas," Molly said. "I heard him tell her to keep her ideas to herself."

"They didn't get along?" Jaimie asked.

"That would be putting it mildly," Molly said.

"Did Dr. McGrath report directly to Wendel Garrett?" Jaimie asked.

"Yes, at least for the last year," Molly said. "Before that, he worked in quality assurance."

"How long did he work in quality assurance?" Jaimie asked.

"For ten years," Molly said. "He had a hard time changing that mentality. You know how quality assurance people are. They have a set of rules and it's their job to make sure those rules are followed. McGrath would crawl up your ass with a microscope to see which ones you violated and spare no effort to inform you of each and every violation. Oh, I'm sorry. I shouldn't have said that."

"That's OK," Jaimie said as she laughed and stared at this new Molly.

"McGrath wasn't very friendly," Molly said. "He wasn't flexible. I shouldn't be saying this. I always talk too much."

"Was McGrath close to anyone here at Sayer?" Jaimie asked.

"Not really," Molly said. "He worked strange hours. He wasn't a morning person and usually didn't come in until the afternoon. Actually, I guess I liked that. There I go again. My husband tells me I talk too much. I was doing so well, too."

"Why did McGrath leave?" Jaimie asked, pretending she didn't know the answer.

"He was murdered," Molly said. "He was the victim of a car jacking and they killed him."

"That's terrible," Jaimie said.

"Yes, it was," Molly agreed.

"Did he seem OK before he was killed?" Jaimie asked.

"Now that you mention it, he was acting strange," Molly said. "He was so nervous all the time. I could tell he was upset. He went to see Garrett a couple of times that last week."

"Did he say anything about what was bothering him?" Jaimie asked.

"No, I tried to ask him but he said it was better if I didn't know," Molly said.

"Is there anybody else he might have confided in?" Jaimie asked.

"I don't think so," Molly said. "Why are you so interested in Dr. McGrath?"

"Just curious about my predecessor," Jaimie said.

Luke Harper looked out the window of his Atlanta hotel room at the lush green plants planted in the courtyard. Harper hadn't conquered his paranoia, but he felt he had it under control. Fifteen years ago, suspicious panic would have left his palms moist with perspiration, his breathing slightly ragged, and the smiles of strangers a source of terror. These days, he managed to disguise most of those reactions.

Solitude had been Luke Harper's constant companion as a child, and to him it felt comforting, unlike the terror of being around other children. Peers were always a problem to be dealt with, and Luke was frequently taunted for some manufactured sin. Alone, surrounded mostly by silence, no one could hurt him. Science was Luke's passion, a passion that was stronger than his mistrust of others and enabled him to go to college and graduate school.

The hallucinations began after graduate school, and Luke started to withdraw even more. By the time he had been at Stanford for several years, Luke's reputation as an outstanding researcher outweighed any concerns about his personality quirks. By the time Luke finished the research and two years of treatment, he was ready for a change.

Wendel Garrett, aware Luke was a brilliant researcher, was ready to promise him anything to get him to work at Sayer. Luke decided he wanted to have his lab on Jekyll Island, so he gave Garrett an ultimatum. It seemed like the ideal place for Luke to have the seclusion he still needed.

Luke's first coup at Sayer had been the development of a new home pregnancy test that was easier to use and more accurate than any other. When it was introduced, it immediately took over the market and the other drug companies could hardly wait for Sayer's patent to expire.

Garrett invited Luke to come to Atlanta to discuss his current project and attend Garrett's party that would include Sayer stockholders and potential investors. Luke understood this was a command performance so Garrett could parade him around the party like a prized heifer. Luke would let him. He still needed the Sayer umbrella, at least until he finished the research Garrett knew nothing about. That was another advantage of solitude; it gave Harper the opportunity to do his research without meddling assistants getting in his way.

The phone rang, and Luke picked up the receiver. The desk clerk informed him the limo that was to take him to Sayer had arrived. Half an hour later, Luke was sitting in Garrett's office, waiting to meet Charley McGrath's replacement. Luke had come full circle. At thirty-eight, he had outgrown the thin, awkward boy he once was. He had gained weight and looked fit. A stylist now cut the unkempt blond hair and he wore contacts instead of the thick glasses. Luke took great care when he shopped for clothes, and he found it ironic that women found his new style and wardrobe irresistible.

Ms. Peterson buzzed, and after Garrett answered, Jaimie entered the room. She wore a black pantsuit with a blue sweater underneath. Both Luke and Garrett stood when Jaimie approached.

"Jaimie Martin, I'd like you to meet Luke Harper," Wendel Garrett said.

"We've met before," Jaimie said.

"We have?" Luke Harper asked. "I'm sorry, I don't think that's possible. I would have remembered you."

"Thank you," Jaimie said. "We met about ten years ago at a conference at Stanford."

The Luke Harper Jaimie remembered was thin, awkward, and wore ill fitting clothes. She was amazed by the transformation as she looked at the tall, well-built man who stood before her with a gleam in his blue eyes.

Dr. Terry White was sitting in Jaimie Martin's office, waiting to speak with her new manager. White felt bitter she had been passed over again while someone with less ability had been given the job that should be hers. Pecking orders and kissing ass were all familiar tasks to anyone intent on climbing the company ladder, but Terry White lacked the ability to perform them. Terry understood the consequences for not observing proprieties; she had been fired from three jobs as a result of her bad attitude. Too stubborn to change, she came to Sayer with the same chip on her shoulder.

At forty-five, White looked to be in her late thirties with a firm body, brown eyes, and black hair. If someone caught a glimpse of White with a smile on her face, they would consider her attractive, but she seldom allowed such a public display. Underneath that facade, she was a surprisingly passionate woman.

White guarded her research carefully and was determined to make Maxicillin a viable option in the treatment of newborn pneumonia. Terry White considered all her bosses administrators who would only get in her way. Fortunately, Terry realized she couldn't go around them, so she tried to put up with their management in order to get the job done.

The door finally opened, and a breathless Jaimie walked into the office followed closely by Molly, who was in the process of giving Jaimie all her messages.

"They called from personnel," Molly said. "You have to get your tax forms in ASAP. Oh, your husband called. He wants you to call him back."

"Thanks, Molly," Jaimie said. "I'll call them all back. I'm sorry, Dr. White. Command performance in Garrett's office."

Terry White's response was a resigned nod.

"He wanted me to meet Luke Harper," Jaimie said. "Have you met him?"

"Yes, I met him about a year ago," Terry White said as she looked away uncomfortably. Jaimie had the distinct feeling there was some history there, and she didn't think it was pleasant judging by the look of pain that appeared briefly on Terry White's face.

"Have you had a chance to look over the data yet?" Terry White asked, changing the subject and ending any further discussion about Luke Harper.

"Yes, I have," Jaimie said. "Did Dr. McGrath ever see this?"

"No, he didn't consider it relevant," Terry said.

"Did you ask him about adding an inhibitor to the formula?" Jaimie said.

"I asked, but he rejected the idea," Terry White said.

"Why?" Jaimie asked.

"Dr. McGrath was very careful," Terry said. "He didn't want to change anything that drastically. We kept trying different strengths of the original formula and got mild sensitivity results, so he wanted to keep trying that approach."

"I want you to try the inhibitor and see if it makes a difference," Jaimie said. "I've reviewed all the data, and I think it's worth a shot."

Something very close to a smile played at the corners of Terry White's lips, and she stayed for another hour to discuss the research. As Terry White was about to leave, Alex called again. Molly stuck her head in the door, unsure if she should interrupt.

"I'm sorry, it's your husband again," Molly said. "He really wants to talk to you."

"I'll get out of your way," Terry White said as she left.

"Alex, I'm sorry," Jaimie said. "It's been crazy here."

"I just wanted to catch you before you left," he said. "I thought you might like to meet me for dinner."

"That sounds good," Jaimie said. "Did you have someplace in mind?"

"How about Garfield's in an hour?" Alex asked.

"OK, I'll see you there," Jaimie said as she hung up and Molly stuck her head in the door of the office.

"I'm outta here," Molly said. "See you tomorrow."

"Molly, were Terry White and Luke Harper ever an item?" Jaimie asked.

"Where did you get that idea?" Molly asked.

"My radar picked it up," Jaimie said. "How is it functioning?"

"Very well," Molly said. "When they were building Harper's lab on Jekyll Island, he stayed here in Atlanta. I worked late one night and caught them doing some, you know, research together. It made me horny just watching them. Not that I watched that long or anything. Oh, you know what I mean."

Jaimie arrived first and the young waiter brought her a glass of wine and lingered a long time to talk with her. She found him impossibly cute, much too young, but enjoyed the flirting. Alex finally arrived and he could tell the waiter was disappointed.

"So, you were flirting with my wife?" Alex asked as he sat down and smiled at the young man.

"Just talking with her, sir," the waiter said nervously.

"I understand," Alex said.

The waiter took Alex's drink order and left immediately.

"How was your day?" Alex asked after he left.

"Very busy," Jaimie said. "I met Luke Harper today."

"Is he like you remembered him?" Alex asked.

"No, actually he's changed," Jaimie said. "He looks a lot better. I didn't remember him being very attractive, but he seems to have undergone a transformation."

"He's not paranoid anymore?" Alex asked.

"I guess not," Jaimie said. "He's pretty reclusive. He has a lab on Jekyll Island and only comes to Atlanta for meetings. You'll get to meet him at the party tomorrow night."

"I'm still doing background investigations on all these people," Alex said.

"My chief research doc, Terry White, had a thing with Harper," Jaimie said.

"How did you find that out?" he asked.

"A little tidbit from Molly," Jaimie said.

"I thought she was quiet," Alex said.

"That's what I thought until today," Jaimie said. "I asked her to talk to me about McGrath and Terry White. All of a sudden, she just spilled her guts."

"Do you think Terry White is involved in this?" Alex asked.

"I don't know," Jaimie said. "McGrath gave her bad performance reviews, but I think he just didn't like her. I've read her ideas and she has great research instincts. Isn't it ironic the company responsible for infecting thousands of mothers might also come up with an antibiotic to treat those infections?"

"Do you think that's possible?"

"Definitely," Jaimie said. "Maybe we'll get Garrett and a treatment."

"Don't forget why you're in there, Jaimie," Alex cautioned.

"I know," Jaimie said. "It's just hard not to want to find a treatment."

"What did Molly say about McGrath?" Alex asked

"Nobody liked him," Jaimie said. "He reported directly to Garrett, so I don't think he told anyone else about the contamination."

"Everything seems to point to Garrett, doesn't it?"

"Yes," Jaimie said.

Rudy Fletcher sat in Wendel Garrett's office, drinking two fingers of Wendel's best bourbon, waiting for Garrett to return. When Garrett came in a few minutes later, Rudy poured them both a drink.

"What do you think about Jaimie?" Garrett asked.

"She seems OK as far as I can tell," Fletcher said. "I think the marriage is out of character, but she answered all the questions satisfactorily."

"You're too suspicious," Wendel said as he sipped his drink.

"That's what you said about Charley McGrath," Fletcher said.

"Point taken," Wendel said.

"I'll do some more digging," Rudy said. "She's bringing her husband to the party tomorrow night, isn't she?"

"Yes, I was very specific about including him when I invited her."

"Good, I want to get a take on him," Fletcher said. "I think a little test for the newlyweds is definitely in order."

Chapter Twelve

Wendel Garrett stood in the shower, changing the settings on the head so the hard spray might relieve the stiffness in his neck and back muscles. He thought about the party, which was a celebration of the success Sayer had enjoyed for the last three years. Wendel Garrett had waited twenty-five years to prove he was a better CEO than Garth Sayer, and nothing was going to spoil his continued success.

Luke Harper had been Wendel's key to success. Garth Sayer, weakened from a stroke for several years before his death, had warned against hiring someone with Harper's jaded psychological history, but Wendel prevailed. The success of the Sayer home pregnancy test validated Wendel's decision.

Poverty was the enduring legacy of Wendel's childhood, so the acquisition of wealth and power were the primary forces that drove him. Growing up in the Atlanta area, Wendel heard stories of Jekyll Island and how some of the wealthiest families in America once lived there. Wendel became obsessed with acquiring land on the island.

It proved to be a difficult proposition. When later generations of wealthy families lost interest in the island, it was sold to the state of Georgia in 1947. Wendel had been forced to hand over a huge block of

Sayer stock to bribe a congressman to sponsor a bill that would open up parts of Jekyll Island to private interests. The property Wendel acquired on the island was where he built his second home.

Luke Harper had shocked Garrett when he requested laboratory facilities on the island. After Harper made extreme salary concessions to get his wish, Garrett reluctantly agreed. It had been three years and Wendel was pleased with the arrangement. Since he seldom saw Harper, he didn't have to deal with any of Harper's psychological problems.

Tonight, they would all bask in the glow of the Sayer success story. Wendel finally got out of the shower, dressed, and went to find his wife, Margo, to discuss the final preparations for the evening.

Carol Fletcher, Rudy's quiet, withdrawn wife, worked as a secretary for a construction company. Blond and petite with unusual green eyes, Carol had worked for her employer for almost twenty years. Carol dreaded the command performance that would be required tonight at Wendel Garrett's party. The last time Garrett had a party, Rudy drank too much and Carol had a difficult time trying to squeeze him into the passenger seat of his truck.

By the time Carol got home she was tired, Rudy was snoring loudly, and she just didn't feel like dragging his sorry ass out of the truck. So Carol left him there with his face plastered against the window of the passenger side, his saliva forming a little stream as it slowly flowed down the side of the glass.

The next morning, Carol woke up to Rudy's first punch which broke her nose, causing a torrent of blood to explode from both nostrils. The blood made Rudy's already unsettled stomach lurch, and he ran into the bathroom.

Carol had given up control over her life so long ago it simply didn't occur to her she had options. The person she once was fled the scene after being married to Rudy Fletcher for two years, replaced by someone who found it easier to take the path of least resistance. Carol Fletcher just went through the motions, trying to avoid her next inevitable failure that would require Rudy's verbal and physical correction.

Several members of White's team stormed into Jaimie's office and were threatening to quit. Molly left the agitated pair sitting in the outer office with their arms folded in silent, stony protest while she went in to break the news to Jaimie.

"Two of Terry White's assistants just stormed in here," Molly said as she approached Jaimie.

"What's wrong?" Jaimie asked.

"They said they couldn't work with her," Molly said. "They want to talk to you or they're gonna walk."

"They're threatening to quit?"

"That's what they said after I got them calmed down," Molly said. "I can't tell you what they said they were going to do to White when they first got here."

"I guess you'd better have them come in," Jaimie said.

Two hours later, after a long discussion with Terry White, a truce and negotiated settlement were in place. Jaimie already had a headache and could barely hope the peace would last. For the first time that morning, Jaimie was alone in her office when the phone rang.

"Jaimie Martin," she said.

"Good morning, wife," Alex said.

"Hi," Jaimie said uncertainly.

"Is that any way to greet your better half?" Alex asked.

"Probably not," Jaimie said.

"I missed you, Jaimie," Alex said. "It's been a long time since I kissed you good bye this morning."

"Yes, it has," Jaimie said tentatively.

"I want you to meet me," Alex said. "I'm in room 209 at the Doubletree Hotel right down the street from Sayer."

"There's a lot going on here," Jaimie said. "I was going to leave early today. You know, because of the party tonight, remember?"

"I know, but I'm a hopeless romantic," Alex said. "I just can't seem to get enough of you."

"I truly don't know what to say," Jaimie said, laughing.

"Say you'll come," Alex said. "There are places I've been neglecting to kiss lately, wife. I have a bottle of champagne on ice. I'll be waiting for you."

The lobby at the Doubletree was crowded with guests and employees. Jaimie walked to the bank of elevators and took one to the second floor, curious about the purpose of this meeting. Jaimie paused at the door to room 209 and then knocked.

"Hi wife," Alex said as he opened the door and Jaimie entered the room.

"What's this about?" Jaimie asked as she looked at Alex.

"I got a phone call this morning from Sara," Alex said as he stepped back.

"I needed to talk with you," Sara said as she came forward.

"I wasn't sure what to think when you called," Jaimie said as she looked at Alex.

"We have to assume your phone at Sayer is bugged." Alex said. "If it is, they'll think you're having incredible sex with your husband right now."

"Instead of incredible sex and champagne," Sara said as she handed Jaimie her lunch with a smile on her face. "Alex got you a sub and a diet Coke."

"Sometimes in life you're better off not responding," Jaimie said as she looked at both of them. "What's going on?"

"Dave's team has finished their preliminary study of newborn pneumonia," Sara said. "Their conclusion from the studies they've done so far is that the mothers were infected vaginally. I brought the print outs so you could look at them. This should help you narrow the focus of what products might have been contaminated."

Margo Garrett was fifty-two with blond hair. Thin, rich, and fit, Margo could feel herself reaching a point in her life where she would have to make a decision. All the excuses she had used over the years to stay married to Wendel time had erased or she had stopped giving them the importance they had never earned in the first place.

Shortly after the birth of their second son, Margo began to suspect Wendel was having an affair. One night, after the nanny put the boys to bed, Wendel told her he had to go back to work, so Margo followed him. The road to Sayer was lined with small businesses and fast food restaurants, but the road to Wendel's mistress's house was dotted with dark, lonely roads Wendel negotiated with practiced haste.

A trust fund and prenuptial agreement left Margo with money of her own, so the private detective she hired quickly determined Wendel had known this woman for several years.

Denial and the endless minutia of the childhood of her two sons replaced the relationship she thought she had with Wendel. In her more honest moments, Margo understood Wendel needed her so he could erase the memories of poverty, but she also realized he didn't love her.

By the time the boys reached high school, Margo looked at the world through the next bottle of whatever brand of liquor she chose to crawl into that day. Margo couldn't remember those years with any degree of clarity. Time just sort of floated by on a river of booze.

It was Garth Sayer's stroke that jolted her back to reality, but she didn't understand why that event had such a profound impact on her. Perhaps it was that the polite, superficial, restrained relationship she had with her father was so similar to the one she had with Wendel. Those words accurately described the characteristics of both liaisons, but they were no substitute for the passion, joy, or even anger that would have been some tangible proof to Margo that either man possessed deeply held feelings for her.

Whatever the cause, by sheer force of will, Margo simply put away the bottle the day after her father had his stroke. She realized her cold turkey withdrawal could be eased with the help of medication, but she felt if she experienced every cold sweat, every uncontrollable shaking episode, and every terror-filled nightmare, she could atone for the painful effects her addiction had on her sons.

Margo didn't sleep for three weeks, barely able to cope with the frequent sweats and the inability to stop shaking. After that, she embarked on a period of physical recovery, trying to allow her body the time it needed to heal. Even then, Margo understood there would come a time when she would have to deal with the rest of her baggage.

The Sayer's second son, Bradley, had finally left home for college, so Margo was free for the first time to think about personal goals. She was no longer terrified and finally learning to live one day at a time. Margo dialed the number of the caterer to make sure the timeframes they had discussed for this evening's event were still appropriate.

Jaimie stood in her bedroom and looked at herself in the mirror, trying to spot any major problems with her appearance. The dress was short, black, and fit her curves in all the right places. She had taken extra care with her hair and make-up and was pleased with the overall effect. Jaimie tried to put the necklace around her neck but couldn't close the clasp despite multiple attempts.

Alex's shirt collar was a little tight and he tried to stretch it a bit as he checked the knot of his tie in the mirror that hung on the wall in Jaimie's living room.

"Alex, could you help me with this necklace?" Jaimie asked as she came into the room.

"Jaimie, you look gorgeous," Alex said as he smiled.

"Thank you," Jaimie said as she came up to Alex, handed him the necklace, and turned around so he could put it on her neck.

Alex had a hard time getting his fingers to complete the task his brain commanded. His senses were bombarded with the smell of Jaimie's hair and the way the dress she wore hinted at but didn't expose the best parts of her figure.

"Finally," Alex said as he hooked the necklace. "The clasp doesn't fit right."

"I know, I need to get it fixed," Jaimie said.

"I guess we should go," Alex said.

The night was dark, cloudless, and somewhat cool but the air smelled of spring; of young, tender plants trying to break free of their winter prison. Alex guided the car through the light traffic.

"Jaimie, remember they think we just got married," Alex said. "We need to hold hands and act like we really care about each other. How did it go after you went back this afternoon?"

"I looked up all the products Sayer makes that are used vaginally," Jaimie said. "Then I got all the data concerning the production facilities and copied all of it onto a disk. When we get together with Sara on Sunday, we can enter all the data into the CDC computer."

"It's a good thing Sara has a terminal at home," Alex said.

"Well, here we are," Alex said as he pulled the car up the circular drive.

Two young, handsome valets approached on both sides of the car, opening the doors and taking Alex's keys while they stared at Jaimie. The car disappeared quickly as Alex walked over to Jaimie and put her hand in his; they began to walk toward the brightly-lighted manse of Wendel Garrett.

The butler at the door smiled stiffly and gestured them toward a path that led into the large, open living room. A live band played a familiar tune while the guests milled about. Wendel Garrett appeared magically out of the crowd, accompanied by an attractive blond woman.

"Jaimie, I'm so glad you could come," Wendel Garrett said. "This must be your husband."

"Yes, this is my husband, Alex Martin," Jaimie said.

"Nice to meet you," Alex said as he extended his free hand to Garrett.

"The pleasure is mine," Wendel Garrett said as he shook hands with Alex. "I'd like you to meet my wife, Margo."

At that moment, the band began playing a much louder song so smiles served as replies. Wendel exchanged additional pleasantries, and then he and Margo began to work the rest of the room with practiced expertise.

Luke Harper came alone and looked somewhat uncomfortable. When he spotted Jaimie, he came over immediately to talk to her. Luke smiled when he noticed Alex felt the need to put his arm around Jaimie as if that were some signal to Luke she was his possession. A few minutes later, Alex asked Jaimie to dance.

"Why did you put your arm around me when Luke came up?" Jaimie asked as they moved slowly around the room.

"I decided to act like I would if we really were married," Alex said as he looked into Jaimie's eyes. "If you were mine, I'd never let another man anywhere near you."

Uncomfortable silence danced with them until the song ended and Alex left to find the men's room. Before the band could strike up another song, Wendel approached and began speaking into the microphone.

"I'd like to interrupt for a moment," Wendel said. "A speech is mandatory on an occasion like this. I'll try to keep it brief."

"I need to talk to you," Rudy Fletcher said as he walked up to Jaimie.

"OK," Jaimie said.

"I was hoping we could go out on the patio," Rudy said. "I need a cigarette."

Rudy led the way, and his gait was slightly unsteady, making Jaimie somewhat apprehensive. The patio was far away from the party and Wendel's speech. They stopped near the stone wall that formed the boundary.

"What did you want to talk to me about?" Jaimie asked.

"I wanted to ask you some more questions," Rudy said as looked intently into Jaimie's eyes.

"What kind of questions?" Jaimie asked suspiciously.

"I want to know what it would be like to fuck you?" Rudy asked as he grabbed Jaimie's arms and put them behind her back, his breath reeking of alcohol.

Jaimie's breathing ceased and then came in quick, shocked gasps as she stared into Fletcher's eyes. Surprise, a measure of fear, and finally rage appeared in her eyes. She began to struggle against his hold.

"You'll never know," Jaimie said. "Let go of me right now, Fletcher."

"How about a kiss?" Fletcher asked as he leaned over while Jaimie turned her head to avoid contact.

"Take your hands off my wife, Fletcher," Alex said angrily.

Fletcher complied reluctantly, turned and stared at Alex, who was so angry Jaimie could see a vein throbbing dangerously on the side of his face. Alex stared back into Fletcher's eyes, ready to attack if threatened or encouraged. The look of murderous rage on Alex's face scared Jaimie, and left her hoping Alex would never direct a similar expression at her.

Chapter Thirteen

Margo Garrett and Carol Fletcher, desperate for a cigarette, arrived at the front door at the same time, holding their cigarettes and lighters.

"Great minds," Margo said, laughing.

"Something like that," Carol said.

They walked around the side of the house until they reached the patio where they decided to stop and light up near several tall bushes.

"Wendel hates it when I smoke in the house," Margo said as she lit their cigarettes.

"Rudy hates the fact I smoke at all," Carol said. "We've had several intense discussions about it."

"It's the only addiction I have left," Margo said as she inhaled deeply. "Rudy's been with Sayer for three years. It seems strange we've never escaped and talked at one of these affairs until tonight."

"I guess it's just fate," Carol said.

That next deep drag had barely reached their lungs when they saw Rudy and Jaimie walk out on the patio. Darkness and the shrubbery made it impossible for Rudy or Jaimie to see them. Margo and Carol watched the scene unfold in stunned silence, taking quick, intense puffs on their cigarettes.

After Rudy released his hold on Jaimie, she immediately went over to Alex, who put his arms around her protectively. The stand off continued until Wendel came out on the patio.

"What's going on?" Wendel asked.

"Your security chief can't keep his hands to himself," Alex said.

Wendel looked at Rudy, who merely looked away without commenting.

"Consider yourself on probation, Rudy," Wendel said. "Jaimie, Alex, I'm sorry this happened."

"I don't think probation is a strong enough punishment," Alex said.

"I promise you I will deal with this," Wendel said. "Rudy won't bother you again. Isn't that right, Rudy?"

"That's right," Rudy said, his speech slightly slurred.

"I really am sorry," Wendel said as he walked up to Jaimie and Alex and escorted them to the door. "Please let me handle this. Rudy has a drinking problem we're trying to deal with. Please try to understand. I'm going to stay out here and explain to him I won't tolerate any more behavior like this."

"Just keep him away from Jaimie," Alex said, moderating his tone.

"I promise," Wendel said as he watched Alex and Jaimie walk into the house.

Garrett walked over to Rudy, who was sitting on the stone wall, looking a lot less inebriated now that Jaimie and Alex were gone.

"What do you think?" Garrett asked.

"She was surprised at first," Rudy said. "Then there was fire and passion in her eyes. I really do want to know what it would be like to fuck her."

"That's not what I meant," Wendel said distastefully.

"I know," Rudy said, laughing. "She may be pretty much what she seems to be. I think we're looking at the wrong person. It's Alex we'd better check out. When he saw me trying to kiss her, he looked at me like he wanted to kill me."

"If he really loves her that wouldn't be an unusual reaction," Wendel said.

"Except for the fact he's supposed to be a computer salesman," Rudy said. "I know he's killed before."

"How do you know that?" Garrett asked.

"I could see it in his eyes," Rudy said as they walked back toward the house.

Neither Carol nor Margo said anything until after Rudy and Wendel left. It was Margo who finally broke the silence, but she took two more deep drags off her second cigarette before she spoke.

"I give up," Margo said. "What the hell was that all about?"

"I don't have a clue," Carol said.

"I hate to be the one to break this to you, Carol," Margo said. "Your husband is a pig. I know that because my husband is also a pig, and they're up to their eyeballs in something bad."

Jaimie stopped in the hallway just outside the living room. Alex pulled her close and wrapped his arms around her, very aware she was still shaking.

"Are you OK, Jaimie?" he asked quietly.

"Yes, I was surprised more than anything else," Jaimie said.

"Fletcher is a pig," Alex said.

"I think there's more to it than that," Jaimie said. "The whole thing doesn't feel right."

"What do you mean?" he asked.

"I don't think he was that drunk," Jaimie said. "It seemed like a test of some kind."

"To check out our reactions?" he asked.

"I guess," Jaimie said. "I thought you were going to punch him out for a minute there."

"I was tempted," Alex said. "When I saw him pawing you like that, I wanted to kill him."

"I could tell," Jaimie said as she moved back slightly to look into Alex's eyes. "It wouldn't be the first time you killed someone, would it, Alex?"

"No," Alex said quietly.

Sunday morning dawned clear and sunny with a temperature in the seventies. Plants that had threatened to bloom for the last week suddenly seemed to find the will as a light breeze blew them back and forth.

The man waited down the street from Jaimie's house in a black Taurus. When Jaimie and Jake left for their early morning run, he decided to stay where he was. Forty-five minutes later, he saw them coming back. The dog's tongue kept dropping out of his mouth as if he had lost control of it sometime during their run.

An hour later, the garage door opened and the red Acura moved slowly down the driveway. The man noticed Jaimie, Alex, and the dog were all in the car so he started the engine and pulled in behind them at a discreet distance.

"Did you have any problem getting access to the production information?" Alex asked.

"No, Sayer doesn't really try to protect information that's a matter of public record," Jaimie said. "Fletcher has beefed up security in the areas that have to do with research and development. The security in my building is really tight. At this point, I can't get access to anything that isn't related to Maxicillin."

"Fletcher had a drinking problem when he was with the CIA," Alex said.

"How did you find that out?" Jaimie asked.

"I called in a favor from a friend," Alex said. "It's possible he was just drunk and obnoxious the other night."

"Maybe so," Jaimie said.

Alex took a sudden right turn and then accelerated at a rapid pace, aware Jaimie was staring at him.

"That car's been behind us for a while," Alex said as he negotiated a sharp turn to the left.

"I don't want to take a chance we're being followed," he said. "It would look odd you stormed out of the CDC after a fight with Sara and then we show up at her house."

Alex took several more quick turns, and when he was satisfied no one was following him, he got on the highway to complete the trip to Sara's house.

The man in the Taurus tried to follow until he realized Alex was trying to shake any possible tail. After the third sudden turn, the man gave up the chase, pulled the Taurus over to the side of the road, and called his superior.

Cori Dalton looked out the glass doors of Atlanta's St. Francis Hospital emergency room, admiring the bank of yellow tulips on the side of the hill. The noise escalated as the chopper approached, and Cori watched it land.

The flight nurse opened the door, climbed out, and smiled at Cori.

"Hi, stranger," she said. "There's a full moon this weekend."

"Don't remind me, Danny," Cori said. "What have we got?"

"MVA," Danny said. "He was going the wrong way down I-65 and hit another car. Forty-five year old with a comminuted right tib and fib fracture. Wouldn't be surprised if he had a couple of busted ribs, too. Vitals stable."

"I want something for pain, dammit," the man on the stretcher screamed.

"You'll need a tox screen and blood alcohol level," Danny said as she smiled at Cori.

Trauma room 1 was Gary King's first stop along his road to recovery. His initial exam, x-rays, labs, and intravenous insertion were all completed while he screamed for pain medication. The staff kept trying to explain he couldn't get anything for pain until they knew what drugs were in his system. Gary King couldn't seem to remember the names of those he washed down with the alcohol he had consumed.

While Cori Dalton waited for the results of King's labs, she went into the second trauma room where Carol Fletcher was lying on the treatment table. Carol was waiting for the results of her x-rays. The films were taken to determine if Rudy had fractured any of Carol's ribs during his latest beating.

Cori sat down next to Carol and pulled the treatment tray over so she could clean Carol's right arm and right eye, where several angry lacerations were visible. Cori opened the surgical pack, put the latex gloves on, and poured betadine into the metal container.

"Do you want to talk about it, Carol?" Cori asked as she began to clean the wounds.

"There's no point," Carol said as she looked away. "You'll just ask me how I could let him do this to me, and why don't I leave him?"

"It's hard for me to admit I was ever that stupid or insensitive," Cori said. "I guess there was a time when I might have said that. I've been working in the emergency room for fifteen years. Now I understand that abuse is both a process and a cycle. For the abuser, it's the repetition of a pattern they learned as a child. For us women, Carol, it's a process in which a strong woman gets lost because she wants to try to do everything possible to fix or hold together a relationship. That strong woman is still inside you somewhere, Carol. She's just hiding in there, and we have to find a way to reach her. I don't want you think about where you need to end up. Today, just think about taking one step. You have to start talking to somebody, Carol. You need to share your feelings with someone."

"It's easier not to," Carol said as the tears welled up.

"It just seems like that because you haven't tried for such a long time," Cori said. "Think about someone I can call for you. Someone you feel you can talk to."

Cori removed her gloves, threw them on the tray, and moved it out of the way. Without saying a word, she sat down next to Carol and put Carol's hand in hers. Carol just stared at Cori's hand, and then she started to cry, the tears quickly turning into uncontrollable sobs as Cori held her.

Jake ran up the steps to Sara's house, unwilling to wait for Jaimie or Alex so he could get Sara's undivided attention. Sara came out before they reached the door and began to pet Jake.

"You're spoiling him," Jaimie said.

"That's my job," Sara said as they all went into the house.

Sara led Jaimie and Alex into her first floor office, followed by Jake. The doors to the terrace were open, allowing a gentle breeze to flow through the room. Sara's elaborate garden, visible through the open doors, represented the other passion in her life.

"This is beautiful," Alex said as he stared at the garden from the doorway.

"I find it very therapeutic to work out here after spending all day in an office," Sara said as she walked over to stand next to Alex. "My one creative impulse."

"It's worth the effort," Alex said as he smiled at Sara. "Is there anything I can do to help?"

"Not at the moment," Sara said. "We'll probably need to brainstorm later. We'll reach a point where we'll get stuck and need a fresh mind."

"Why don't I take Jake outside?" Alex asked.

"Good idea," Sara said.

"Where should we start, Jaimie?" Sara asked as she sat down, turned on the computer, and accessed the database at the CDC.

"Let's get into Dave's testing results," Jaimie said as she sat down beside Sara. "Then we can add the information I got from Sayer."

"The team was able to match the symptomology and clinical course exactly as soon as they introduced the strep-A vaginally," Sara said. "There were major differences with the clinical course when they tried other modes of transmission."

"Sayer produces a wide range of possible sources," Jaimie said as she entered the product list into the database. "They make pregnancy tests, condoms, IUD's, spermicides, diaphragms, and then there is a whole range of prescription drugs that are available for use vaginally."

The afternoon waned as they continued to correlate data, only stopping briefly when Jake and Alex came in with a snack and drinks.

"How's it going?" Alex asked.

"Slow and very frustrating," Jaimie said.

"Are you sure you can figure out what was contaminated this way?" Alex asked.

"The answer is here," Jaimie said. "We just need to think of the right question to ask the computer."

"Why don't we go back into the stats?" Sara asked. "Then we can look at the percentage of infected newborns in relation to the total number of births. We can use the projection for the market share that Sayer holds."

A few minutes later, the computer began to spit out the data as they all crowded around Sara's terminal.

"We've eliminated all the prescription drugs," Sara said. "Sayer doesn't have big enough share of that market."

"What's left?" Alex asked.

"All the birth control products," Jaimie said.

"And the tampons and douche products," Sara said.

They entered frequent commands into the computer, but nothing seemed to provide the answer. Frustrated and hungry, they decided to take a break to fix dinner.

The pace in the emergency room declined, and Cori Dalton was relieved. Her scheduled twelve-hour shift was all she could tolerate today. Gary King was still waiting in a trauma room, but this time it was for the orthopedic surgeon, who was on his way to the hospital. Gary's fractures were going to require surgery to repair the shattered bones. King remained obnoxious, threatening, and had kicked or punched several members of the staff.

"Good news, Gary," Cori said as she entered the room.

"Yeah, what?" Gary asked.

"Dr. Taylor said I could give you a pain shot," Cori said.

"Well, where the fuck is it?" Gary asked.

"First things first, Gary," Cori said. "You're going to be a patient here for a while so we're going to attempt a little behavior modification on you. In order to get your pain shot, there are three things you're going to have to remember."

"Or else what?" Gary asked nastily.

"Or else you better hope the syringe with Demerol in it grows legs, walks in here and jumps on your butt, because that's the only way you'll get it."

"I'll do anything," Gary finally said quietly.

"I want you to remember the family you hit while you were driving the wrong way on the highway is in as much pain as you are," Cori said. "The second thing you have to remember is not to kick or punch any of the staff who work here. Are you still with me, Gary?"

"Yeah," he said weakly.

"Now for the third thing," Cori said as she leaned over and looked Gary King squarely in the eyes. "Don't ever call me a fucking cunt again."

"I've been a real asshole, huh," Gary said timidly.

"Yes, you have, Gary," Cori said as she pulled the syringe out of her pocket and gave Gary the injection.

"Try to remember we're just trying to help you," Cori said.

"I will," Gary said.

"That's a lot better, Gary," Cori said. "You might just be trainable after all."

Cori paused at the door, walked into the hall, and almost ran into a blond woman who looked as if she would rather be anywhere but the emergency room at St. Francis.

"I'm looking for Cori," she said.

"I'm Cori," she said. "You must be Margo Garrett."

"Yes, I am," Margo said.

"Let's go in the lounge for a minute," Cori said as she led the way.

The sun shone brightly in the small, deserted room as Cori closed the door.

"From what you told me on the phone, I take it Rudy beat Carol up," Margo said.

"Yes, and it's not the first time," Cori said. "I think this has been happening for a long time."

"I don't know Carol that well," Margo said. "I'm not sure I can help her."

"She desperately needs someone to talk to," Cori said. "We can fix the broken bones and sew up the lacerations. Those injuries will heal. But we can't even put a Band-Aid on that big gaping wound inside. She needs help."

"I'm not very good with things like this," Margo said. "I don't think I'm the right person to help her."

"Are you afraid to try?" Cori asked. "Or, are you worried you might have to cancel a golf game at the club?"

"Doesn't anyone in medicine have any tact anymore?" Margo asked.

"No, usually I don't have the time," Cori said. "I guess when I have the time, I don't seem to have the energy."

"I crawled out of the bottle three years ago," Margo said. "How can I possibly help anyone else?"

"We're all recovering from something," Cori said. "I won't let her leave until she promises to talk to somebody. Will you be that someone?"

"I'll try," Margo finally said as Cori smiled.

"Oh, Carol," Margo said when she walked into the treatment room and saw Carol's face, which was bloody, bruised, and filled with tears.

"We need to tie Rudy to the back of your truck," Margo said. "Then we need to drag his sorry ass through a couple of states."

Chapter Fourteen

The shadows cast by the late afternoon sunlight played around the crowded vegetation in Sara's garden. Alex grilled steaks, and they ate outside by a bed of spring plants. Their diversion over, they headed back to Sara's study and turned on the computer to access the CDC program.

"You've eliminated all the prescription products?" Alex asked.

"Yes, Sayer doesn't have enough of the market share of any of those products," Jaimie said.

"None of the other products match the percentage of infections?" Alex asked.

"Not so far," Jaimie said. "Maybe we've been trying to look at the big picture too much."

"What do you mean?" Alex asked.

"We asked the computer to match total production with the percentage of infections," Jaimie said.

"What happened?" Alex asked.

"Nothing even came close," Sara said.

"Why don't we try to break it down?" Jaimie asked. "I'll enter the units manufactured at individual facilities and have the computer identify any patterns."

"The home pregnancy test," Sara said when the answer finally appeared on the screen.

"The ones produced here in Atlanta," Jaimie said. "It's too close a match to be a coincidence."

"That's the source of the infections?" Alex asked.

"Yes, Sayer took over the market when they introduced this test," Jaimie said. "It's produced at five different facilities. Four in the U.S. and one overseas."

"What's so special about the Sayer test?" Alex asked.

"It's easier to use and more accurate," Sara said. "A long Q-tip is dipped into a solution and then inserted into the vagina. It's so accurate, hospitals routinely use it instead of a blood or urine test."

"The data indicate it must have lasted about a month," Jaimie said. "Those were the peak dates of exposure. Then the reported cases began to drop which makes sense. There are still isolated cases but those tests were probably purchased and not used for a while. The only drawback to the test is that the shelf life is only sixty days. But that may be what saved us. After sixty days, they pull the unsold tests off the shelves."

"Look at this," Jaimie said. "Sayer sponsored a promotional campaign in the D.C. area a week before the test went on the market. They gave away a bunch of free samples."

"That's why the first reports came from that part of the country," Sara said.

"What caused the problem?" Alex asked.

"Contaminated solution is the most likely culprit," Jaimie said. "I wonder how Charley McGrath discovered it?"

"What do you mean?" Alex asked.

"He was supposed to be working on Maxicillin," Jaimie said.

"Maybe someone told him about it," Alex offered.

"From what Molly told me, I didn't get the impression anyone had that much contact with McGrath," Jaimie said.

"Wouldn't they check those tests for contamination?" Alex asked.

"I would think so," Jaimie said. "We need to get in the production facility and see what kind of quality control procedures they have in place."

"Wouldn't they have changed them when they discovered the contamination?" Alex asked.

"Probably," Sara said. "Can you identify the manufacturer of the equipment? If we had that information we could call them to see if any changes have been made."

Jaimie entered the commands, and they discussed their options while they waited for an answer.

"I'm not sure we should sneak into the production facility," Alex said.

"That information isn't included in the data base," Jaimie said as she looked at the screen. "I can get the name of the manufacturer and the serial numbers while I'm in there. Maybe I can figure out how it could have happened by looking at the way the line is set up."

"I think she's right, Alex," Sara said.

"OK, but how are we going to get in there without being noticed?" Alex asked. "You can't use your pass to access the building. If Garrett or Fletcher find out we've been snooping around in there, they'll know what we're looking for."

"I'll have to steal someone else's pass," Jaimie said.

"Where are the tests produced?" Alex asked as Jaimie entered instructions into the computer.

"The tests are produced in building A," Jaimie said. "Right now that line is only running two shifts."

"So we go in at night," Alex said.

"Are you sure you should go?" Jaimie asked. "I might be able to explain my way out of being there. If they catch both of us the game's over."

Margo Garrett took a sip of club soda and smiled at Carol Fletcher, who seemed uncomfortable. Three days had made a tremendous difference in Carol's appearance. Most of the swelling and discoloration had disappeared.

"You look a lot better," Margo said.

"I heal fast," Carol said. "Rudy usually avoids punching me in the face."

"How nice of him," Margo said sarcastically.

Carol cringed at her remark.

"I'm sorry," Margo said.

"I think this was a bad idea," Carol said. "I don't think anyone can help me."

"I promised that nurse I would try," Margo said. "Why did you ask for me?"

"I've always admired you," Carol said. "You seemed to have it all. Money, looks, a husband who loves you, kids. The whole package."

"Things aren't always what they seem to be," Margo said as she laughed.

"What's so funny?" Carol asked.

"I'm married to a man I know for a fact doesn't love me," Margo said. "I'm still trying to get over a drinking problem that almost destroyed my kids. Every day is a struggle to stay sober."

"Wow," Carol said.

"Yeah," Margo said. "When I first stopped drinking, I thought reality really sucked. Now, I'm about ready to make some major changes."

"Like what?" Carol asked.

"I'm going to leave Wendel," Margo said. "I've been planning it for a while. It took a long time for me to figure out what I needed to do, and then I had to make sure Wendel couldn't do anything about it."

"What do you mean?" Carol asked.

"The thing that terrified me about leaving was the possibility that Wendel would get custody of my sons," Margo said. "With my alcoholic history, what judge would give me custody? I've spent the last three years trying to make Margo a whole person and tearing down all the barriers my sons built to protect themselves from their alcoholic mother. Now that they are both over eighteen, custody is no longer an issue, so I guess it's time to make a move."

"I don't know what to say," Carol said.

"There's nothing to say," Margo said. "It wasn't wasted time, Carol. I had a plan, a purpose, and now I'm strong enough to survive anything. Even being alone. Why did Rudy beat you up?"

"I asked him about that scene we saw the other night," Carol said. "It just set him off and one thing led to another."

"Have you ever thought about leaving Rudy?" Margo asked.

"Sometimes I think about it," Carol said. "It scares me more than staying. How did you begin planning to leave?"

"I retained my own lawyer," Margo said. "One that Wendel doesn't know about. I already had a prenuptial agreement, so I had access to money. When my father died, Wendel wanted me to let him invest my inheritance but I refused, thank God. Then I got an investment counselor who is a genius."

"We don't have the kind of money you do," Carol said.

"Do you have any property or assets you could get to without Rudy finding out?" Margo asked.

"My father left me a house and some cash," Carol said. "He died a couple of months ago. Rudy said he'll figure out what to do with it when he has more time."

"Why don't we help him with that?" Margo asked.

"What do you mean?" Carol asked.

"I want you to see my lawyer," Margo said. "I'll go with you if you want me to."

"I don't know," Carol said guardedly.

"My lawyer can help you figure out how to separate your assets," Margo said. "Maybe if you felt some financial independence you would consider getting out. My investment counselor can invest whatever cash you can get your hands on. What do you think? Why don't we start planning your escape, Carol?"

"Rudy will kill me if he finds out," Carol said quietly.

"Rudy's going to kill you anyway, Carol," Margo said.

Alex was hiding in the back seat of Jaimie's car when she went through the security gate at Sayer Pharmaceuticals. One of the members of White's team was notorious for misplacing security passes, and Jaimie possessed his most recent loss.

As she began to drive down the road to her office, Jaimie paid no attention to the black Jeep that pulled in behind her. Jaimie parked in her usual spot outside the research and development building. The driver of the Jeep hesitated and then drove away.

"We're here," Jaimie said as she turned off the ignition and removed the key.

"I'll meet you in the woods back there," Alex said.

Alex sat up and watched Jaimie enter the building. Then he scanned the area carefully. When he was satisfied no one was around, he grabbed his back pack, got out of the car, and went to wait in the nearby woods.

Jaimie moved her security pass through the slot and opened the door when the light turned green. A security desk was manned constantly during the day, but at night, the guard made rounds frequently. Elmer Turner, a guard Jaimie had met her first day at Sayer, was standing by the desk.

"Late work, huh Dr. Martin?" he asked as he smiled.

"Yes, sometimes there isn't enough time in the day to get it all done," Jaimie said.

"Happens to all of us," Elmer said.

The elevator stopped at Jaimie's floor and she got off, using her security pass to access her office. She turned on the lights, walked over to her desk, and picked up the phone to call Alex.

Alex watched the driver of the black, late model Jeep check out the cars in the parking lot. The driver was far enough way that Alex couldn't tell if he had blond or gray hair. He parked the vehicle several rows behind

Jaimie's car. Alex could still see the exhaust coming out of the tailpipe and thought, "What the hell is he waiting for?"

A security car passed by, and the guard noticed the driver of the Jeep was just sitting there. The guard backed up and entered the lot as the man pulled out, waving to the guard as he drove away. Alex felt the vibration of his cell phone so he opened the flap.

"Alex, is it OK if I come down?" Jaimie asked.

"Just give it a minute," Alex said. "There's a security car here. I want to make sure they're gone before you come out."

"OK," Jaimie said.

"They're leaving," Alex said a few minutes later.

Jaimie said good-bye to Elmer Turner and scanned the parking lot as she went out the door. When she reached her car, she put her briefcase inside, and then locked the door again. One more look convinced her no one was around so she joined Alex in the woods.

Alex was waiting by a large tree, and he handed Jaimie a dark jacket he had pulled out of the backpack. As Jaimie put it on, Alex pulled communication devices out of the pack.

"There was a guy in a black Jeep," Alex said. "He pulled into the parking lot and was just sitting there until he saw the security patrol. I hope he wasn't following you."

"Did you recognize him?" Jaimie asked.

"No, he has blond or gray hair, medium build," Alex said. "Does that description sound familiar?"

"No," Jaimie said.

"Maybe we should abort this tonight," Alex said.

"It won't be any different tomorrow night," Jaimie said. "If he is following me, we'll still have to shake the tail."

"I guess you're right," Alex said.

Jaimie placed the set on her ears and put the microphone in place. Alex placed the other set in his ears and adjusted the microphone as he nodded at Jaimie.

"Let's go," Alex said as they began the short hike to the next cluster of structures where building A was located.

The man pulled the black Jeep back into the parking lot. To avoid any more problems with the security patrol, he decided to leave the vehicle and wait in the woods. He pulled the cell phone from his pocket to check in with his employer.

"Martin is in her office," the man said.

"Are you sure?" the voice asked.

"As sure as I can be," the man said. "I saw her go in and she hasn't come out. Her car is still in the lot."

"I'll call the guard and verify she's in there," the voice responded. "I'll call you right back."

The man leaned against a tree, stretching his knee in order to relieve the stiffness. He had torn all the ligaments during a pursuit last year, so there wasn't much cartilage left to cushion the joint. His doctor told him if he had one more injury his knee was finished. The pain he felt was constant, and he was massaging the offending limb when he felt the vibration of his cell phone.

"The guard said she left a couple of minutes ago," the excited voice said. "Get to the group of buildings to the north of your position as fast as you can. Call me when you get there."

Alex and Jaimie paused at the thicket of trees next to building A. Jaimie pulled the stolen security pass from her pocket.

"Jaimie, I don't want you to take any chances in there," Alex said as he grabbed her hand. "Do you understand?"

"Yes, I'll be careful," Jaimie said.

"Talk to me the whole time," Alex said. "If you stop talking, I'll assume there's someone close to you. If you need me, just say abort."

Alex reluctantly let go of Jaimie's hand and watched her as she put the pass through the slot and entered the door of Building A.

"I'm standing in the middle of a large open building, Alex," Jaimie said quietly as she began to move forward. "I don't see anyone around. This building can't be more than four or five years old.

"I'm going to look around a little," Jaimie said.

Jaimie walked past the first large area where the production line started but didn't see anyone. She moved down the line until she spotted several men across the other side of the factory who were working on a large machine.

Jaimie retraced her steps and returned to where the production line began.

"Alex, I'm going into a clean room where the solution is mixed," Jaimie said as she entered the room.

"Everything is state of the art in here," she said as she began to write down names and numbers. "The cleaning procedures for the mixing machines are plainly posted in several places. A checklist hangs on the wall and has to be signed by three people at the beginning and end of each shift. Any leftover solution is dumped and not reused. The dates indicate the machines were manufactured four years ago with only one small machine added since then."

Jaimie continued walking down the aisle, looking at the system that was in place to deliver the solution into the plastic tubes. A sheet prominently displayed indicated a culture of the solution was to be taken at the beginning and end of every shift. The same precise, multiple check system was in place for this phase of the operation. Jaimie frowned when an unpleasant reality occurred to her.

The man moved through the woods as quickly as his injured leg would allow, scanning the area for any signs of Dr. Jaimie Martin. He stopped abruptly when he realized he was approaching building A and phoned his supervisor.

"I'm in front of building A," the man said. "I don't see her anywhere. What do you want me to do?"

"Search building A," the tense voice said. "I'm on my way."

"Alex, I just had a terrible thought," Jaimie said.

"What do you mean?" Alex asked.

"This equipment was installed three years ago," Jaimie said. "I don't know what procedures were in place when the contamination occurred, but unless they were a whole lot different back then, there's no way this contamination was an accident."

"Do you realize what you're saying?" Alex asked.

"Someone intentionally infected all those mothers," Jaimie said.

"Jaimie, that man from the parking lot is approaching the door to building A," Alex said nervously. "I think he's looking for you."

Chapter Fifteen

The man limped noticeably as he approached the door to building A. As he put his security card through the slot, he vowed to make someone pay for his crushing, intolerable pain. After the door closed behind him, he pulled his gun out and looked around.

His next step was accompanied by a loud popping noise and a string of muttered curses. He bent over to massage the rapidly swelling knee, trying to keep most of his weight on his only viable lower extremity. The realization it was time for his total knee replacement made him swear to exact a brutal revenge.

The agony that washed over the man's face scared Jaimie as it quickly turned to a powerful rage. Jaimie knew the consequences would be deadly if the man found her, and she said a quick, silent prayer.

When Alex told her the man was approaching, Jaimie begged him not to come in. It would blow their cover and any chance at solving the mystery. Now, as Jaimie watched the furious man attempt to drag his useless limb behind him, she doubted she'd made the right decision.

Her position inside the clean area was fine as long as he didn't enter the room and proceeded down the main aisle of the plant. She watched as the man put a small amount of weight on his leg to test its strength. The misery rolled across his face, but he put more weight on his leg and began moving forward with the gun pointed in front of him.

While he began moving down the main aisle, he looked in the direction of the clean room. Jaimie dropped below the level of the glass. She became convinced the man was moving in her direction.

Her instincts screamed for her to find a hiding place, so she looked around anxiously. She spotted a steel cabinet under the production line that had a sliding door. Jaimie was able to squeeze into it and close the door as she heard the man's tortured voice.

"If I get my hands on you, Jaimie Martin," the man said ominously as he entered the room. "I'm going to kill you. No one will be able to stop me. You just caused me to blow out what little cartilage I had left in my knee. I'm going to make sure you hurt as much as I do.

"Where are you, Jaimie?" the man asked nastily as he pounded his fist on the steel cabinet over her hiding place.

"I'll find you," he said as he hobbled down the aisle.

"I was just supposed to follow you," he said as he laughed hideously. "But you pissed me off. I killed the last person who did that.

"Where the fuck are you?" the man screamed as he reached the other end of the clean room and walked into the main production area.

Jaimie opened the sliding door slowly and saw the man dragging his leg behind him as he left the room. She knew the pain would slow him down but the rage was a strong factor in his favor. Forcing herself to count to ten, she left her hiding place and crawled over to the windows of the clean room. She took a deep breath and raised herself up until she could see out the bottom of the window.

The man was moving down the aisle of the main production line. Jaimie crawled down the aisle to the door closest to the main entrance. When she reached the doorway, she glanced quickly at the man.

About thirty feet down the aisle, the man stopped, listening intently for any signs of movement. Jaimie looked longingly at the front door of the building, so far and yet only ten feet away. She peeked out the door and waited until the man began to move forward. Jaimie thought she could hear him muttering obscenities and her name in the same string of sentences.

Jaimie waited ten more seconds, took several deep breaths, and then bolted for the door. She was almost there when she heard the shouted command to stop followed by the pinging sounds as he fired at her.

Alex waited impatiently, convinced he should ignore Jaimie's request and enter the building. The seconds seemed like hours, and Alex tried simple breathing exercises to relax. From somewhere in the distance, he thought he heard the tires of a vehicle squealing. His anxiety increased when he heard the vehicle approach at a high rate of speed.

If that sound represented reinforcements, Alex would have no choice but to intervene and rescue Jaimie. The noise of squealing tires escalated. Alex drew his weapon about the same time he heard the sound of a gunshots and saw Jaimie burst out of building A, running at full speed toward him.

"Let's go," she screamed as she reached the woods and the door burst open behind them.

"I'll get you," the man screamed as he stood by the door and the Trooper exploded into the parking lot. The driver of the vehicle stopped by the man, but Alex and Jaimie didn't pause long enough to see if they could recognize the driver.

"We've got to get to my building before they do," Jaimie said as they ran at top speed through the woods. "I'll go back to my office. You'll have to wait in the woods."

"What if the guard is sitting there?" Alex asked.

"Then we're screwed," Jaimie said. "Can you think of a better idea?"

"No," Alex said as they reached the end of the woods.

The squealing of tires filled the night as Jaimie pulled her security pass out, ran it through the slot, and entered the research and development building. She ran through the deserted lobby, thanking God or fate for Elmer Turner's absence. As she entered the elevator, she could hear a vehicle screech to a halt in front of her building.

Jaimie forced herself to breathe normally on the elevator, aware someone would be hot on her trail and very suspicious.

"Alex, I've reached my office," Jaimie said. "I'll leave the mike on. You should be able to hear the conversation. If I need you, I'll work the word abort into the conversation."

Jaimie put her card through the slot in her door, entered her office, and left the door ajar. She took the jacket off and draped it behind her chair with the microphone under one of the arms. She sat down and pretended to be reviewing a stack of print outs while her heart felt like it was going to explode inside her chest.

The elevator door opened, and Jaimie heard deliberate footsteps approach her office. Rudy Fletcher burst into the doorway of her office and glared at her.

"How long have you been here?" he asked angrily.

"I don't know," Jaimie said, pretending to look relaxed and surprised. "I wasn't aware I had to report my whereabouts to you, Fletcher."

"Someone broke into building A," Rudy said as he stared at Jaimie.

"It's your job to take care of security, Fletcher," Jaimie said nastily. "Can't you do it properly instead of harassing innocent employees?"

"The guard said you left," Rudy said.

"I did, but I forgot something so I came back," Jaimie said.

"What did you forget?" Rudy asked.

"I'm not answering any more questions," Jaimie said as she walked over to her door.

"No more games, no more questions," Jaimie said as she glared at Fletcher. "You can be sure Garrett will hear about this the first thing in the morning.

"Now get the hell out of my office," Jaimie said as she slammed the door in Rudy Fletcher's red, angry face.

Dr. Jekyll was becoming increasingly concerned Jaimie Martin wasn't what she pretended to be. There was nothing specific he could point to as a basis for his belief, but his instincts rarely failed him. The plan he had devised and executed just seemed to breeze along until Charley McGrath discovered the contamination and derailed the whole operation. Now, the possibility existed the contamination would be revealed and spoil his plan to achieve the bigger objective.

As he sat in his car, Dr. Jekyll thought about the reason he became involved. He realized Jenny Morgan's eerie, haunting confession that cold, rainy night became a turning point for him. The anger he felt turned to rage every time he remembered the insane, maniacal look in his grandmother's eyes. Eventually, he harnessed the anger and began to plan a revenge that would satisfy the sense of outrage he felt.

His first tentative, clumsy attempts to organize and develop the current plan were a distant memory. Now, the implementation of the plan that had evolved over the last few years was threatened. The premature revelation could mean the end of everything.

Involving others in his scheme had been a necessary but difficult decision for Dr Jekyll. He worried about the possibility of exposure and limited the number of people within the organization he built who knew his real identity.

The larger plan still needed to be protected; and since Jaimie Martin was a doctor and possibly something more, she would be a worthy adversary. There had to be a way to send her a message, one that would require intelligence to solve. The message must be clear to her but subtle enough she wouldn't be able to prove it was anything but what it appeared to be on the surface. Dr. Jekyll enjoyed games that allowed him to match wits with others as much as he believed in the master plan.

Alex built a fire in Jaimie's bedroom while she made coffee. Jaimie brought the hot mugs upstairs and they sat on the thick rug in front of the fireplace to sip the hot brew.

"You could have been shot, Jaimie," Alex said.

"We were lucky the guard wasn't sitting by the desk," Jaimie said.

"Yes, but Fletcher thinks it was you," Alex said.

"But he can't be positive I was the one in building A," Jaimie said.

"Maybe not, but he was already suspicious because he had that guy following you," Alex said. "So far, you've been lucky."

"I meant what I said in there, Alex," Jaimie said. "They've had a very sophisticated delivery system in building A for the last three years. I can't imagine this was an accident."

"That's a big leap, don't you think?" Alex asked.

"Maybe so," Jaimie said. "I got the name of the manufacturer and the serial numbers off the equipment."

"I'll go see the manufacturer tomorrow," Alex said.

"There's something else that's bothering me," Jaimie said.

"What is it?" Alex asked.

"If Charley McGrath was as detail oriented as he seemed to be, maybe he didn't believe the contamination was an accident," Jaimie said. "Are you sure there wasn't anything at his house about this? I can't believe he didn't leave some kind of a record."

"I have the inventory of everything they found there," Alex said as he walked out of Jaimie's bedroom.

"Let's look at the list again," Alex said as he came back into Jaimie's room, sat down, and handed her the list.

"I was there when they searched Charley's house," Alex said. "I got into his computer records. Everything on the computer had been deleted and I mean everything. He probably did leave a record of what he found, but someone broke into his house and deleted all the computer files."

"Alex, there's a case of home pregnancy tests on this list," Jaimie said. "Maybe that's how he found out. Maybe those tests were contaminated."

"I'll go and get them tomorrow," Alex said. "We can send them to Washington for analysis."

"There's another question we haven't addressed," Jaimie said. "Why would anyone do this intentionally?"

Although Wendel Garrett was nearly blinded every time he looked out his office window at the brilliant sunshine, he could never resist the urge. Another stand of tulips had popped up overnight on the hill behind his building. Wendel admired the view as he drank his third cup of coffee. His secretary announced Rudy Fletcher's arrival, and Wendel sighed, remembering a very angry Jaimie Martin who had already paid him a visit.

Rudy strode into the room with a nasty look on his face, and he only paused long enough to pour himself a cup of coffee.

"We have to do something about Martin," Rudy said.

"That's exactly what she said about you," Wendel said.

"She's lying," Rudy said.

"Did you actually see her in building A last night?" Wendel asked.

"No, and the guy I had following her didn't either," Rudy said. "But I know it was her. I can feel it."

"Well, feelings aren't enough," Wendel said. "I need her so I can get Maxicillin out before the competition comes up with something."

"If she figures out the contamination happened here there might be nothing left to protect," Rudy said.

"There's nothing left to find, remember?" Wendel asked.

"Maybe not, but I think we should get rid of her," Rudy said.

"I just told you I can't right now," Wendel said. "She's close to finding a treatment for newborn pneumonia. As soon as we get Maxicillin viable, I'll get rid of her."

"Why don't I send her a little message?" Rudy asked.

"I think you should just follow her," Wendel said.

"I think a subtle message to back off would do wonders," Rudy said.

"You have to go out of town, don't you?" Wendel asked.

"Yes, but that's not a problem," Rudy said. "Messages can be delivered in many ways."

Sleep claimed Jaimie reluctantly, and when it did, her dreams were filled with chases and a man with a damaged knee threatening her. Jaimie began her day feeling weary, and her long diatribe in Wendel Garrett's office about Rudy Fletcher's behavior enhanced the fatigue.

By the time she left Sayer, it was already dark. She couldn't reach Alex at her house, so she called ahead and picked up a pizza on her way home. The smell of pepperoni, bacon, sausage, and mushrooms filled the kitchen when Alex walked in.

"That smells good," Alex said. "I'm starving. I didn't have time to grab lunch.

"How did it go with Garrett?" Alex asked.

"I was properly outraged," Jaimie said. "I'm not sure he totally bought it, but he's concerned about developing Maxicillin. I checked on the results of the latest sensitivity tests before I went to see him. For the first time, we have a positive reaction using the inhibitor. He knows we're getting close, so he's not going to dump me until we've completed work on the new drug."

"I'm more concerned about what Rudy might do," Alex said. "I went to see Martin Dempsey this afternoon. He's the president of the company that manufactured the machines in building A. Charley McGrath called him and said he was concerned about the possibility of contamination. Dempsey told Charley it was impossible unless all the cleaning procedures were ignored. McGrath asked him to modify the machine and add another cleaning process as a back up. Dempsey did the work, but he told me there was no way that solution could be contaminated."

"That's what I was afraid of," Jaimie said. "The pizza is ready. Why don't we go out on the porch?"

Alex sat on the swing next to Jaimie and a small candle on the table provided the only light. After they finished eating the pizza, Alex pulled a small tape recorder out of his pocket and laid it down next to Jaimie.

"I went back to Charley McGrath's house this morning," Alex said. "I looked through the case of home pregnancy tests. I was just going to send the whole box to the lab in D.C., and then I decided to look through all of them."

"You found a tape?" Jaimie asked.

"Yes," Alex said.

As the swing continued to move back and forth slowly, Alex pressed play and the frightened voice of Charley McGrath filled the air.

"I've never been this frightened before," Charley said nervously. "I think I'm being stalked by several people. I can't figure out how to get myself out of this situation."

The tape stopped abruptly and then Charley began to speak again. "Sorry, I had to answer the phone. I'm meeting an FBI agent tonight named Alex Tanner. I don't see any other way out. I wanted to leave some kind of record about how I found out about the contamination at Sayer. I left this information on my computer, but I'm afraid someone might delete it, so this is a back up."

Another long pause followed, and about the time Jaimie began to give up on hearing any more dialogue, Charley began to speak.

"I wish I had never looked into that case of pregnancy tests," Charley said. "I took it home because I was doing some marketing. I was cleaning out my basement and looked in one of the boxes. The solution was cloudy instead of clear. When we originally tested that solution, it never became cloudy even after the expiration date had passed. I had to know why it was cloudy. When the culture results came back, I freaked."

The sound of a soft drink can being opened exploded from the small player and startled Jaimie.

"Sorry," Charley said. "I took the culture results to Garrett, and I could tell he didn't want to believe me. I told him we had to do something but he said those tests had expired so it didn't matter. I guess I bought that until I heard the first reports of newborn pneumonia. I went to see him again. He kept promising to call the FDA and tell them. That's when I could tell someone was following me. I checked with the manufacturer of the machines and checked on the cleaning procedures in building A. That's when I realized there was no way the contamination was an accident. I guess if someone besides me is listening to this tape, I'm dead. If that's the case, then I sure hope it's you, Alex Tanner."

CHAPTER SIXTEEN

For three days, Logan Carpenter had been feeling weak and tired. This morning, he accepted the flu he had been trying to elude had tackled him, and now held him firmly in its grip. His temperature hovered near 102 degrees, and he had to force himself to drink fluids.

Logan Carpenter's brittle diabetes made the flu potentially life threatening so he checked his blood sugar. Then he would lower his morning dose of insulin to compensate for his inability to eat. Later in the day, he would repeat this process so he could adjust his evening dose of insulin.

The weakness he felt overwhelmed him, so he decided to go back to bed, leaving his glass of fresh squeezed orange juice on the counter. An hour later, his restless, achy sleep was interrupted by the ringing of the phone.

"Hello," Logan said softly after he picked up the receiver.

"Dad?" Jaimie asked. "Are you OK?"

"I've got the flu," Logan said.

"You sound terrible," Jaimie said. "I didn't think you'd be home. I expected to leave a message."

"Well, you got me instead of the machine," Logan said as he coughed.

"I just wanted to see how you were," Jaimie said.

"I've been better," Logan said.

"Maybe you should call Dr. Howard," Jaimie said.

"I will if I don't feel better this afternoon," Logan said.

"Please do," Jaimie said. "It doesn't take much to throw your blood sugar off."

"Yes, Doctor," Logan said.

"I can't help it, Dad," Jaimie said. "I'm a doctor as well as your daughter. I worry about you."

"I know," Logan said. "I'll be OK, Jaimie."

"Promise me you'll call Dr. Howard," Jaimie said.

"I promise," Logan said.

"Well, I guess I should let you get some rest," Jaimie said. "I'll call back later. I love you, Dad."

"I love you too, Jaimie," Logan said.

Jack Connelly had arrived in Atlanta on an early morning flight and was waiting for Jaimie and Alex to join him at his downtown hotel. It was a rainy, dreary morning that started with a landing delayed by the fog that hung over the city. By the time the plane pulled up to the gate, Jack had a headache and was grousing about the enormous amount of time he wasted flying.

Jaimie and Alex should be completing their evasive maneuvers and would be joining him momentarily. Jack looked at the steady rain and breathed in the fresh smell of it that hinted of the summer that was almost upon them.

Alex had seemed genuinely upset about the events that occurred several nights ago, particularly the shots that had been fired in Jaimie's direction. Jack was concerned about Jaimie but fearful that Alex might care more for Jaimie than he was willing to admit.

At this juncture, Jack wanted to see how they acted around each other. That first and only time he met with them he had sensed a certain amount of tension that he wouldn't describe as totally negative. Since the atmosphere seemed so charged in the beginning he needed to know how things were now that they had spent some time together.

Jack didn't object to them having a relationship per se, he just worried it would interfere with what they were supposed to accomplish. Since this latest revelation raised the danger level, he wanted to be sure Alex stayed focused on determining who orchestrated the contamination.

The coffee was fresh, a subtle mixture of several flavors that blended together well. As Jack drank his second cup, he felt relaxed, savoring the solitude.

The knock startled Jack although he had been expecting it to occur at any moment. Alex and Jaimie were still feeling the rush from their early morning adventure.

"I'm glad our tour of Atlanta is over," Alex said as they entered the room.

"I hope they got as wet as we did," Jaimie said as she laughed.

"How about some coffee?" Jack asked as they nodded and walked over to get a cup. They sat down next to each other, talking and laughing in a comfortable, relaxed way. Jack didn't think they had slept together yet, but he realized they were attracted to each other and given their situation, it might be inevitable.

"The coffee is great," Jaimie said.

"I know, I was thinking the same thing before you got here," Jack said.

"What's going on?" Alex asked.

"The preliminary test results are back," Jack said. "They confirm the presence of strep-A in those pregnancy tests you found in McGrath's house. The tape McGrath made should be enough to nail Garrett and Fletcher for covering up the contamination. If we arrest them now, we might never figure out who contaminated the tests and murdered McGrath."

"We were thinking the same thing," Jaimie said.

"On the surface, Garrett doesn't seem to have a motive," Alex said. "The pregnancy test made him millions, and the contamination had the effect of dropping the demand for the tests as well as Sayer stock prices. What motive would he have for contaminating them?"

"I agree, that's why we have to make the investigation more comprehensive," Jack said. "We need to change the focus."

"We were wondering if this might be some vendetta against Garrett or Sayer," Jaimie said. "Maybe a disgruntled employee or someone who hates Garrett."

"I've had agents gathering that kind of information," Jack said. "I brought their reports so you could review them. Alex, you can do some of the follow up interviews that are in the vicinity. Jaimie, you need to snoop around inside Sayer and see if you can get a take on who might hate Garrett enough to do this."

"I can ask my secretary," Jaimie said, laughing. "She seems to know most of the juicy gossip."

"I'll have agents helping you," Jack said. "The director wants us to pounce on this."

"Is it possible there's some other explanation for this?" Alex asked.

"What do you mean?" Jack asked.

"The most obvious answer is some kind of revenge directed at Garrett," Alex said. "It just seems to be such an extreme act of retaliation. Someone killed a lot of innocent babies. It's hard for me to imagine they did it just to get back at Garrett or Sayer."

"You think someone might have a bigger agenda?" Jack asked.

"I think it's possible," Alex said. "I think we should consider all the possibilities."

"OK, I'll get the word out for everyone to check with their sources about any possible foreign or domestic terrorist groups who might have had a hand in this," Jack said. "I want you to be careful. The stakes are higher now, and I think both of you are in danger."

"We'll be careful," Alex said.

"Three agents will be arriving tomorrow to help you," Jack said. "Alex, I need to speak with you alone for a few minutes."

"Why don't I wait downstairs?" Jaimie asked as she stood up.

"I want to thank you again for helping us," Jack said as he took Jaimie's hand and walked her to the door.

"What did you want to talk to me about that she couldn't hear?" Alex asked after Jaimie left and they sat back down.

"I want to remind you how vulnerable she is in this situation," Jack said.

"You think I don't know that?" Alex asked angrily.

"Yes, but I also want you to realize how vulnerable you are," Jack said. "You're in a very dangerous situation, and it's perfectly reasonable that you'd be attracted to her."

"I haven't slept with her, Jack," Alex said angrily.

"She's a beautiful, bright woman," Jack said. "Don't insult my intelligence by telling me you haven't thought about it. I want you to stay focused on your job so you won't do anything that might distract you or end up hurting her."

Logan Carpenter was finally beginning to feel better now that his doctor had prescribed antibiotic therapy. Though he felt Logan had a viral infection, Dr. Howard wanted to err on the side of caution due to possible complications from Logan's diabetes.

This morning Logan felt better, and he didn't know whether to credit the antibiotic or the healing effects of time for his improved status. His appetite still hadn't returned to its pre-illness level, so he continued to adjust his insulin. He was working on a paper he was supposed to present at a conference when the phone rang.

"Hi, Dad," Jaimie said.

"Hi, Jaimie," Logan said.

"How are you?" she asked.

"A lot better," Logan said. "I went to see Dr. Howard, and he put me on an antibiotic. I feel pretty good today. I'm going back to work tomorrow."

"I'm glad," Jaimie said. "I was going to catch a flight out there if you weren't better by today."

"Well, maybe that's not such a bad idea," Logan said. "You could bring Alex. That's probably the only way I'll get to meet him."

"I could feel that zinger coming," Jaimie said. "We're both really busy right now. We'll come out when things settle down a little bit."

"Is that a promise?" Logan asked.

"Yes," Jaimie said.

"I'm going to hold you to that, Jaimie," Logan said. "I want to meet the man who was able steal your heart. He must be a very brave man."

"It would take a brave man to put up with me?" she asked.

"Yes, but if it's any consolation, I think you're worth the effort," Logan said.

Margo Garrett picked up Carol Fletcher early for their lunch date. Margo wanted to visit her son, Bradley, who was attending classes at St. Dominic's, a small private college located on the fringes of Atlanta.

"I hope you don't mind the detour so I can see Bradley," Margo said.

"It's not a problem," Carol said.

"Something is wrong with Bradley," Margo said. "I can hear it in his voice."

"How do you know that?" Carol asked.

"I'm not sure I can put it into words," Margo said. "Since I stopped drinking, I've made it my mission in life to make sure my sons are as whole and happy as I can make them. When you have that kind of relationship, it isn't really the words that are spoken that tip you off. I guess you can hear it in the tone of their voice, in those subtle little cues that live between the words. It's like you have a little devil sitting on your shoulder who annoys the shit out of you until you check out the situation."

"Your little devil has been tormenting you?" Carol asked, laughing.

"Mercilessly," Margo said.

St. Dominic's campus was spread out over acres of rolling, green hills that glistened in the glow of the sun. Margo had been impressed with the setting when they toured the college. Bradley's dorm was called Horner Hall and it was the newest facility on the campus.

"His room is on the third floor," Margo said as she got out of the car.

"Are you sure you want me to go with you?" Carol asked.

"Yes, maybe you'll pick up something I miss," Margo said.

The third floor was noisy with occasional pockets of furious activity that indicated which residents had no classes at the moment.

Margo and Carol walked down the long corridor that led to Bradley's room. They could hear music screaming from the end of the hall. When they reached the last door, they realized it was Bradley's room and the source of the blaring clamor. The door, attached loosely to the frame, literally shook from the vibration of the rap music. Margo looked at Carol and knocked tentatively.

"What?" the tall boy with long, dark hair and a goatee asked impatiently when he finally answered the door.

"I'm Margo Garrett," she said as she entered a room darkened by drawn curtains.

"I'm Nicholas," the boy said. "I'm Brad's roommate. He went to the library to study. He should be back soon."

"OK," Margo said hesitantly as they all stood in the smoke filled room.

"I'll turn the music down," Nicholas offered as Margo stared at the incense burning in a small bowl.

Carol looked at Margo strangely, trying to figure out why she was hesitating. The smell that permeated the room was sickly, sweet, and made Carol nauseous. Nicholas sat down on a small couch, looking nervously at Margo and then at Carol.

"OK, I guess I should probably just stay out of this and let Bradley handle it," Margo said. "I have a problem with that since that it's my fault he's having a difficult time figuring out what to do."

Nicholas and Carol looked at Margo as if she were totally deranged.

"This is how this is going to come down, Nicholas," Margo said as she walked over and got right in his face. "I realize you want to sit in here and smoke pot and think about how much reality sucks and how much nicer it is to get high and pretend you're on another, better planet. And for you, Nicholas, that's fine. Frankly, I don't give a damn."

"I don't know what you mean," Nicholas said weakly.

"Yes, you do," Margo said "I've been there, done that, so I know exactly what's happening. Bradley barely survived my addiction, and I won't let him try to survive yours. I'm going to pack his bags and get him another room. I don't want there to be any consequences for him, so I'll make you a deal. Bradley quietly gets a new room and we all keep our mouths shut. But if you hassle him, I'll call the Atlanta cops and have them pay you a visit. What do you say, Nicholas?"

"I'll help you pack," Nicholas said as he stood up.

"Mom, what are you doing here?" Bradley asked when he entered the room. "What's going on?"

Two hours later, Bradley had been moved into a private room on another floor of Horner Hall, and Margo and Carol were having lunch at a restaurant they spotted on their way back to Atlanta. Their salads had been ordered and they sipped mint tea while they waited.

"You're really something, Margo," Carol said. "I didn't realize that was pot. I thought you had totally lost it. I thought that smell was just really bad after shave."

"You're not as old as I am." Margo said. "I was a teenager in the sixties. You would have had to be in a coma or have slept through the decade not to know what pot smells like."

"I could tell you were mad," Carol said. "But you handled everything very calmly and firmly. I wish I could do that."

"Don't you ever get mad, Carol?" Margo asked. "Don't you ever just want to scream or beat the shit out of Rudy or something?"

"I've been afraid to open that door," Carol said quietly. "I guess I've tried to store all those feelings in this little, private closet. I open the door just enough to shove them in there and then close it as quickly as I can.

I'm afraid if I open it all the way, all those feelings will come tumbling out, and I won't be able to control them anymore."

"It's time to open that door, Carol," Margo said.

Aunt Sam hit a burst of creative energy early in the morning that extended throughout the entire day. Fatigue hovered but Sam knew the best light was waning, so she continued working her brushes furiously. It was impossible for her to explain these spurts to someone who had never experienced the phenomenon. Intense moments of passionate fury drove her as if someone had cast a spell over her.

The creative monster would sweep her away and she was powerless to resist its impulses. Everything came together in an explosion of pure expression and made her feel consumed but totally satisfied. The ringing of her phone intruded about the time she realized the light was gone, so she reluctantly picked up the receiver.

"Aunt Sam?" Jaimie asked.

"Hi, Jaimie," Sam said. "How are you?"

"I'm fine," Jaimie said. "I was wondering if you've seen Logan today?"

"No, I haven't," Sam said. "I went over there yesterday, and he still seemed weak but he said he was better."

"I called him this morning," Jaimie said. "I left a message for him to call me when he got home from the university but he hasn't called. I was wondering if you would mind going over there to check on him for me."

"Sure, I'll go right now," Aunt Sam said. "He probably just went out for dinner. I'll go check and call you right back."

"Thanks, Aunt Sam," Jaimie said as she pressed talk and looked at Alex.

"I'm sure he's OK," Alex said as he handed Jaimie a glass of tea.

"You're probably right," Jaimie said as Jake came up to her and began to demand some attention.

"Let's go out on the porch," Alex said. "We can take the cordless with us."

"OK," Jaimie said as they walked outside, trailed by Jake, who had a large rawhide bone in his mouth.

"Molly told me about a woman who had an affair with Garrett," Jaimie said after they sat down on the swing. "She worked at Sayer for a couple of years. Molly said she was asked to leave last year after her affair with Wendel ended. According to Molly, she made a lot of threats against Wendel."

"What's her name?" Alex asked. "It's worth looking into."

The phone rang before Jaimie could answer as a look of relief washed over her face.

"Hello," Jaimie said.

"Jaimie," Aunt Sam said tentatively.

"Aunt Sam," Jaimie said. "What's wrong, Sam?"

"Jaimie, sweetheart," Sam said as she started to cry. "I'm as sorry as I can be, baby. Logan's dead, Jaimie."

Chapter Seventeen

When she wandered into Aunt Sam's studio, the sea commanded Jaimie's attention until her eyes finally landed on the partially finished canvas. A gentle breeze blew the smell and feel of the ocean into the room, but her old friend brought Jaimie no comfort.

Sam's phone call the previous evening became a kind of dividing line in Jaimie's life as if all of her feelings would now be defined in terms of those that came before her father's death and those that would come after. Although she had been frantic making travel arrangements for San Diego, she was fortunate that she had very few unoccupied moments.

Alex and Jaimie had boarded flight 288 bound for San Diego while the last gasp of black, empty night surrounded them, but Jaimie thought the darkness fit her mood completely.

Wendel Garrett had tried to extend his sympathies, but Jaimie sensed he was hesitant to let her leave. The Maxicillin research was at a delicate stage, so, reluctantly, Jaimie had promised to keep in touch with Terry White to accommodate Garrett's concerns.

Since their arrival in San Diego, Jaimie felt as if all the events were happening in some altered concept of time. Minutes seemed like hours and hours like minutes, but then nothing felt right or normal.

The arrangements for her father's autopsy, funeral, and frequent phone calls to speak with Terry White to coordinate the Maxicillin research had consumed most of her time.

Jaimie studied Sam's painting and realized Sam's talent had finally matured. Her early work had lacked this kind of intricate detail but now time, creative flair, and a certain amount of courage made the canvass take on a life of its own.

The painting was nearing completion. Jaimie's expression changed abruptly when she looked closely at the two people walking along the beach, astounded that she was the woman in the painting and it was Alex holding her hand. Aunt Sam couldn't possibly have known what Alex looked like.

She had been so occupied with the concerned but hovering Aunts that she had taken no time to deal with her father's death. Tears welled up and Jaimie let them fall without trying to stop them. Her guilt was almost a physical ache. She should have flown out to check on her father, but she was too confused to know if she felt real guilt or the inevitable loneliness of being the one left behind.

Death was no stranger to Jaimie. Medical school, internship, and several years of residency made it a frequent, unwanted companion. Jaimie finally understood the feelings of survivors after death claimed someone they loved. None of those survivors had ever verbalized this notion that there was a physical manifestation of grief, so Jaimie believed she might be the only one to feel the dull pain centered in her chest.

Jaimie was so lost in thought she didn't realize Sam was standing next to her until she felt Sam's hand reach for hers. They let the silence remain unbroken while they looked at Sam's painting.

"I should have gone over to check on Logan earlier," Sam finally said.

"I should have flown out to make sure he was OK," Jaimie said. "I think we both know feeling guilty isn't going to change anything."

"Did you talk to Dr. Howard?" Sam asked.

"Alex and I are going to see him," Jaimie said.

"I like Alex, Jaimie," Sam said. "He seems like a very nice man."

"He's the man with me, isn't he?" Jaimie asked.

"Yes, he is," Sam said. "After you called to tell us you got married, I knew the painting must involve two people instead of one. It was only yesterday I painted in the details of their features. By noon I realized the woman I had been painting was you, and Alex just seemed to take shape after that."

"How did you know what he looked like?" Jaimie asked.

"Intuition?" Sam asked. "I don't know for sure. I can't explain a process I don't understand. I just know it happens."

Alex and Grace came into the studio as Sam and Jaimie turned around.

"Are you ready to go?" Alex asked as he came up beside Jaimie and reached for her hand.

"Yes," Jaimie said as she smiled at him.

"There's one good thing that came out of this," Grace said. "Sam and I finally got to meet Alex."

"We're going to see Dr. Howard," Jaimie said. "Do you want to go somewhere for dinner after that?"

"Sure, why don't you call us after you see him and we can make plans?" Sam asked.

The drive to Dr. Howard's office took them along the coast highway so they caught glimpses of the ocean in between the structures. Alex continued to hold Jaimie's hand and Jaimie appreciated the gesture.

"I'm sorry you're getting dragged into my personal life like this," Jaimie said. "Maybe we should just tell them the truth."

"It's OK, Jaimie," Alex said. "I don't think we should tell them. It's only a couple of days."

Dr. Howard's office was located in a strip of offices located near the medical examiner's office where Logan's autopsy had been completed. Ray Howard looked young, weary, and seemed to be dealing with another crisis by phone as his secretary showed Alex and Jaimie into his office. Ray Howard stood up and smiled at them as he ended his call.

"Hi, Jaimie," he said as he came around the desk to hug her.

"Hi, Ray," Jaimie said. "I'd like you to meet my husband, Alex Martin."

"Logan told me you got married," Ray Howard said as he shook Alex's hand.

"I guess he told you how shocked he was," Jaimie said.

"Of course," Howard said, laughing. "Actually, he seemed happy about it. I didn't want to talk about this over the phone, Jaimie, that's why I asked you to come over."

"I appreciate that, Ray," Jaimie said.

"The results of the post are back," Ray Howard said. "It was a diabetic coma like we expected. I guess he must have had a relapse of that flu. He came to see me a few days ago and I put him on an antibiotic. He called me the next day and said he was better."

"Was that the last time you talked to him?" Jaimie asked.

"No, he called yesterday," Ray Howard said. "He said he took his morning dose of insulin and checked his blood sugar at noon. He was concerned it was still so high. I told him the flu probably made it unstable. He was supposed to take an extra dose of insulin and call me back if he had any problems. I tried to call him later but didn't get an answer so I assumed everything was OK. Maybe I should have gone over there."

"Aunt Sam and I already went on this guilt trip," Jaimie said. "I don't think any of us realized how sick he was."

"I think the flu just threw his blood sugar off," Ray Howard said. "He probably passed out, and his blood sugar just kept rising until he went into a coma."

"It's hard for me to accept that," Jaimie said. "Logan was always so careful."

"He was getting older, Jaimie," Ray said. "A lot of my patients have been getting this flu and Logan wasn't the only one it claimed."

Cascades of yellow roses covered Logan Carpenter's casket as his mourners gathered at a grave located high on a hill overlooking the ocean. Logan had requested a single, short service at his grave instead of visitation at an impersonal funeral home or a church service. So, a colleague from the university gave Logan's eulogy as his family and friends stood nearby. It was early enough that the dew still covered the ground, and Jaimie thought it looked like an endless expanse of stars.

Logan would have appreciated this setting, and Jaimie tried not to think about how much she was going to miss him. That such a strong, vital man had lived in such a frail body was a source of irony for Jaimie. Her father's gentle strength had shaped much of her personality, and she recognized his subtle influence in many of her actions. Where she might have acted hastily, he had shown her a calmer, more thoughtful course. Jaimie always thought his best legacy was the smoothing out of all her rough edges. Alex stood by her side, holding her hand throughout the brief service.

Alex surveyed the small crowd that had gathered and noticed a woman he could easily have mistaken for Jaimie but for the gray that streaked her auburn hair. He glanced away but was drawn back to her eyes, so much like Jaimie's. He saw that she, too, was drawn to Jaimie's eyes, as if she might be trying to gauge the impact of Logan's death on his daughter.

Occasionally, Alex noticed she also studied him when she thought he wasn't watching. No one had to tell him she was Jaimie's mother.

When the service was over, Aunt Sam invited everyone to come to her house. Alex saw Jaimie's mother standing in Sam's studio, studying Sam's painting. Candace Carpenter looked across the room at Alex. Alex could sense the invitation in her eyes, the same large brown eyes he thought were one of Jaimie's most attractive qualities. The impulse became irresistible so he walked across the room.

"You must be Alex," Candace said as she reached for his hand.

"You must be Jaimie's mother," he said.

"Candace," she said simply. "How is Jaimie doing?"

"She seems fine on the surface," Alex said. "I don't think it's really hit her yet."

"I think you're right," Candace said. "I'm glad she's found someone. It will make this easier for her."

"I hope so," Alex said.

"So, Alex Martin," Candace said. "I want you to take good care of my daughter for me. I never thought she'd let anyone into her heart, but now that she has, maybe she'll be able to find a place in it for me as well."

"I don't know what to say," Alex said.

"I know," Candace said. "I don't expect you to say anything. Just know that I love Jaimie, and if there's anything I can do for her, please call me."

"I will," Alex said as Candace walked away.

Alex watched as she went up to Jaimie and began talking. They were kind to each other like casual acquaintances might be but he thought their greeting lacked a typical mother and daughter intensity. Candace kissed Jaimie and Alex saw Jaimie flinch as if the advance seemed more like a surprise then an unwanted gesture.

Jaimie smiled at her mother with that same guarded smile Alex had been given when he first met Jaimie. He suddenly realized that reserved smile had given way to one that seemed to betray a warmth and sincerity that lit up Jaimie's entire face.

Night came reluctantly to San Diego as the guests scattered, and those who had loved Logan Carpenter were left alone to fill in the gaps his death left in their lives. Jaimie and Alex returned to Logan's house. Jaimie pleaded fatigue and went to bed early, but her room seemed to be inhabited by old ghosts who refused to let her sleep.

Jaimie sat by the open windows, listening to the ocean, willing that familiar cacophony to fill the void she felt surrounding her. Sleep wouldn't claim her, so she ruminated about the minutiae of the life she had shared with Logan Carpenter.

Finally, she could feel exhaustion approaching, so she drew back the bedspread and tried to find a comfortable position on her bed. Not even a restless sleep could penetrate the endless parade of detail that floated through her consciousness.

From somewhere in the distance, Jaimie heard a voice. She got up and went into the hall, briefly convinced the sound had come from Logan's room. For a moment, Jaimie was excited about seeing Logan until she remembered the events of the last two days. The voice called out again and she realized the sound emanated from the guestroom where Alex was sleeping.

Unsure if she should intrude, Jaimie realized Alex must be dreaming when she heard pleas for help escape his lips. Jaimie went in and saw Alex in the moonlight, moving about the bed as if he were being attacked.

Jaimie placed her hand on Alex's shoulder as he began to mumble unintelligible sounds. Her hold became a shaking motion until Alex jumped, sat up, and finally seemed to be fully awake.

"I'm sorry I woke you," Alex said, his breathing ragged.

"That's OK," Jaimie said. "It seems strange in here."

"What do you mean?" Alex asked.

"This is the only room in this house that isn't filled with memories," she said.

"Are you having trouble sleeping?" Alex asked.

"I can't even manage the restless sleep you seemed to be having," Jaimie said. "Do you want to talk about your dream?"

"I don't think it'll help," Alex said.

"It might," Jaimie said. "We're third level friends, remember?"

"I keep dreaming about those little girls that were murdered," Alex said. "Sometimes I think I should leave the bureau. There are times when I'm not sure I want to keep seeing and doing some of the things I have to do to get the job done."

"I guess we all have our demons, don't we?" Jaimie asked.

"Yes, we do," Alex said. "I'm so damn sorry about your father, Jaimie. Tell me what you're feeling?"

"I don't know how I'm going to make it without him," Jaimie said as she began to cry.

"It's OK," Alex said as he pulled her close. "Go ahead, Jaimie. Cry it out. I'll hold you."

"I never realized it would hurt like this," Jaimie said. "I feel like I have this weight in my chest. I don't want to feel this anymore."

"Is there anything I can do?" Alex asked.

"Make me feel something else for a while," Jaimie said as she put her arms around his neck and kissed him gently.

"I don't think we should do this," Alex said.

"I've been imagining what it would be like to kiss you," Jaimie said as she kissed him again, this time molding her mouth along the contours of his.

"Sometimes, once in a great while," Jaimie said as she moved her lips across his chest, "you kiss someone and everything just seems to come together perfectly."

"Jaimie, you're very vulnerable," Alex said as his breath caught. "I don't want to take advantage of that."

"It's OK, Alex," Jaimie said as she pulled back slightly, lifted the nightgown over her head, and pressed her body close to Alex's. "We're married, remember?"

The fragments of a dream floated through Alex's consciousness when he felt Jaimie's nipples brush against his bare chest. The intensity of the contact and their immediate, hungry arousal startled them both. They kissed again, their mouths searching first for comfort and then something more as the sounds of the ocean became merely background noise.

Alex remembered all those places he had thought about kissing Jaimie and then set out to accomplish the task. They rolled over each other frequently, taking turns leading the way, watching each other's reactions and then letting the perceived cues dictate the next move. The guestroom, where no ghosts haunted Jaimie, represented a source for new memories. For the first time, Jaimie was able to forget about Logan's death, Maxicillin, dying babies and anything but the soothing harmony of moving in perfect synchronization with Alex. When they were sated and exhausted, sleep finally claimed them.

CHAPTER EIGHTEEN

Jaimie stirred reluctantly, unwilling to surrender the warm, safe cocoon provided by the soft hair on Alex's chest. The rise and fall of his thorax accompanied the comforting, soothing rhythm of each heartbeat.

She looked at Alex's face, peaceful and innocent in slumber and took note of the details. Overnight, his beard looked dark and coarse. Jaimie blushed when she remembered the feel of the stubble on his chin and his lips when he moved them over her body.

Alex's arm was around Jaimie and his hand rested possessively on her left hip. Jaimie wondered if last night's events represented her neediness from her father's death or her underlying feelings for Alex.

The phone rang and startled them both but Alex only stirred slightly. Another strident ring and Alex was fully awake, looking at Jaimie with a confused stare and then reaching for the phone which was on the table by his side of the bed.

"Hello," Alex said weakly after he picked up the phone.

"Good morning, Alex," Jack Connelly said. "I guess it's pretty early there. I wanted to see how Jaimie was doing."

"I'll get her for you," Alex said as he put his hand over the receiver. After a couple of minutes, he handed Jaimie the phone and got out of bed.

"Hi, Jack," Jaimie said as she took the phone from Alex, who avoided looking into her eyes.

"I'm OK, Jack," Jaimie said. "I appreciate your concern."

Alex watched her as he pulled his jeans on, zipped them up, and walked across the room. Jaimie had a sheet draped over her lower body, but Alex could see her bare back and the curve of one breast as he stood in the doorway.

The memories they made in the guestroom followed him while he walked into the kitchen. He took a plastic jug of orange juice out of the refrigerator, taking a long gulp as the guilt hovered and then settled in his consciousness. Alex realized that making love to Jaimie was a mistake, and he accepted the fact it was his fault. He ran his hand through his hair and remembered Jack's warning about sleeping with her. He wanted to kick himself for letting it happen.

He remembered the feel of Jaimie's skin, and how each touch seemed to be charged with an electric current that escalated into the body rush and finally, the exquisite release. Alex pushed those thoughts aside as he considered what he should do now.

The web that surrounded them seemed to have an ever-widening reach. Their lives might depend on finding the answer inside Sayer, not in exploring what they felt for each other. Alex concluded that Jack was right, but he also understood it was a little late to come to that conclusion.

"Alex," Jaimie said tentatively as she came into the kitchen wearing a robe.

"Last night was a mistake, Jaimie," Alex said as he turned around and glared at her. "It's not ever going to happen again."

"OK," Jaimie said.

"I mean it," Alex said. "We're not married. We'll just have to pretend last night never happened."

"I get it, Alex," Jaimie said.

"Good, we have a job to finish," Alex said. "Last night isn't going to change what we have to do or what happens when the job's over. That's all it is, Jaimie. Just a job."

"You're right, Alex, we're not married," Jaimie said. "I think you should go back to Atlanta today. I want to make the rest of the arrangements here by myself. I'll come back tomorrow like I planned."

"Are you sure that's what you want?" Alex asked.

"I'm positive," Jaimie said. "I need some time alone. There are some things I need to do by myself."

"OK, I'll pick you up at the airport tomorrow," Alex said.

"Whatever," Jaimie said as she left the kitchen and walked down the hall to her room. When she reached it, she slammed shut its door as well as the one to her heart.

Two hours later, Alex was on his way to the airport, and Jaimie was cleaning out Logan's refrigerator wishing the freezer wasn't self defrosting so she could attack it with an ice pick. Tears welled up when she thought about Logan and then Alex, who left without any additional comments.

He had called last night a terrible mistake, and Jaimie could tell by the look on his face that he meant every angry word he uttered. So much for men and the possibility of third level friendships. She tried not to let the romantic glare from last night rule her thoughts, but in unguarded moments, Jaimie understood she already missed her friend.

The possibility of withdrawing from the investigation flashed through Jaimie's mind. She wouldn't have to face Alex or deal with what might become a very unpleasant situation. Guilt accompanied those thoughts along with the images of the dead babies, but Jaimie decided to consider that option until she returned to Atlanta.

When she finished cleaning all the shelves, Jaimie turned her attention to the items in the door of the refrigerator. There were several bottles of insulin sitting there, and fresh tears came to Jaimie's eyes as she threw them in the trashcan. As she watched the bottles land, she realized something was wrong but wasn't sure what was bothering her.

Jaimie thought her father had been taking NPH insulin, and she was puzzled by the fact that NPH usually appears cloudy after it is shaken. Both of the bottles in the trash can still looked clear. Her father might have been taking another type of insulin, so she picked up both bottles from the trash to check the labels. The NPH sticker was prominently displayed, but she began to shake when she read the manufacturer's label.

The words Sayer Pharmaceuticals were prominently displayed on both labels, and Jaimie's fear turned to rage when she thought about what might have happened. She picked up the phone in the kitchen, dialed the number, and waited for the phone on the other end of the line to ring.

Ray Howard paced and mumbled to himself, convinced Jaimie must be experiencing some kind of paranoid episode associated with her father's death. He was waiting for her at Kelleher Labs where he had made arrangements for the bottles of insulin to be tested. Jaimie looked pale and shaken when she joined him half an hour later.

"Hi, Ray," Jaimie said.

"Hi, Jaimie," Ray Howard said. "How are you doing?"

"I'm not paranoid, Ray," Jaimie said. "I'm involved in something I can't discuss. I think someone is trying to send me a message."

"It might be a pretty deadly message," Ray said.

"Actually, I hope I'm wrong," Jaimie said.

"Let's have them analyze the contents of the bottles," Ray said as he led the way into the lab. "Then we'll know for sure."

The technician looked at her strangely when Jaimie asked her to wear gloves to remove a sample from each bottle but she complied. Jaimie and Ray Howard were drinking Dr. Peppers in a small waiting area when the technician walked in with the bag containing the bottles of insulin and a computer print out.

"Both bottles contain water," the tech said with a surprised look on her face as she handed both items to Jaimie.

"Thanks a lot," Jaimie said as the tech walked away.

"What are you involved in, Jaimie?" Ray Howard asked.

"Nothing illegal, Ray," Jaimie said. "I need for you to keep this information confidential for a while."

"If Logan was injecting himself with water instead of insulin his death was no accident," Ray said. "It all makes sense now. That's why his blood sugar got so high. He was still weak from the flu so not getting any insulin was enough to send his blood sugar into orbit."

"Someone removed the insulin from the vials and substituted water," Jaimie said.

"Logan was murdered," Ray Howard said. "The coroner has to be notified."

"We can't do that right now," Jaimie said. "I'm working with the FBI, Ray. I need for you to keep this confidential. I'll have someone from the FBI contact you."

"Do you have any idea who did this?" Ray asked.

"It's all connected," Jaimie said.

"Are you in danger too, Jaimie?" Ray asked quietly.

"I guess I am," Jaimie said. "I didn't really think about it until now. Maybe I should have given it more thought before I got involved. If I had, Logan might still be alive."

"You said before someone might be trying to send you a message," Ray said. "Is the message back off or else?"

"Yes, but I have a personal stake in this now," Jaimie said. "There won't be any backing off."

Dr. Marc Grant's North Atlanta office was crowded with patients; the doctor had an emergency. The fact he routinely instructed his staff to book patients every ten minutes didn't help. There were no empty seats left in the crowded waiting room.

His infected sinus passages throbbing mercilessly, Daryll Connor sat with the rest of the patients. Daryll came to Marc Grant's office hoping he could get an antibiotic so he could survive another spring allergy season.

Daryll wore jeans, boots, biker gloves, and a denim jacket with the sleeves ripped out. The tattoo "Born To Be Wild" on Daryll's exposed forearm caught the attention of the old lady who was sitting next to him. Then she looked at the dangling earring hanging from Daryll's left ear lobe.

After the nurse came out and took someone back to an exam room, the old woman got up and moved to a different seat. It made Daryll's day when he realized the woman was disturbed by his appearance.

The magazines were two years old, but those who waited picked up discarded copies as soon as they were relinquished. Several old copies of People occupied Daryll until he was called to begin his wait in one of the rooms in the back. Daryll checked his watch and realized he probably had another hour to wait. A simple equation of doubling whatever time was spent in the waiting room usually worked when trying to figure when Marc Grant would appear in the exam room.

The nurse escorted Daryll into room 5, took his blood pressure, temperature, and assured him Dr. Grant would be with him soon. Daryll grunted, realizing his perception of soon was very different from hers. The tall man with dark hair who walked into exam room 5 wore a white coat but didn't look familiar to Daryll.

"Hi, Daryll," the tall man said as he shook Daryll's hand and sat down across from him on the stool. "I'm Alex Tanner. I'm an FBI agent."

"I'm outta here," Daryll said.

"Hang on, Daryll," Alex said. "I know you talked to Agent Petersen in Nashville before you moved here. He told me the last time you talked you said they were watching you and you couldn't call anymore."

Daryll looked at Alex with a guarded, surprised look on his face.

"I have an ID, Daryll," Alex said as he pulled it out of his pocket. "Petersen said if I called you 'Scooby' you'd know I'm with the FBI."

"OK, I believe you're with the FBI," Daryll said. "I didn't expect to ever talk to you guys again. They watch me constantly. There's no way I can get to a phone."

"That's why I'm here, Daryll," Alex said. "We've been trying to contact all our sources recently to see if there's anything going on we should know about."

"There's a shit load of stuff going on," Daryll said. "I keep trying to figure out a way to get out, but I know they won't let anyone go, at least not alive."

"What's going on?" Alex asked.

"This group wasn't into much until a couple of years ago," Daryll said. "I got in it because of my brother. He's the one who's really into this shit. In the beginning, it was just a lot of bullshit talk. We always had a lot of guns and we talked about blowing things up and shit like that. That's all it really was, a lot of big talk. Just a bunch of guys drinking and shooting off guns in the woods."

"What changed?" Alex asked.

"We got a new leader," Daryll said. "He came in and took over and suddenly everyone got real serious. That's when I got scared and started talking to Petersen. They started following me, and I told Petersen I couldn't call anymore."

"What's going on now?" Alex asked.

"These people are talking about getting even in a big way," Daryll said. "I only hear bits and pieces. They aren't talking about bombs and guns anymore. I heard them talking a couple of months ago about causing some kind of illness. I didn't think much about it until those babies started getting sick. They know something about that. I think they did it. I think they're planning something else, something bigger."

"What?" Alex asked.

"I don't know," Daryll admitted. "Most of the time, I just stay drunk and do what they tell me to. I'm scared. If they find out I talked to you guys, I'm a dead man."

"We need to keep in contact with you, Daryll," Alex said.

"You need to fucking get me out of there," Daryll said.

"Let's get you out today," Alex said.

"No, I have to talk to my brother first," Daryll said.

"I'll have them give you a follow up appointment in a few days," Alex said. "That should give you enough time to talk to your brother. I'll be here when you come back. See what you can find out in the meantime. What's the name of your group?"

"We call ourselves the Reapers," Daryll said. "Isn't that a load of shit? I just want out. These people scare the piss out of me."

"What do you know about the new leader?" Alex asked.

"Nothing much," Daryll said. "I've never seen him and I don't know his name. The only thing I know is that he's some kind of scientist or doctor or something like that."

Grace Collier was weeding the flowerbed in front of her house. The weeds were a constant source of irritation for Grace, who was considering covering all the beds with mulch.

"You don't seem to be enjoying your gardening," Jaimie said as she sat down on the steps.

"I used to. That's when I was younger and had more patience. Now it just feels like another task I have to complete. How are you doing?"

"OK, I guess. It just seems so strange."

"I know what you mean. I find myself thinking about going over to see Logan, and then I realize he isn't there."

"Aunt Grace, did you see anybody hanging around Logan's house the last couple of days?"

"What do you mean?" Grace asked.

"Did you see any strangers recently?" Jaimie asked.

"I don't think so," Grace said. "Wait a minute. There was a guy coming down Logan's front walk the day before he died."

"What did he look like?" Jaimie asked.

"I was looking into the sun when I talked to him," Grace said. "I don't remember much. He said he had the wrong address and left."

"You don't remember anything, Aunt Grace? Think. What color was his hair? Was he tall?"

"I kept having to look up to see him, so I know he was tall," she said. "He had light hair and wore sunglasses. Oh, and I remember he walked with a limp."

Chapter Nineteen

Jaimie tried to pick out familiar landmarks as her plane descended to William B. Hartsfield's-Atlanta International Airport. Alex's last icy glare lingered in Jaimie's memory, so she hoped be wouldn't be waiting when the plane landed.

Now that Jaimie knew Logan had been murdered, a fire burned in her heart. Any thought of bailing out or concerns regarding her uncomfortable relationship with Alex would now be a secondary consideration.

Alex saw Jaimie first and a rush of tender emotions washed over him. He had destroyed the carefully built bridge of trust between them because he felt it was the only way to salvage their mission. Now, as he watched Jaimie walk toward the arrival area, he wasn't sure he could continue to pull off the act.

Jaimie spotted him and looked disappointed. Alex cringed when he realized she had resurrected that guarded smile, but he accepted his fate. When Jaimie reached him, he hugged her tightly.

"Someone followed me to the airport," he whispered. "How was your flight?"

"It was fine," Jaimie said.

"We need to get your bags," Alex said as he reached for Jaimie's hand.

When they reached the car, Jaimie pulled her hand away. It wasn't until they reached I-85 that Alex broke the silence.

"There are some new developments here. I talked with an informant yesterday. He told me about a new paramilitary group that might be involved. Supposedly, their leader is a doctor or scientist. He thinks their group might be responsible for spreading newborn pneumonia."

"Do you think that's a possibility?" Jaimie asked.

"We're taking it seriously," Alex said. "They're a new group, and we don't know much about them, but we're looking into it."

"I have some information, too," Jaimie said as she pulled the plastic bag containing the insulin bottles out of her purse.

"When I was cleaning out my father's refrigerator, I found these insulin bottles," she said. "The insulin in this bottle should be cloudy but it isn't. I had both bottles tested and they contain water."

"What are you saying?" Alex asked.

"I'm saying someone murdered my father," Jaimie said. "Logan injected himself with water instead of insulin, and that's what made his blood sugar soar."

"You think it's someone connected to this?" Alex asked.

"These bottles have Sayer labels on them," Jaimie said. "Aunt Grace saw a man with light hair and a limp at my father's house the day before he died. I think someone was trying to send me a message."

"Do you think it's the man who chased you through building A?"

"He was the first one I thought of," Jaimie admitted.

"I'll send the bottles to the FBI lab in Washington," Alex said. "They can verify the test results and check the bottles for prints."

*

Luke Harper was experiencing an episode of severe ankle pain. His Achilles tendon was inflamed, and the inflammation caused his pronounced limp. He stretched his foot to relieve the stiffness.

Garrett had insisted Luke remain in Atlanta while they complete the formal application process to the FDA for the new drug Luke had developed. At least his current stay in Atlanta seemed more palatable than the last one. When Garrett was building the lab on Jekyll Island, Luke had lived in Atlanta for several months but never really felt comfortable.

Terry White had worked in the same building and accounted for most of Harper's distress. Their relationship had ended so badly last year Luke dodged White whenever possible. The sex had been intense, frequent, but they were unable to communicate on any other level. Luke began to search for reasons to avoid contact.

The three flights of stairs he walked down increased his ankle pain sequentially. By the time he reached the last set, he almost ran into Jaimie, who was coming up the steps two at a time. They mumbled courtesies and Luke noticed that Jaimie stared at him strangely when she realized he was limping.

Jack Connelly got another cup of coffee and sat down at his desk in D.C. to review the reports from field agents who had been interviewing informants. When his phone rang, he welcomed the diversion.

"Jack Connelly," he said.

"Jack, Jaimie and I are here," Alex said.

"Good," Jack said. "How are you, Jaimie?"

"Better, thanks," Jaimie said.

"I wanted to have this conference call so we could talk about where we are," Jack said. "I've had agents out completing interviews."

"What have they come up with?" Alex asked.

"We're still looking at this from two possible angles," Jack said. "The revenge motive as well as the possibility of domestic terrorism."

"We haven't been able to dig up much on the Reapers," Jack said. "They have been quiet and very careful. Some of these groups are vocal and make a lot of threats but that isn't the case with this group. I wish I could tell you I find that comforting but I can't. There's always the possibility they believe in deeds instead of words."

"Do you have anything concrete?" Alex asked.

"All we know is that they are based somewhere near Atlanta," Jack said. "We had another informant confirm their existence. He was with them briefly but they tossed him out. He met with them several times. Those meetings were in the woods, so he doesn't know anything else except he thought they were pretty spooky."

"We need to get Daryll Connor out of there," Alex said.

"Yes, we do," Jack said. "We'll have more agents at Dr. Grant's office. Daryll isn't going to have a choice this time. He's the only link we have so we'll take him into protective custody."

"What about that Sayer employee Wendel had an affair with?" Jaimie asked.

"Katherine Carter lives in Florida now," Jack said. "The agent who interviewed her said she seemed angry but he thought she had gone on with her life. She seemed delighted the FBI was looking at Garrett, so I'm sure she's hoping we find something to bury him with."

"What about the guy with the limp who works for Fletcher?" Alex asked.

"We haven't been able to come up with an ID on him," Jack said. "Fletcher has been out of town and the guy with the limp seems to have disappeared."

"What do we have on Fletcher, Garrett, and Harper?" Alex asked.

"Fletcher worked for the CIA for a while," Jack said. "They dumped him when he couldn't control his drinking. He's worked for Garrett for three years. Apparently, he beats his wife. She's been in the hospital several times."

"What about Garrett and Harper?" Jaimie asked.

"Both of them went to medical school and then into research," Jack said. "Strangely enough, they have similar personal histories. They were only children who ended up being raised by an elderly relative. We're not going to be able to get anything from either one of those ladies."

"Why not?" Alex asked.

"One of them died two years ago," Jack said. "The other one is confined to a private sanitarium. The agent talked to the administrator. Apparently, this woman is delusional and hears voices. The agent didn't see any point in doing a personal interview."

"Is there anyone else we could interview?" Alex asked.

"I'm going to send an agent to a small town in Georgia to interview Garrett's former neighbors," Jack said. "He lived there for about ten years. Harper grew up right there in Atlanta."

"I'll interview his neighbors," Alex offered.

"I'll fax you their names and addresses," Jack said.

"There's something else that's been bothering us," Jaimie said.

"What is it?" Jack asked.

"McGrath must have told Garrett the contamination was intentional," Jaimie said. "Why didn't Garrett just report it? Why would he cover it up?"

"Maybe he was worried about the effect news reports linking Sayer to the contamination might have," Jack said.

"Would he go that far to protect them?" Alex asked.

"Greed and arrogance get a lot of people in trouble," Jack said. "Are you suggesting Garrett had some other motive?"

"Maybe he just had a different agenda," Jaimie said.

"Like what?" Jack asked.

"What if Garrett has some connection to the Reapers?" Jaimie asked.

"That's an ugly thought," Jack said. "We'll look into it."

"Jack, did you find any other prints on those insulin bottles?" Alex asked.

"No, the prints they could identify belong to Jaimie and her father," Jack said. "The tests confirmed the fact both vials contained water. I'm sorry, Jaimie."

"Thanks, Jack," Jaimie said.

"This is getting very dangerous," Alex said. "Maybe you should throw in the towel, Jaimie? No one would blame you if you did."

"I was thinking the same thing the other day," Jaimie said. "At least until I realized they killed my father. Now I won't quit until I figure out who did it."

Alex approached the brightly painted condo, a clone lost in a cluster of similar units. Several frustrating days had elapsed since Alex began trying to locate any friends or former neighbors of Luke Harper.

Yesterday he found the address of the house Harper lived in for the first fifteen years of his life. The vacant lot, which was now inhabited by a sparse collection of weeds, seemed to be all that was left of that part of Harper's life. Former neighbors had scattered, and Alex hadn't found anyone to interview who was alive or remembered Harper.

Alex approached the condo where Harper had lived after he left Stanford. Alex read the number and walked up the steep steps. He rang the bell and hoped this effort wouldn't lead to another dead end. The woman who finally answered the door sounded surly as if he had disturbed her, and she opened the door reluctantly.

The chain only allowed the door to open a few inches, so all Alex could see was an unruly mass of gray hair.

"What do you want?" the woman asked.

"I'm Alex Tanner, FBI," he said as he stuck his ID into the partially open door.

"Really?" the woman asked as she inspected Alex's ID. "What do you want?"

"I wanted to talk to you about a former neighbor," Alex said.

"This isn't about me?" the woman asked.

"No," Alex said.

"Cool," the woman said as she removed the chain and opened the door. "Come in."

Alex looked around the tidy condo, which was decorated with every conceivable kind of country craft item. The woman pointed to a chair.

When Alex sat down, he found himself staring into the face of a very large stuffed pig sitting on the table next to him.

"Who did you want to ask me about?" the woman asked.

"Luke Harper lived next door to you for a while, didn't he?" Alex asked.

"Yes, he did," the woman said. "He wasn't very friendly. I tried to talk to him but he always avoided me and everyone else around here."

"Is there anything you remember about him?" Alex asked.

"Mostly that he was so unfriendly," the woman said.

"Did you ever see anyone else?" Alex asked. "Did he have any friends or did anyone ever come by?"

"No, I really don't remember anyone," the woman said.

"Any idea what he did in his spare time?" Alex asked.

"He used to go away on weekends," the woman said. "I can remember seeing him pack up his car, and then he would leave for a couple of days at a time."

"Any idea where he went?" Alex asked.

"Not exactly," the woman said. "But he must have gone someplace in the woods."

"Why did you think that?" Alex asked.

"He wore fatigues," the woman said. "I figured he was out in the woods somewhere with one of those groups that shoot each other with paint balls or something."

Jaimie was running with Jake, who was trying to keep pace at her side. She had just gotten her second wind so her lungs no longer burned.

The details of the Maxicillin research kept flashing through her mind as she approached the open expanse of road that wound along the woods. She wore reflective clothing as a precaution though there was never much traffic along this stretch.

Jake was huffing more than usual and Jaimie realized how quickly both of them had gotten out of shape. He looked up at her occasionally begging for mercy, but Jaimie only smiled and encouraged him to keep going.

The headlights appeared from behind and Jaimie moved a little closer to Jake to accommodate the car. The driver put the headlights on high beam, and left them on high as the car approached.

Jaimie kept her pace steady until the driver appeared to floor the vehicle. When she realized the car was racing toward her at a high rate of speed, she stopped and decided to wait until the car passed. All Jaimie could see when she looked to the side was the steep embankment dotted with trees.

Jake whined as the car and the blinding lights headed right for them. Jaimie looked, convinced the driver of the car would see them and move to the middle of the road. She glanced at Jake and then at the lights again as the vehicle veered even farther to her side of the road, speeding up as it bore down on them.

Alex looked through the reports while he drank a glass of tea. He had expressed his reservations to Jaimie about her run, but he could tell by the look of intransigence on her face there would be no discussion. Since that last morning in San Diego, the atmosphere surrounding them had been thick with anger, regret, and unexpressed, hidden feelings.

Jaimie had been distant since she returned, and Alex was no longer convinced he could continue the charade. The brutal truth was that he missed her warm smile and the closeness they had shared. She had truly become a third level friend, the only one he had ever had. Every night he dreamed about making love to her, and he couldn't conceive of his soul being free of her regardless of what happened with the investigation.

Alex wandered about Jaimie's house, looking at the pictures of Logan and her aunts on the walls. The minutes crawled by and increased Alex's anxiety. He continued to pace around, playing various scenarios that could have detained Jaimie and Jake.

Unable to stay in the house any longer, Alex picked up the car keys and jumped into Jaimie's car. As he drove through the deserted neighborhood, his eyes scanned the area to see if he could see a runner or a golden retriever.

Jaimie's immediate neighborhood led to a dark stretch of road. When he rounded a corner, Alex spotted the flares that had been placed by the side and his heart stopped. There was no sign of Jaimie, but he could see Jake being restrained by a police officer.

Alex pulled the car to the side of the embankment and walked quickly toward the officer. Jake pulled hard on the rope the officer held and broke free when he saw Alex. The officer approached as Alex bent down to pet him.

"Is that your dog, sir?" the young officer asked.

"Yes, my wife always takes him with her when she runs," Alex said nervously. "Where is she?"

"It was a hit and run," the officer said. "The driver probably came around the corner too quickly and couldn't see her until it was too late."

Chapter Twenty

The soft, soothing lighting captured Rudy Fletcher's attention when he walked into the office. Garrett was sitting behind the massive desk, a thoughtful expression resting comfortably on his face.

Rudy Fletcher never had unguarded moments, Wendel concluded as he watched Fletcher's cloaked, observant eyes scan the room. Rudy's belief that Wendel's only goal was the acquisition of wealth suited Wendel's purposes perfectly. Wendel realized Rudy had lost any passion he might have felt for causes. Now, Rudy sold his experience to the highest bidder without any moral concerns.

"How was your trip?" Wendel asked.

"Everything went well," Rudy said. "How are things here?"

"The research on Maxicillin is about to pay off," Wendel said. "If Jaimie can keep White's team together, I think we'll get what we want."

"Then we can get rid of her," Rudy said.

"That's the plan," Wendel said. "I've decided to have a meeting at Jekyll Island this weekend. I want the entire team to get the message we're going to rap up the research there. It will be a mandatory meeting. I wasn't going to invite spouses."

"I think you should," Rudy said. "Then we can keep an eye on Alex Martin."

"Are you sure you want him there?" Wendel asked.

"Yeah, I'm sure," Rudy said. "Now that I'm back, I'm going to do a little more snooping around into his background. Maybe I can come up with something before we leave for the weekend. I sent Jaimie a message like I said I would. Hopefully, she got it and she'll back off."

"I suspected you were involved in her father's death, but I don't want a confirmation," Wendel said. "I'll be glad when this weekend is over and we can be done with this mess."

Alex pulled the car into the St. Francis emergency room parking lot, talking constantly to Jake in a nervous attempt to convince them both Jaimie wasn't severely injured.

Jake wanted to follow Alex, who rebuffed his advance and ordered him to stay. Jake sat down in the back seat and placed his massive head on his front paws in a pose designed to look extremely forlorn. Alex got out of the car and whispered soft assurances to Jake his ploy wasn't working.

The driveway to the emergency room was lined with harsh spotlights. A loud swish signaled the opening of the automatic doors, the first in a series of furious noises that accompanied the activity going on at the desk. Several secretaries manned the station and were in the process of speaking with relatives or answering the phones.

Alex approached an older secretary who was heavily engaged in a terse conversation on the phone. A kind smile crossed her face when she saw Alex, and she raised a finger as if to say she would be with him soon.

Alex waited patiently, dreading the news he might have to hear if he hurried the response. The conversation finally ended and the woman smiled at Alex.

"Can I help you?" she asked.

"I think they brought my wife here," Alex said weakly.

"What's her name?" she asked.

"Jaimie Martin," Alex said.

"Yes, she's here," the secretary said. "I think your wife's in x-ray right now, Mr. Martin. Why don't you wait in the waiting room? I'll tell the nurse you're here and try to get her to come and talk to you."

"Thanks," Alex said as he walked toward the crowded waiting room.

Alex breathed a little easier when he realized Jaimie must be alive since they were taking x-rays, but her injuries could be extensive. He paced aimlessly around the room with other distraught relatives.

An old movie was playing on the t.v. that was attached to the wall. Most of the other inhabitants of the room seemed to be watching it intently. It wasn't clear if they were having the same strange, disjointed thoughts he was experiencing at the moment.

After what seemed like an eternity, a nurse wearing scrubs came into the waiting room as twenty pairs of eyes became riveted on her.

"Alex Martin," she said as she scanned the room.

"Yes," Alex said as he walked over to her.

The nurse smiled when she saw the sick expression on Alex's face.

"Your wife is fine, Mr. Martin," she said as she led him back to the trauma room. "She has a nasty bump on her head, and we had to put in a few stitches, but the skull films are negative. The doctor is with her."

The nurse stopped by the third trauma room and directed Alex inside with a wave of her arm. Alex entered and saw Jaimie sitting on the side of the exam table, a thick dressing and an ice bag covering the right side of her face.

Alex smiled, raced across the room, and wrapped his arms around her. Jaimie returned his gesture with an equal amount of intensity.

"I was scared," Alex finally said as he backed up slightly and put his hands on Jaimie's face. "When you didn't come back, I went looking for you. I came around that corner and saw Jake. A cop told me they brought you here."

"Where is Jake?" Jaimie asked.

"He's in the car," Alex said. "He's fine, but I think he's mad I left him out there."

"Mr. Martin, I'm Dr. Brown," the tall, thin doctor with the wire rimmed glasses said from the other side of the table.

"I'm sorry," Alex said as he reached over the table to shake the doctor's hand.

"That's OK," Dr. Brown said. "Your wife has a slight concussion. She sustained a pretty good blow to the back of her head. The skull films are negative but she's a little dizzy and she's having some nausea. Those are symptoms of a concussion. We can either keep her overnight for observation or you can take her home but you'll have to wake her up every two hours to make sure she's all right."

"She's coming home with me," Alex said quickly, ending any further need for discussion.

Daryll Connor guided his Harley around the dark, lonely corners of the old interstate that led to the safe house owned by the Reapers. The rush of the pot Daryll had smoked was only partially diminished by the alcohol he had consumed.

The Reapers were far too intense to suit Daryll's tastes, and he would be glad when his involvement with them was over. He hated having to pretend he shared their goals, whatever the hell they were.

Bright headlights from behind startled Daryll. They were the only source of light he had seen for the last half-hour. Daryll finally relaxed, convincing himself the vehicle wasn't close.

Dr. Jekyll had a difficult time keeping up with Daryll Connor; Daryll didn't follow the rules. Instead of waiting at traffic lights, Daryll eased his bike between the other cars so he could be the first one through when the light changed. If anyone objected with a honk, Daryll would just stick up his middle finger and take off.

The turn off to the old interstate came up so quickly Dr. Jekyll missed it, so he had to turn around and come back. He had only been to this safe house twice, and both times it had been during the day when Daryll had been sent away on an errand. Jekyll made up lost time on this last stretch of winding, hilly, deserted road. He caught a glimpse of Connor's Harley around the next bend and began to feel the rush that came with pursuit.

Daryll Connor had been a liability from the outset, but Jekyll needed Daryll's brother, so he had waited to take care of the problem. Now the time had come for tying up all the loose ends. Daryll's departure marked the beginning of the climax that would get rid of anyone who posed a potential threat.

Jaimie Martin and her pesky husband would have to be dealt with, but Jekyll needed a more elaborate plan to get rid of them. A smile crossed his face as he considered the message he had already sent and his options for the final solution. For the moment, when Jekyll saw the taillights of Connor's Harley, he forgot all about Jaimie Martin.

The adrenaline rush took over as he approached Connor's Harley and bumped the back of it gently. Fear appeared on Daryll's face as he looked back at the car, increasing Jekyll's enjoyment. Daryll tried to speed up but the sleek sports car kept pace, bumping the rear end of the Harley repeatedly.

Daryll was no longer enjoying the rush from the pot or the ride. At the moment, he was feeling nothing but complete and utter terror while he tried to think of a plan that might spare his life. The driver of the vehicle behind him was toying with him, but Daryll understood he would eventually grow tired of the game. As he rounded the next corner, Daryll felt the Harley begin to slip out of his control.

Dr. Jekyll decided he had played with Connor long enough. He floored the vehicle, striking the Harley broadside, which caused it to lift off the ground and become airborne on the crest of a very large hill. Jekyll braked forcefully, jumped out of the car, and watched the Harley fly down the side of the hill with only Daryll's high pitched scream to accompany its flight.

At first, the Harley seemed suspended in mid-air until it finally landed in dense vegetation and disappeared. Jekyll could hear the sound of the fragments landing at the bottom of the hill. Jekyll breathed in the cool, crisp air as his adrenaline rush reached fever pitch. He looked around and realized no one would be able to see what was left of the Harley from this vantage point. Everyone would believe Daryll had finally bolted just like his brother had predicted he would.

Somewhere in the distance, he heard the sound of a coyote howling and suddenly he joined the forlorn animal in a long deep howl followed by his insane laughter. He might be just as crazy as Jenny Morgan but he was far more dangerous.

Jaimie looked sleepy when she walked into her kitchen the next morning, picked up a mug, and poured herself a cup of coffee. Soft music from a local radio station played in the background. Alex was reading the newspaper but chuckled when he looked at Jaimie and saw the expression on her face.

"You look like you've got a hangover," Alex said.

"That's an appropriate description of how I feel," Jaimie said. "Did you wake me up last night? I have vague memories of someone shaking me."

"Yes, I did," Alex said. "You scared me at four a.m. I kept shaking you but you didn't respond at first. Finally, you told me to leave you alone."

"I'm sorry," Jaimie said as she blushed slightly. "Thank you for taking care of me."

"I'm just glad you're OK," Alex said. "I guess there's no point trying to convince you to quit, is there?"

Before Jaimie could respond, the announcer on the radio station began to read the morning news.

"In a sad development, Senator Ted Drew announced this morning he was withdrawing from the Presidential race. Officially, he spoke of devoting more time to his family. Unnamed sources confirm that Drew's wife recently attempted suicide as a result of her depression over the death of their son. Sources within the party expressed sympathy but disappointment at the withdrawal of a candidate they expected to win the election in November."

"He came to see me at the hospital after his son died," Jaimie said sadly. "He wanted me to be sure I remembered the pain in his eyes so I would find the answer."

"Is that why you agreed to get involved in this?" Alex asked.

"It was part of the reason," Jaimie said. "I can't quit now, Alex. If I do, then it means that Logan and the rest of them all died for nothing. We have to stop them."

Carol Fletcher met with Conrad Morton, Margo Garrett's attorney, at his spacious downtown office. Conrad Morton was fifty, nervous, and didn't look like he enjoyed much of anything, including the practice of law. Carol met with Morton while Margo waited in Morton's outer office.

"I hope you don't mind if I smoke," he said.

"I don't mind," Carol said as she lit a cigarette of her own.

"I think I have everything I need," Morton said nervously. "Is it true that your husband has violent tendencies?"

"Yes," Carol said.

"Do you think he would hurt you if he suspected what you were doing?" Morton asked.

"I think Rudy would hurt anyone who got in his way," Carol said.

"I'll remember that," Morton said. "I talked with Margo's investment counselor. The property your father left you should be worth a fortune, so we're going to set up a separate account in your name. He's going to arrange to sell the property. Then he'll invest the money."

"Are you sure Rudy won't be able to get his hands on it?" Carol asked.

"Hopefully, he won't find out until it's a fait accompli," Conrad said. "When it's sold and invested, you should think about filing for divorce. I'll get a restraining order."

"I'm not sure that will stop Rudy," Carol said.

"Maybe you should consider filing and leaving town," Conrad said. "He can't hurt you if he can't find you."

After her meeting with Morton, Carol left his office with Margo. Lunch was next on the agenda as they got in Carol's blue Honda Accord. Carol wasn't particularly hungry, but she wasn't sure whether it was fear or anger that was causing her gastric distress. Carol guided the Honda onto the entrance ramp that led to I-85.

Carol tried to weave into the interstate traffic, but the driver of a black pick up was traveling at the same rate of speed to her left and seemed intent on blocking Carol's access to the highway. Resigned to entering the lane after the pick up went by, Carol slowed down to allow it to pass. Instead of passing her, the driver also slowed down, confusing Carol, who assumed the driver was slowing down to allow her access to the lane. When Carol speeded up, the other driver followed suit, again blocking Carol's access.

Out of room on the ramp, Carol made a complete stop. The driver of the pick up finally flew past her, honking and giving Carol the finger as a parting gesture.

"What an asshole," Margo remarked as Carol finally pulled the Honda on the highway.

A boiling, escalating rage consumed Carol Fletcher as her hands tightened around the leather wrapped steering wheel. All attempts to control her anger utterly failed until Carol floored the Honda and began to weave in and out of the traffic. Carol was only vaguely aware that Margo was staring at her.

Carol approached the rear end of the black pick up truck. She remained close to his bumper and noticed he looked at her frequently in his rear view mirror. Suddenly, Carol turned the wheel of the Accord sharply to the left and came alongside the driver's side of the pick up. When Carol looked over, she saw the emblem "Go Braves" prominently displayed on the hat the driver wore, but that only seemed to increase Carol's rage.

"I hate that chop thing they do at Brave's games," Carol said furiously as she floored the Honda.

"Chop this, asshole," Carol screamed as the Honda flew past the pick up.

Carol forced the black truck off the road. Both vehicles came to a screeching halt as Carol jumped out and ran to the driver's side of the truck. She opened the door and grabbed the young driver by the collar while she screamed obscenities at him.

Her hands imbedded in the soft padding of the dash, Margo Garrett watched from the Honda. She breathed gulps of air to ease the shock that coursed through her body and considered her options. When she saw the driver of the truck reach for something under his seat, Margo realized she had to act.

Margo jumped out and ran over to the truck.

"You red neck son of a bitch," Carol yelled as Margo came up beside her.

"Carol, listen to me," Margo said as she looked at the frightened truck driver, whose right hand was hidden.

"You can't do this again, Carol," Margo said. "You can't castrate this one like the last guy. They won't care that you're crazy this time."

Carol still held on to the driver's shirt collar, but she looked at Margo with a confused expression on her face. The driver pushed her hands away, closed the door, and shifted the truck into reverse. When he was far enough behind the Honda, he rolled down the window and floored the truck so he could get around them.

"You're fucking crazy, you know that?" he screamed as he flew passed them.

Margo took Carol by the hand and led her back to the Honda, helping her get into the passenger side of the vehicle. Margo got into the driver's seat and pulled the Honda back on the highway while total silence prevailed inside the vehicle.

Carol looked pale and shaken but finally managed to say something.

"Why did you say that about castrating that guy?" she asked.

"I saw him reach under the seat," Margo said. "I didn't know what he was reaching for. It was the only thing I could think of that might scare him enough to make him leave."

"I've never done anything like that before," Carol said. "I can't believe I did that."

"I think it's good that you're finally getting some of that anger out," Margo said. "We're just going to have to figure out a way to keep you from killing anyone while you get it out of your system."

"OK," Carol said weakly.

"I realize you might take offense at this," Margo said. "Until we get you past some of this anger, I think I should drive."

"Sure, I get it," Carol said.

"Look at it this way, Carol," Margo said. "That red neck son of a bitch will think twice before he does that again."

Chapter Twenty One

Dr. Marc Grant's schedule was overbooked, so a sea of angry patients occupied his waiting room. The captives seemed restless and surly, so Grant's office staff was convinced a full moon must be influencing their behavior.

Alex wore a white lab coat and stayed in Grant's office while he waited for Daryll Connor to make an appearance. Daryll was already an hour late, and Alex checked with the agents watching outside frequently to see if they saw anyone who fit Daryll's description.

Jaimie believed the weekend trip to Jekyll Island would result in making Maxicillin a viable treatment option, and Alex could sense a climax approaching for the investigation inside Sayer.

Alex had difficulty sleeping, and he could hear Jaimie moving about her house at night as if they shared the same problem. Jaimie still seemed distant, and Alex wasn't sure if the Maxicillin research, the investigation inside Sayer, or her father's death consumed her.

When Jaimie got up for her nighttime walks, Alex decided not to approach her. She still maintained a discreet distance from him although he sensed she was no longer directing her anger toward him. Alex was surprised when he realized her indifference frightened him more than her wrath. At least the fury indicated some depth of feeling even if those feelings were all negative.

The afternoon waned, as did Alex's hope that Daryll Connor would attend his scheduled appointment. The last patient came and went as Grant's staff prepared to wrap up their day. Alex waited until everyone left the office before he phoned Jack Connelly.

"Connelly," the tired voice said.

"You sound like you've had the same kind of day I've had," Alex said.

"Daryll didn't show, huh?" Jack asked.

"No, I wish I could say I thought Daryll had ridden off into the sunset to find a better life but I think he's toast."

"I'll put an APB out for him just in case," Jack said. "But I think you're probably right."

"I wish this group was as vocal as some of them seem to be," Alex said.

"These quiet ones scare the hell out of me, too," Jack said. "They have a deliberate, deadly agenda and they don't brag about it, they just do their dirty work very quietly and efficiently."

"Do you have any more data on the Reapers?" Alex asked.

"No, we're looking at all the satellite transmissions to see if we can come up with anything," Jack said. "So far, we have zip. I did get some info on Rudy Fletcher from a source inside the CIA."

"Anything interesting?" Alex asked.

"Yeah, it's interesting," Jack said. "He went to medical school while he was with them. He graduated and got his M.D. but didn't complete an internship or residency. Supposedly, he did some biological work for them but that's all they'll tell me. I got totally stonewalled when I asked if the only reason he left was alcohol abuse."

"What do you think that means?" Alex asked.

"The last time I got that answer it turned out the guy had killed someone," Jack said.

"His resume didn't include anything about his medical training," Alex said. "I wonder why?"

"I'm not sure we'll ever know," Jack said. "How's Jaimie?"

"Quiet and very tense," Alex said.

"She's got a lot to cope with," Jack said.

"I know, I'll be glad when this is over," Alex said. "After the episode the other night, I've been having someone follow her when I can't. Actually, I'd better get going so I can follow her tonight."

Candace Carpenter walked through the doors of the restaurant wearing a long dress with a shawl carelessly wrapped around her shoulders. As she came down the aisle toward Jaimie's table, she smiled and waved at her daughter. Even at fifty, she remained a striking woman. The fact Jaimie looked so much like her had been a source of comfort for Logan but a definite source of irritation for Jaimie.

"I'm sorry I'm late," Candace said when she reached Jaimie's table.

'That's all right," Jaimie said as Candace sat down and the waiter took their drink orders.

"How have you been, Jaimie?" Candace asked.

"OK, I guess," Jaimie said.

"I know how hard Logan's death must be for you," Candace said. "It's good to see you."

"You said there was something you wanted to talk to me about," Jaimie said, trying to divert the conversation away from the subject of Logan's death.

"Yes, I met someone several years ago," Candace said nervously. "We've been together a long time, and I wanted to tell you I was getting married again."

"You're kidding?" Jaimie asked incredulously.

"No, I'm not kidding," Candace said quietly. "Why are you so surprised, Jaimie?"

"The women in our family don't have a very good track record with marriage," Jaimie said.

"What do you mean?" Candace asked.

"You ran away from your marriage," Jaimie said. "Aunt Grace and Aunt Sam never had the nerve to take the plunge. I would have thought your first attempt was such a dismal failure you wouldn't want to try it again."

Candace blushed noticeably but tried to hide her embarrassment.

"I used to think that was true," Candace finally said quietly. "I don't believe that anymore. I was young and scared when I married your father. It was my mistake, Jaimie. I ran away and I know I hurt you both. I really believed that you would be better off if your father raised you alone so I pursued my career."

"So what changed?" Jaimie asked.

"I changed," Candace said. "Or maybe I just finally grew up. I don't know for sure. Maybe it was just the toll of all those lonely years or maybe I just wasn't ready until now. I only know that I love Adam. He stormed into my life, and I'm never going to be the same. I had hoped since you got married you might understand, but I can see nothing has changed."

When Candace spoke of Adam, Jaimie noticed the gleam in her mother's eye and the way her face softened when she said his name. Jaimie didn't understand why her mother's revelation made her so angry, but nothing after Candace's announcement seemed to quell Jaimie's mounting fury.

"I think this was a mistake," Candace said a few minutes later when she got up to leave. "Alex was wrong. You aren't ready to deal with us yet."

Confusion assailed Jaimie as she watched Candace walk out of the crowded restaurant. Suddenly, Jaimie wanted to know what Candace meant by that remark about Alex and desperately wanted to talk to her mother. Since she was five years old, Jaimie had allowed her anger to get in the way of any meaningful conversation Candace attempted.

Jaimie jumped up, threw several bills on the table, mumbled apologies to the surprised waiter, and ran out the front door.

"Candace," Jaimie yelled.

Candace turned around as Jaimie approached.

"What does Alex have to do with this?" Jaimie asked.

"He called me, Jaimie," Candace said. "He told me he thought you needed to talk to someone about what was going on. He thought that someone should be me. I'm not so sure."

"Do you still want to be that someone?" Jaimie asked quietly.

"That's what I've always wanted, Jaimie," Candace said quietly.

"I don't know how to start," Jaimie said as the tears welled up. "I don't know how to talk to you."

"Tell me how much you miss Logan," Candace said.

"I'm not sure I can talk about him," Jaimie said as she started to cry. "I'm so lost without him."

"Let me help you, Jaimie," Candace said as she smiled.

Jaimie looked at Candace, walked over to her, and voluntarily embraced her mother for the first time.

"It's OK, honey," Candace whispered as she held her daughter. "I left you once but I won't ever do it again. I'm here for you, Jaimie."

The waves rolled toward the shore, and the sound felt comforting to the little boy as he walked along a stretch of beach on Jekyll Island, searching for his identity. This place had cast a spell over him though he could only visit the island in his dreams.

Years later, when he realized he must a descendant of one of the rich and powerful men who had lived there, he finally visited Jekyll Island. His imagination, enhanced by the sense of childhood longing only resulted in a deep-seated rage looking for a means of expression. Tonight, he dreamed the Jekyll Island dream again, that familiar fantasy in which his rich, caring parents were smiling at him.

The next scene began with the tortured, demented face of Jenny Morgan begging him to understand that her rape had destroyed their lives. Jenny told him how she wanted to love him but every time she looked at his face, it was replaced by the sneering, menacing, evil visage of the old man.

When he saw that twisted face coming toward him, Jekyll woke up with a start and sat up at his desk, grateful to be awake as a cold sweat rolled off his body. He stood up and walked over to the window, watching the gentle rain fall. Jenny was always more agitated this time of year so it was entirely appropriate that the climax should occur now.

The upcoming meeting on Jekyll Island might provide the perfect opportunity to get rid of Jaimie Martin and her husband. A tragic accident on Jekyll Island seemed like a very appropriate message to send the establishment. If Jaimie and her husband were their agents, their death would represent the first salvo in the continuing battle. The irony of killing them where Jenny Morgan was violated also appealed to him. Jekyll continued to watch the rain as he considered his plan of action for the weekend.

Alex watched the scene unfold outside Giusseppe's and was relieved when he saw Jaimie embrace her mother. A light rain began to fall with no warning as Jaimie and Candace ran back into the restaurant. The confused waiter returned them to their table and took their dinner orders reluctantly. They laughed when they realized he was watching them intently to see if they would bolt again.

They shared a bottle of wine as Jaimie poured out her heart to her mother regarding all the details of the investigation and Logan's death. The wine and the bearing of her soul had a relaxing, cleansing effect on Jaimie. Several courses later, they managed some lighthearted moments, mostly at the crabby waiter's expense.

"I feel better than I have in a long time," Jaimie said. "This is all so ugly and I haven't been able to talk to anyone about it."

"It's easy to see why you got involved in this," Candace said. "Guilt is a powerful motivator, Jaimie."

"I got involved because babies were dying," Jaimie said. "Now I feel guilty that I'm responsible for getting Logan killed."

"Don't do that to yourself, Jaimie," Candace said. "You had the best intentions imaginable. There was no way you could have known they would kill Logan."

"On some level I know that," Jaimie said. "Loss and guilt seem to go hand in hand when someone dies."

"Logan called to tell me you got married," Candace said. "He seemed very happy about it."

"Did you talk to him a lot?" Jaimie asked.

"Yes, we ended up being good friends," Candace said.

"Tell me about Adam," Jaimie said.

"I met him when we worked on a special project," Candace said. "We were kind of thrown together, and when the project ended, he refused to let me run away. The women in our family aren't very good at relationships, Jaimie. You're not wrong about that. But I never met anyone like Adam before. He was a friend before anything else happened."

"I thought Alex was a friend," Jaimie said sadly.

"I think he still is," Candace said. "I really believed you and Alex were married until tonight."

"Why did you believe that?" Jaimie asked.

"I can tell he cares about you, Jaimie."

"I think he's just good at pretending," Jaimie said. "He's certainly much better at it than I am."

"I don't think so," Candace said. "I saw something in his eyes in San Diego. There's something there, Jaimie."

"Maybe you're just hoping," Jaimie said.

"When he phoned me, he wanted to make sure I would call you," Candace said. "He was very concerned about you."

"He's just worried about solving the mystery," Jaimie said.

"I think there's more to it than that," Candace said. "Is it possible you're letting your fear get in the way?"

"I guess it's possible," Jaimie said. "I'm not sure how I feel about anything right now. There are just too many things going on."

"Does that include trusting me?" Candace asked.

"No, that part feels right," Jaimie said.

Wendel Garrett was working late, listening to the opera in his office as the soprano's voice reached a crescendo. Usually humorless, it suddenly occurred to him it was entirely appropriate the fat lady was singing with so many things reaching a climax this weekend. With any luck, all his goals would be met and he would be able to survive. As the soprano hit the highest, final note, his phone rang.

"Wendel, it's Rudy," the voice said.

"What have you found out?" Wendel asked.

"Mostly, I've run into a lot of dead ends," Rudy said. "Alex Martin checks out at least as far as I can tell. I'm trying to run down someone from the small town where he grew up to see if anyone remembers him. There are some things I need to do tomorrow but I thought I'd go visit that town on Saturday."

"That should be OK," Wendel said. "There isn't going to be much going on at Jekyll Island until late Saturday night. It'll take most of the day tomorrow for everyone to fly to Savannah and drive to Brunswick. I've chartered boats to take them to Jekyll Island from there."

"That should work out well," Rudy said. "I can drive to Valdosta early Saturday morning. After that, I can drive to Brunswick and catch a boat out to Jekyll Island. Have you given any more thought to what you want to do if we find out Alex Martin isn't who he seems to be?"

"Yes, if he turns out to be some kind of fed, we won't have a choice," Wendel Garrett said. "We'll have to get rid of both Jaimie and Alex."

CHAPTER TWENTY TWO

Luke Harper wore shorts, a sleeveless tee shirt, and no shoes as he walked along the beach on Jekyll Island. It was very warm, and this weekend would probably represent the first hot spell of the summer.

The inner sanctum Luke had created was about to be invaded by the Maxicillin team, who would be using Luke's lab facilities for the weekend. Luke had expressed his displeasure to Wendel Garrett, who finally ended up reminding Luke that Sayer had paid for all the facilities.

The team would have a meeting Friday night and begin again at dawn on Saturday. Garrett's wife had arranged for a buffet dinner and hired a local band to play on Saturday night. The itinerary for Sunday included another long day unless the team pulled all the data together early.

Luke checked his watch and began walking back to his lab. He still had a few hours left before the team arrived, and there were things he needed to accomplish before the invasion began.

Jaimie dropped Jake off at Ellen's house and got into the passenger seat of her car. Alex backed out of the driveway so they could complete the first leg of their trip to Brunswick, Georgia. From there, they would board a boat that would take them to Jekyll Island.

Terry White and her team were flying to Savannah and then driving to Brunswick, where boats had been chartered for them. When that option had been presented to Jaimie, she promptly opted to drive rather than accompany the rest of the team.

Jaimie relaxed and thought about her dinner with Candace. That encounter represented the first time Jaimie had spent time with her mother that wasn't marred by some kind of cold or angry retreat. Jaimie wanted to thank Alex for calling Candace but didn't know how to broach the subject.

As Alex guided the car through the light traffic, Jaimie looked over at him and realized how confused she was about her feelings for him. Those nights she had spent pacing around her house had seemed like torture. Several times she was tempted to storm into his room and confront him, but the plan she envisioned quickly evaporated. Her anger left her confused and empty. She craved more than friendship though he had made it clear that was all he wanted.

The gulf that separated them seemed impossibly wide, and Jaimie could think of no way to restore the emotional closeness they had shared. The physical desire was another issue; she wanted to feel his lips and hands move over her again, to explore all those secret places no one else had ever reached. Jaimie could no longer separate her emotional and physical needs. They had become one aching hunger that frightened her.

Alex had slammed the door in her face, and she couldn't afford to forget that the end of the investigation was also the end of their marriage. So Jaimie kept her armor firmly in place, guarding her heart so she could remain aloof and distant. Damage control was safer than risking another close encounter with Alex.

The cell phone rang, interrupting her thoughts. Alex took it out of his pocket and opened the flap.

"Tanner," he said.

"Alex, this is Jack," he said. "How's the drive going?"

"We're making good time," Alex said.

"I've got some news," Jack said. "We ran a check on Daryll Connor's brother and found out he owns a house outside of Atlanta. I've had several agents watching the place. One of them spotted some wreckage at the bottom of steep hill. We checked it out and very quietly recovered the remains of Daryll Connor and what was left of his Harley."

"I hate it when we're right," Alex said.

"I know," Jack said.

"Do you think Daryll's brother had anything to do with his death?" Alex asked.

"I don't know," Jack said. "We're keeping Daryll's body on ice for now, so we haven't notified his next of kin. We've got a tap on the phone lines at the house."

"Have you intercepted any communication so far?" Alex asked.

"There was a call yesterday from a man who sounded like he was running the show," Jack said.

"Did this guy identify himself?" Alex asked.

"No, he didn't," Jack said. "Whoever answered the phone seemed to recognize his voice. We tried to trace the call but all we could nail was that the call was made from Atlanta. We're following anyone who leaves."

"It's the first break we've had," Alex said.

"Yes, it is," Jack admitted. "It couldn't have happened at a better time."

"What do you mean?" Alex asked.

"The Director is getting impatient," Jack said. "The day before we intercepted that message, he talked about pulling the plug on the undercover investigation. He thought we should just arrest Garrett and Fletcher and be done with it."

"How does he feel now?" Alex asked.

"He's willing to give it a little more time," Jack said. "But we'd better get something soon."

"Hopefully, the guy will call back," Alex said. "I don't expect much to happen this weekend."

"I know," Jack said. "You'll have a little down time since all you can do is keep an eye on Wendel and Rudy."

"Luke Harper will be there," Alex said. "I thought I'd try to spend some time with him since he isn't working on Maxicillin."

"That's a good idea," Jack said. "Did you remember to bring our new toy?"

"Yes, I did," Alex said. "I haven't had a chance to try it out yet."

"I used it a few months ago when I went on a cruise," Jack said. "The phone was specifically developed for maritime use. The top of the briefcase actually is the antenna. The signals are bounced off a satellite so you can call me from a boat or anywhere on the island."

"It's not exactly a small unit," Alex said.

"That's because there's only one satellite up there right now," Jack said. "Sometime next year they're supposed to put up more satellites and they won't be as far away. Then the phones will be the size of the one you're holding in your hand."

"Something else to look forward to," Alex said.

"Don't you find it comforting to know I can reach you anywhere?" Jack asked.

"That's one of those trick questions," Alex said.

"Yeah, I guess it is," Jack said. "I'll let you know if we intercept any other messages. Tell Jaimie I said hello."

Carol Fletcher and Margo Garrett were standing at the dock in Brunswick, Georgia, waiting for a boat to take them to Jekyll Island when Alex and Jaimie approached.

"I was sorry to hear about your father, Jaimie," Margo said.

"Thank you," Jaimie said quietly as Alex reached for her hand, a gesture that made Margo smile.

"Are you going to be able to get this new drug up and running this weekend?" Carol asked.

"I sure hope so," Jaimie said.

"Wendel said there were a lot of personality conflicts," Margo said.

"He wasn't exaggerating," Jaimie said. "I'm not sure how much longer I can keep the team together."

"I'm looking forward to a nice relaxing weekend," Carol said. "That's why I agreed to tag along."

"When is Rudy coming?" Alex asked.

"He said he wouldn't be coming until tomorrow afternoon," Carol said.

"He should be here by the time the party starts," Margo said. "I hired a band to play. I thought it might take everyone's mind off the stress for a while."

"It can't hurt," Jaimie said. "We'll probably need to unwind after a long session tonight and all day tomorrow."

Garrett's house was huge, spread out from the middle where a massive entry area led into a large room. The outer perimeter faced the ocean, with three sets of wide French doors that opened onto a large porch that wrapped around that side of the house.

Small tables with chairs were positioned against the walls and a raised stand was set up near the French doors to accommodate a band. The view outside the doors and windows allowed them to see blue water as far as possible in every direction.

Margo indicated their room was on the second floor, so Alex carried their bags up the sweeping staircase and down the wide hall. At the end, Margo opened the door and ushered them in. The room was painted a light cream color with green drapes and a floral bedspread. French doors led to a small porch where they could see the same panoramic view visible from the first floor.

Jaimie saw the king size bed and realized she hadn't given the fact she would be sleeping with Alex any consideration. She took a deep breath and sighed as she considered this new reason the next three days could be very difficult.

Alex noticed Jaimie's sigh and realized its source must be the sleeping arrangements. He wanted to tell her his thoughts mirrored hers. Alex's recurring dream haunted him, making him dread every sunset.

An hour later, Alex and Jaimie went down to the ballroom where a buffet had been prepared. After filling their plates, they wandered around inside by the French doors. From there, they could see the porch, where the lighted candles on the tables seemed to seduce them.

Margo spotted Jaimie and Alex, waved, and invited them to join her and Carol at their table. Wendel was no where in sight and Margo indicated he would be arriving later.

Terry White and the rest of her team sat in tight knit little groups, whispering to each other occasionally. When they had finished eating, Margo took Carol and Alex for a walk on the beach while Jaimie gathered her team for the first meeting.

Luke Harper's lab, which adjoined his quarters, was out of sight of the main house but within walking distance. The only member of White's team who had a sense of humor told a joke on the way. It seemed to decrease the tension as they entered the lab, turned on the lights, and began to discuss the technical problems they still had to solve.

Alex thought Margo and Carol were good friends. They teased each other, and Carol Fletcher seemed more talkative than the last time Alex had seen her. When they returned from their walk, they took cold drinks out on the porch and continued talking. Eventually, they traded the conversation for the solitude of their rooms. Alex read for a while but the long drive and the sound of the water moving back and forth across the beach lulled him to sleep.

Jaimie's meeting finally broke up at midnight, and she was tired but excited by the significant progress they'd made. White had suggested a slightly different approach that Jaimie thought might represent the answer. A technician stayed behind to mix the new variable of the formula and test it on the culture.

The team walked to Garrett's house and most of the members seemed animated as if they could feel the answer was within their grasp. When Garrett first suggested this idea, Jaimie told him this group might end up killing each other before the weekend was over, but things seemed to be going well.

Garrett's house was dark and deserted when they returned. All conversation ceased as they walked up the wide stairs. Jaimie entered her room tentatively, aware of the darkness first and then Alex's even, steady breathing.

Jaimie was relieved when she realized Alex was asleep, and she tiptoed into the bathroom to get ready for bed. She thought about Maxicillin and how close they were to an answer. If the team could come up with an antibiotic no more babies would die from strep-A. Jaimie considered the development of Maxicillin as important as determining who was responsible for spreading the strep in the first place.

When Jaimie sat down on the bed, Alex stirred slightly. She put the travel alarm she had set in the bathroom on the table by her side of the bed. Alex's breathing was the only thing Jaimie heard after her head hit the pillow. Eventually, a soothing symphony invaded her consciousness. She could hear the crickets, the call of several different kinds of birds, and the waves moving against the shore as she fell asleep.

Saturday began violently with frequent flashes of lightning that interrupted the black night. A proximate flash startled Alex, but his arms were wrapped around Jaimie and he felt safe. He could smell her hair and feel the curve of her hips as she rested against his chest with her back to him.

Jaimie had moved slightly with the last strike, but she still slept and seemed to burrow in a little deeper against Alex's chest. The storm moved away, and Alex had almost drifted off when he heard Jaimie's alarm begin to beep.

The second series of beeps caused Jaimie to jump and finally, to lean over and turn off the alarm. Jaimie sighed as if she hadn't had enough sleep and then got up and walked into the bathroom.

Luke Harper sat on the deck that faced the ocean, drinking a glass of lemonade while he admired the view. The early morning storm blew away, but as the afternoon progressed, the air reeked of static energy while angry banks of clouds hovered. Luke had successfully avoided contact with any of the invaders but he knew his luck had run out when he saw Alex. Sweat rolled off Alex's face and he looked wilted as if he might be returning from a long walk.

"Good afternoon," Alex said.

"How are you?" Luke asked quietly, hoping his look conveyed his displeasure with the surprise visit.

If Alex realized Luke was unhappy, he hid it well as he sat down in the wicker chair.

"How long have you lived on the island?" Alex asked.

"Almost two years," Luke said.

"Do you like it here?" Alex asked.

"Yes, I do," Luke said. "I don't like to be around people very much."

"You picked the wrong weekend to come back," Alex said.

"I know," Luke said with some impatience.

"What are you working on?" Alex asked, ignoring Luke's attempt to get rid of him.

"I'm trying to complete a drawing of Jekyll Island," Luke said. "These old maps show where all the original estates were located on the island."

"That's fascinating," Alex said as he picked up one of the maps. "I didn't realize this place had such a history."

"In the early part of this century, Jekyll Island was home to all the East Coast millionaires," Luke said as he forgot all about the intrusion. "Carnegie,

Mellon, Rockefeller, all the big names from back then had estates on the island. They even formed a club called The Jekyll Island Club."

"Really?" Alex asked as he picked up a map. "What did the club do?"

"They had meetings here on the island," Luke said. "I can't find much information other than they used to meet at one of the estates. Apparently, they conducted quite a bit of business at those meetings. There are some notes mixed in with some of those old maps but they don't give any clues about anything else that might have taken place."

"This map shows Garrett's estate, doesn't it?" Alex asked as he handed it to Luke.

"Yes, it does," Luke said. "Garrett's house was built in the same location as the original main house."

"Your house and the lab are where the stables used to be," Alex said.

"Yes, they are," Luke said. "There are storage sheds where these old guest houses used to be."

"What about this one?" Alex asked. "I saw the other buildings while I was out walking. Where is this one?"

"I don't know," Luke said. "It's probably in that grove of trees behind the shed where they store the mowers."

"You mean the big one that looks like it's just been painted?" Alex asked.

"Yes, that's it," Luke said. "I've never been back there. I think that building was torn down. The woods are really thick in there."

Valdosta, Georgia looked like a typical sleepy Southern town. Rudy Fletcher guided the rented Jeep through the light afternoon traffic and stopped at a local restaurant that looked like it had been in business for years.

The permanent residents stared at Rudy. Valdosta was a small town so they were curious and wanted to determine if Rudy represented some long lost son or just a lost soul. Rudy ordered the special, which was an amazingly good steak sandwich with fries and a salad. The iced tea he washed it down with was freshly brewed although Rudy thought it was a little too sweet.

Rudy talked to the waitress, modifying his usual gruff manner to solicit information from her while she snapped her gum.

"Have you lived here long?" Rudy asked.

"Too long," the woman answered as she laughed. "Have you come to take me away from all of this?"

"No, I'm looking for a family named Martin," Rudy said.

"There are several families in town with that name," she said.

"Do any of them have a kid named Alex?" he asked.

"I don't know for sure," the woman said. "You might want to try Dale Martin. He lives out off route C. The turn off is about a mile past the stop sign. He's the only Martin who's young enough to have any kids. The other ones are in their eighties. How old is this kid?"

"He's in his thirties," Rudy said.

"I don't know," she said uncertainly. "I've only lived here about ten years. I know Dale was married. His wife died a couple of years ago, but I don't know if they had any kids."

Rudy paid the bill, left a generous tip, and waved to the waitress as he walked out the door. A few minutes later, he pulled the Jeep onto Route C and followed the woman's directions.

Dale Martin was sitting in a comfortable rocker on his front porch, sipping a beer and reading the local newspaper when Rudy pulled up in front of his house. Dale stared at Rudy long and hard as he got out of the Jeep, and the big yellow lab barked deeply when Rudy approached.

"Sit, Casey," Dale ordered as the dog complied but continued to stare at Rudy nervously.

"Are you Dale Martin?" Rudy asked.

"Yes, I am," the man said. "What can I do for you?"

"I'm looking for someone who used to live in Valdosta," Rudy said.

"Who?" Dale asked.

"His name is Alex Martin," Rudy said. "He's a member of the Martin family that used to live on Main Street."

"I used to live on Main Street," Dale said as he looked at Rudy strangely.

"Is something wrong?" Rudy asked when he noticed the expression on Dale Martin's face.

"I had a son named Alex," Dale Martin said. "He died when he was five."

Chapter Twenty Three

Scarlet clouds streaked across the western sky, dominating the horizon as the sun fell into the ocean. Alex stood on the small porch off their bedroom, admiring the view. The weather had decided it would be a member of the cast of characters for the weekend, orchestrating a storm with a brief respite before the next attack.

Jaimie came out on the porch wearing a navy dress dotted with small yellow flowers. Sandals completed her attire and she looked stunning in the strange glow cast by the last remaining light.

"You look great," Alex said as she approached him.

"Thank you," Jaimie said. "It's starting to feel sticky out here again."

"We're supposed to have storms on and off all weekend," Alex said.

"There's something I've been wanting to say to you," Jaimie said nervously.

"What is it?" Alex asked as he looked into her eyes.

"I wanted to thank you for calling my mother," Jaimie said.

"I thought you needed to talk to someone," Alex said.

"I did," Jaimie said as that genuine smile lit up her face. "I told her about everything that's been going on."

"I assumed you would," Alex said. "It's OK, Jaimie. This has been very difficult for you and you needed to share that with someone."

"I appreciate the fact you called her," Jaimie said.

"You're welcome," Alex said quietly.

"I guess we'd better join the party," Jaimie said.

The spotlights in the ballroom provided a soft, pleasing glow that was enhanced by the candlelight. The candles on the tables flickered and danced to the whisper of the intermittent breezes that blew through the French doors. The band was just beginning to set up their instruments when Alex and Jaimie walked in the room.

The atmosphere was as charged as the weather, thick with anticipation and a certain excitement that Maxicillin would soon become a reality. Jaimie felt exhilarated by their progress while she thought about the importance of their success.

A mountain of intricate details still needed to be worked out, but Jaimie figured all the preliminary data should be wrapped up by the next afternoon. Tomorrow would mark the beginning of another process that would involve testing Maxicillin for side effects.

Wendel Garrett arrived and spent several minutes alone with Jaimie discussing the team's progress. He was elated with the news that Maxicillin was almost a reality and promptly visited every table with Margo by his side to congratulate all the members of the team. Then he ordered the waiters to bring out bottles of champagne to celebrate.

The band began to play and they were amazingly good for a small, local group. Another storm approached as streaks of lightening flashed across the sky but no one seemed to notice. The champagne, the weather, and the success provided an excuse for letting go of all of the real and perceived slights of recent weeks.

Rudy Fletcher arrived, immediately took Carol out on the deserted porch and began screaming at her. Frequent blasts of thunder masked most of their dialogue, and when the rain began to fall in earnest, they retreated inside to separate corners of the ballroom. The storm moved away, changing the tempo of the evening. When the band started playing a series of slow songs, Alex asked Jaimie to dance.

"How does it feel to have developed a treatment for something?" Alex asked.

"It feels great," Jaimie said. "We still need to work on the formula but the sensitivity reaction is strongly positive."

"Now, all we have to do is figure out who contaminated those tests in the first place," Alex said.

"How soon do you think Jack will pull the plug on this?" Jaimie asked.

"I don't know," Alex admitted. "Are you anxious to get rid of your annoying husband?"

"I didn't say that," Jaimie said.

Alex thought about the end of the investigation as he held Jaimie and they moved slowly around the dance floor. The band played a popular ballad about love and loss. Alex felt hypnotized by the play of the lightning flashes, the flickering candles, and the glow from the soft lighting. He could see the reflection of all the illumination in Jaimie's eyes.

Jaimie presented him with her warm smile, and when he smiled back, he couldn't stop looking at her. Alex remembered Jaimie's reluctance in the beginning and his own halfhearted agreement to be a third level friend. That bargain led to a relationship that terrified him but at the same time made him feel whole. None of Alex's previous liaisons, weighed down by the games or the necessity of hiding what he really felt, had ever been like this one.

Alex could no longer ignore the possibility that he rejected her not to avoid putting them at risk but, more likely, to avoid his own feelings. His dreams were filled with the sound of Jaimie's voice, the feel of the warmest touch he had ever known, and Jaimie's smile, a look that could reach into his soul.

Holding Jaimie had a narcotic effect on Alex, who finally faced a simple truth. When Jaimie looked up at him and smiled, Alex realized he loved her.

When the rain stopped, Margo and Carol escaped to a corner of the porch. The glow of their cigarettes and the flashes of lightning in the distance provided the only relief from the black night.

"What was Rudy so mad about?" Margo asked.

"The real estate agent handling the sale of my parents house called," Carol said.

"Oh, oh," Margo said. "Does Rudy know you're trying the sell it?"

"No, she was smart enough to tell him she was just checking to see if we were interested in selling the property."

"That's good," Margo said.

"You're not kidding," Carol said, laughing. "He was mad that I even talked to her. I didn't tell him I just signed a contract yesterday and it's a done deal. Rudy really would kill me if he knew that."

Margo lit another cigarette as she watched Alex and Jaimie dance.

"Look at the way Alex looks at Jaimie," Margo said. "He really loves her. You can see it in his eyes. Did Rudy ever look at you like that?"

"I don't think so," Carol said quietly. "I don't think he's capable of loving anyone."

"You realize the cigarettes have to go next, don't you?" Margo asked.

"Oh, come on, Margo," Carol said. "I think all this self improvement bullshit has gone far enough. For the first time in my life I'm exercising four times a week and trying to eat better."

"That's just a start, Carol," Margo said. "We need to be fit, thin, and rich when we dump the boys. That's the best possible revenge."

"I know, I know," Carol said. "But I have to give up my vices one at a time. This weekend, I've decided to give up Rudy. While we were out on the porch, he told me we were going to have a talk when we got back to Atlanta. That means he's literally going to pound his point across. I'm done with that. He's never going to hurt me again."

"I'm glad," Margo said.

"It's about time, right?" Carol asked.

"You had to leave when you were ready," Margo said.

"I need a drink, and I don't want to hear anything about giving up alcohol," Carol said as she stamped out her cigarette and they headed back into the ballroom.

Margo flirted with the young waiter at the bar while he poured her a diet Coke. Another waiter walked by with a tray of champagne so Carol grabbed a glass. When Margo turned around, they toasted Carol's escape just as the band announced they were playing their final song for the evening.

"What were Rudy and Carol arguing about?" Alex asked as they finished their last dance.

"I don't know," Jaimie admitted. "We know Rudy beats Carol and Wendel fools around on Margo so neither one of them have much of a relationship."

"Not all relationships are like that, Jaimie," Alex said.

"Most of them seem like it," Jaimie said.

"Does that reinforce your decision not to get married?" Alex asked.

"Yes, it does," Jaimie said.

"You'd better be careful, Jaimie," Alex said as he looked into her eyes. "You can only hide your heart for so long. Love just might come searching for you when you least expect it."

Rudy Fletcher stood against the wall, nursing a drink with a sour expression on his face. As the band finished playing, he spotted Wendel and walked over to speak with him.

An hour later, little pockets of light were visible from under only a few doors. Fatigue and champagne accounted for most of the casualties but the others had schemes to discuss. Wendel and Rudy were talking in Garrett's first floor study.

"What did you find out?" Wendel asked.

"Alex Martin's ID is a fake," Rudy said. "It's a typical scenario. They search for a child who died at birth or in childhood. After they get the birth certificate, they build an identify from there. It becomes impossible to trace unless you can go back and interview parents or friends."

"Who is he?" Wendel asked.

"Probably FBI," Rudy said.

"Dammit, I don't like this," Wendel said.

"We can't take a chance," Rudy said.

"If they had enough evidence wouldn't they have arrested us already?"

"Not necessarily," Rudy said.

"How are we going to do it?" Wendel asked.

"I thought we could have them come back on your boat," Rudy said. "We'll rig the boat so the engine dies. Then we'll shoot them and dump their bodies in the ocean. I thought we could fake an explosion to make it look good. We'd be the only survivors."

"OK, take care of it," Wendel said.

"No way, Wendel," Rudy said. "We're going to do this together. We'll rig the boat tomorrow afternoon. You're coming with me. I'm not taking the fall for this by myself if something goes wrong."

"There's some down time in the afternoon," Wendel said. "I told the team they could rest and pack. We can go then."

"I want to keep tabs on Alex and Jaimie," Rudy said. "I'll plant a bug in their room in the morning to make sure they're not following us."

"Did you hear something?" Wendel asked.

"No, I didn't hear anything," Rudy said as he put his fingers to his lips and moved to the door.

When Alex heard Wendel's last question, he moved away from the door of the study and ducked into a small closet on the other side of the hall. Alex breathed sparingly while he waited to see if Rudy would find him. He heard footsteps move past his position and then there was only silence. A few minutes later, Alex heard the footsteps return, pause by several doors, and move away.

The space in the closet was cramped but Alex forced himself to wait for several minutes before going back upstairs. Alex realized he had only heard the end of Garrett's conversation with Fletcher.

All Alex was sure of was that Garrett and Fletcher were going somewhere in the afternoon and Fletcher was going to plant a bug in their bedroom. Alex had to figure out a way to follow them without making Fletcher or Garrett suspicious. The scenario he imagined involved returning to their room after lunch and having a discussion about taking a long walk. He weighed the pros and cons and worried one of them might stay behind to keep an eye on them if they heard that conversation. Other possibilities crossed Alex's mind such as taping a conversation tonight he could replay tomorrow while they followed Garrett and Fletcher.

Alex decided he had waited long enough so he peeked around the door of the closet. When he couldn't see anyone, he ran up the winding stairs two at a time, still considering the options.

Jaimie was in the bathroom when Alex walked in their room so he went to his suitcase and pulled out a small tape recorder. Alex put it on the table by his side of the bed and sat down while he waited for Jaimie. The door of the bathroom opened and Jaimie walked over to him with a shy look on her face.

"The zipper on my dress is stuck," she said as she smiled at him.

Alex stood up and fumbled with the zipper, his eyes lingering on Jaimie's bare shoulders. Another scenario occurred to Alex but he knew Jaimie would never agree or feel comfortable with the activity he was considering taping for replay tomorrow.

Alex continued to toy with the zipper, considering his options. He finally decided Jaimie need never know he was taping this encounter. In every way that mattered to him, Jaimie was his wife and he had no intention of ending the marriage when the investigation was over.

Reaching over, Alex pressed the record button and began to attack the stubborn zipper in earnest. Jaimie looked back to check on his progress.

"It's really caught in the material," Alex said.

"I thought that might be the problem," Jaimie said.

Alex spotted the freckle on Jaimie's neck and realized the first time they had made love, it was dark with only the glow of the moon to light their way. His other senses had been so consumed with the smell and feel of her that he hadn't really utilized any visual input.

The soft kiss Alex placed on Jaimie's neck caused her to stiffen. Jaimie didn't seem to be breathing and stood there motionless while Alex traced soft kisses across her shoulder. He put his arms around her as he worked his way up to her neck.

Jaimie began to speak but Alex turned her around and delivered a blistering kiss on her lips to keep her from saying anything. They only stopped kissing long enough to change the position of their mouths for the next attack.

Alex moved Jaimie slowly to the side of the bed and sat down, pulling her down on his knees. The stubborn zipper was finally freed as Alex unzipped the dress and began kissing Jaimie's neck and chest while she ran her hands through Alex's hair. She wasn't aware her bra was gone until she felt Alex sucking and gently biting her breasts.

"I can't seem to resist you," Jaimie said, her breathing heavy and uneven.

"I've missed you, wife," Alex said as he kissed her mouth.

Jaimie pulled Alex's polo up and began kissing his chest, finally pushing the shirt over his head and throwing it on the floor. Alex stood up with Jaimie's legs wrapped around his waist and kissed her while she slowly lowered her legs to the floor. Jaimie fumbled with the belt and zipper on Alex's pants as he peeled off the rest of her clothing.

In unspoken agreement, they made the bed the next battleground as they rolled over each other, touching and kissing unexplored areas. They searched for reactions, seizing the more intense ones as the process continued. Jaimie reached a point where she seemed to be slowly inching away from Alex.

"Where are you going, Jaimie?" Alex asked as he laughed softly.

"It's so good I can't stand it," Jaimie said. "You're very good at this."

"You bring out the best in me, Jaimie," Alex said as he stopped kissing her and looked into her eyes. "I want you to remember what I'm saying to you. I love you, Jaimie. I've never loved anyone the way I love you. I want my third level friend back."

"What about....?" Jaimie began as Alex kissed her mouth and began moving his hands over her, ending any need for conversation.

Dr. Jekyll stood alone on the beach, looked back at the dark house, and thought about his grandmother. Another bank of menacing clouds were gathering in the distance, poised for another assault. The flashes of light caught his attention while he considered how ironic it was that the weather patterns would be so similar.

Jenny Morgan, barely into her teenage years, was violently raped on a hot summer weekend almost identical to this one. He remembered her haunting description of the way the storms had gathered and attacked. Jekyll could feel that a violent confrontation of another sort was imminent.

The master plan was in jeopardy and Jekyll realized he would have to give up his real identity in order to hide from the authorities. The money he had stashed away in various accounts under different names would provide financial security.

Jekyll understood the safest option was to kill anyone who might be a threat and disappear. The contamination inside Sayer was only a test, a first strike to herald the beginning of a war that would change history. Jekyll wasn't sure the contamination would work but the results had been dramatic and the panic he had created excited him.

A gentle rain began to fall and Jekyll raised his hands, believing the rain was some kind of omen, some signal to kill all those who represented a threat. He had been hearing the voices for a long time. With increasing frequency, they warned and advised him, but their whispered alarms no longer terrified Jekyll.

Chapter Twenty Four

Sunday dawned amicably on Jekyll Island. Not a single cloud obscured the sun as the celestial body made its way up the horizon. Warm temperatures, scant winds, and brilliant sunshine promised an end to the series of violent, unpredictable storms. The air was full of expectation and change as the Maxicillin team gathered. A new phase would begin today, and everyone accepted some members of the team would scatter now that this stage of the research was ending.

Rudy Fletcher waited impatiently in the small linen closet at the end of the hall. It was the only place on the second floor where he could get a view of Jaimie and Alex's room without being spotted. The heat and humidity made it extremely uncomfortable in the small, enclosed space and Rudy cursed Alex and Jaimie repeatedly for their sluggish start.

Rudy pulled a face towel from the shelf to wipe away the little pool of sweat on his forehead. Then he lifted up his shirt to catch the little stream that was flowing down his back. Rudy considered his current task and the other activities for the day. He felt no apprehension about the fact he would kill. To Rudy it felt like it had been several lifetimes since the first time he was called upon to perform that act. Nor would he feel any remorse at performing just another chore.

Alex's first awareness was the feel of Jaimie's soft, bare skin against his body. He tried to temper his response but failed miserably. Wonder washed over him while he stroked Jaimie's back, convinced he had never touched skin that soft before.

Jaimie stirred, sensing Alex's proximity and then feeling his caress; contact that stirred strong feelings of warmth and happiness. She snuggled closer to Alex, aware every inch of him was awake and aroused.

"I guess we need to get going," Alex said, disappointment creeping into his voice. "If we don't get downstairs, we'll miss breakfast."

"There are all kinds of hunger," Jaimie said as she turned around and started kissing him.

"I like this agenda better," Alex said, succumbing without further protest.

A few minutes later, Jaimie sat at the dressing table brushing her hair. Alex watched intently, amazed such a simple act could stir all those vague, powerful emotions.

"Why do you keep staring at me?" Jaimie asked.

"Just lingering in the afterglow."

"Well, you'd better get moving, husband," she said. "I've decided I'm hungry after all."

"So soon?" he asked as he came up behind her and began kissing the back of her neck.

"Different kind of hunger," she said, laughing as she looked at him in the mirror.

"See, you're tired of me already," he said.

"Hurry up," she said, feigning hungry moans.

"OK, OK," he said as he shook off the spell and began to walk toward the shower.

Jaimie was barely dressed by the time he stood next to her, fully clothed. "Let's get going, wife. A man could starve to death waiting for you."

"I just need to finish putting my make-up on," Jaimie said.

"You were the one who wanted to hurry, Jaimie. Besides, you don't need any enhancements."

"Aw, that's so nice of you to say that," she said sincerely.

"Impending starvation will make a man say almost anything," he said, blocking Jaimie's playful slap.

Laughing and touching each other intimately on the way to the door, they finally opened it but paused in the threshold for a passionate kiss.

Rudy felt cooler air pouring through the small crack in the door. He had left it open to determine when Jaimie and Alex vacated their room. Rudy heard them before he saw them, their soft laughter echoing down the hall as he heard their door close. Rudy cursed when he looked and saw them stop outside the door to kiss. Finally, they held hands and proceeded down the hall.

The claustrophobia and heat overwhelmed Rudy, but he continued to wait for several minutes, aware Jaimie or Alex might return if they had forgotten something. Finally, Rudy opened the door to the closet and stepped out into the hall where the fresh air assaulted him. Though he was aware he shouldn't loiter, he breathed in the air and enjoyed the breeze.

Rudy scanned the area, went back into the closet to pick up a ladder, and left his prison for good. It was even cooler in their bedroom and Rudy savored the relief. The switch was by the door. Rudy turned it off and moved the ladder into position under the ceiling fan. Five minutes later, Rudy had accomplished his task, folded the ladder, and looked around to see if he had disturbed anything.

Convinced he couldn't hear anything, Rudy opened the door and stepped out in the hall. After he stowed the ladder back in the linen closet, he took the steps two at a time and joined the others for breakfast.

Jack Connelly walked into the communications section of the FBI, which was located on the fifth floor of the Hoover Building in Washington,

D.C. Several large overhead screens showed the placement of the satellites while information flashed across the computer terminals.

Jody Green, communications specialist, was entering commands into a terminal as he approached. Jody was thirty-six with short, brown hair that didn't have the effect of making her look masculine. She wore clothes that were functional rather than stylish but her delicate features, soft blue eyes, and ready smile made her seem extremely feminine.

When Jack saw her, he noticed all those things as if he were realizing them for the first time though he had known Jody for five years. That insight occurred to him just as Jody looked up, saw him, and smiled.

"Hi, Jack," Jody said. "I guess you want to hear the conversation we taped?"

"Yes," Jack said, surprised by the way her casual smile charmed him.

"We taped this conversation about thirty minutes ago," Jody said. "The call was made to Connor's house in Atlanta. I'll play it back for you."

"Hello," the steady voice said.

"Who is this?" the nervous voice asked.

"This is Dr. Jekyll," the gruff voice proclaimed as it was magnified through the speaker.

"Oh, I'm sorry," the voice answered apologetically. "I didn't recognize your voice at first."

"Maybe you shouldn't answer the phone," Jekyll replied rudely.

"I'm really sorry," the scared voice said.

"I wanted you to know I'm leaving here today," Jekyll said. "I'm abandoning our base here. I suggest you do the same thing. I'll contact you in the manner we discussed previously. Good luck."

The sound of a dial tone filled the speakers.

"That's all there is?" Jack asked.

"Yes," Jody said.

"Can you tell where the call originated?" Jack asked.

"Watch the screen," Jody answered as she entered commands into the computer.

Jack watched as four satellites picked up the transmission, triangulated the coordinates until they all centered on one location. The screen changed as the coordinates were placed over a huge map of the southeastern U.S. Each enhancement narrowed the focus until only the state of Georgia could be seen. The augmentation continued until a dot began to flash in red as the name of the location was printed on the screen.

"Jekyll Island, Georgia," Jack said as he read the words.

Alex finished breakfast and watched Jaimie leave with the rest of her team for another session in Harper's lab. The group seemed intent, focused, and excited about their progress. Jaimie looked confident as if she expected they would finish their preliminary work early.

After the team left, Alex was alone on the porch with Rudy Fletcher, who stared at him and spoke sparingly. Alex finally became restless so he excused himself to take a walk along the beach. His surroundings seemed calm and peaceful, but Alex began to feel increasingly anxious as the morning progressed. He couldn't identify the source of his tension and the cloudless blue sky offered no hint of any danger.

An hour later, Alex returned to the house and decided to go upstairs to phone Jack Connelly. If they followed the plan they had talked about earlier, Jaimie would finish her morning meetings, and after lunch, they would follow Garrett and Fletcher. Alex entered his room, picked up the briefcase and took it out on the porch.

The French doors provided a barrier between the phone and Rudy's bug. Alex set up the unit on the ledge farthest away from the doors where there should be no interference from the house. Alex opened the top and the first thing he noticed was the blinking green light that indicated Jack had tried to reach him. The keyboard indicated the caller's ID and phone number so Alex pressed the numbers and touched enter.

"Connelly," the impatient voice said.

"Jack, this is Alex," he said.

"I was starting to get worried," Jack said. "I tried to reach you about an hour ago."

"I took a walk," Alex said.

"Jody picked up a phone call to Connor's house," he said. "The caller identified himself as Dr. Jekyll."

"Do you think he's the leader of the group?" Alex asked.

"It sure sounded like it," Jack said. "He said he was going to close up the safe house and disappear. He advised them to do the same. That's not the best part."

"What do you mean?" Alex asked.

"The call was made from Jekyll Island," Jack said.

"Can you tell where on the island the call was made from?" Alex asked.

"Yes, we can," Jack said. "Jody wants you to turn on the navigational system that's built into your unit."

"OK," Alex said as he turned on the system. The small screen came to life while Alex watched it carefully.

A light simultaneously appeared on the screen at the command center in Washington as Jody Green entered a new series of commands. The huge screen displayed the four satellites as they changed position to compensate for all the variables. The point of origin moved back on forth on the detailed map of Jekyll Island.

"The satellites have lined up the coordinates," Jack said as one steady point began to blink. "Can you tell where it is coming from?"

"Yes, I saw a map of the island yesterday," Alex said. "That location is behind one of the storage sheds in the woods."

"Jody is zeroing in on it now," Jack said. "The woods are so dense we can only make out the shape of part of the building. Is that building still on Garrett's estate?"

"Yes, it is," Alex said. "Luke Harper indicated a guest house used to be back there."

"Dr. Jekyll indicated it was some kind of safe house," Jack said.

"I guess Jaimie and I should go check out that house," Alex said. "That might be more productive than following Garrett and Fletcher."

"I think so," Jack said. "If Garrett or Fletcher turn out to be Dr. Jekyll, that's probably where they're headed anyway. If it's not one of them, maybe you can nail Dr. Jekyll."

"I agree," Alex said.

"If you call when you get close, Jody can have the satellite guide you right to the building."

"That sounds good," Alex said.

"There's another problem you need to be aware of," Jack said.

"What's that?" Alex asked.

"There's a storm approaching the island," Jack said.

"It's clear and sunny right now," Alex said.

"That's going to change shortly," Jack said as he watched another screen where an angry red mass appeared to be bearing down on Jekyll Island.

"How bad is this storm?" Alex asked.

"Jody thinks this storm could involve tornado activity," Jack said. "It should hit Jekyll Island in the next hour or two."

"We'll have to try to get to the house before it hits," Alex said.

"That's the best option," Jack said. "I called to try to get a chopper out there but there are storms pounding the Atlanta area so everything is grounded. I don't think I can get one out there until the weather clears. I have several agents driving to Brunswick but the storm will probably keep them on the mainland for a while."

"I'll do the best I can," Alex said.

"There's a team about to hit Connor's house," Jack said. "Be careful and keep in touch, Alex."

Jaimie was exhilarated by the time they finished the last session. The team joked and laughed as they waited in the buffet line for lunch savoring the positive results of the sensitivity tests. Wendel Garrett attended the session and was so jubilant he announced there would be an early dinner to celebrate before everyone returned to Brunswick.

Rudy Fletcher approached Wendel, and they spoke in hushed tones and left the porch, disappearing into the bowels of the house. Alex appeared from the same general direction and seemed nervous and distracted when he joined Jaimie.

"I've got to talk to you," Alex whispered as he pulled her away from the others.

"Jack intercepted a phone call this morning," Alex said. "It was made from Jekyll Island to Connor's house in Atlanta. Jack thinks the caller is the leader of the paramilitary group. He calls himself Dr. Jekyll."

"Is that a reference to Jekyll Island?" Jaimie asked. "Or do you think it refers to the Dr. Jekyll-Mr. Hyde thing?"

"I don't know," Alex admitted. "I'm more concerned with locating the source of that message. The satellites have pinpointed the exact location. We're going there instead of following Fletcher and Garrett."

"Do you want to go now?" Jaimie asked.

"Yes, Jack says there's a storm coming," Alex said as they both looked at the sky which looked fairly benign until they spotted the black, swirling clouds.

"I just need to go up to our room for a minute," Jaimie said.

"That's not a good idea," Alex said. "Fletcher put a bug in there this morning. I'll go get the briefcase and come right back. That phone I brought also has a navigational device that will help us find the exact location."

Jaimie used the restroom on the first floor and waited for Alex at the bottom of the stairs. When she looked at her shoes, Jaimie realized they were totally unsuited to any kind of a hike. The soles were slick and they could represent a hazard especially if the terrain became wet. Reluctantly, Jaimie began to climb the stairs.

The hall was deserted but when Jaimie stopped outside the door to their bedroom, she was sure she heard voices. Jaimie turned the doorknob slowly, unsure what to expect when she entered the room. When Jaimie walked in, she saw Alex standing by the table on his side of the bed, listening to the words coming from a tape recorder.

A gust of cool, brisk air whistled through the room, bringing with it a dark atmosphere as if the black clouds had suddenly arrived. Jaimie shivered as she thought about how stark and cold it felt. She recognized the dialogue from last night's encounter with Alex, and her trepidation was replaced by anguish.

As Alex turned to leave, the first thing he saw was Jaimie's pained look, but other emotions soon joined the procession that marched across her face. Her initial expressions of hurt and shock were quickly replaced by anger, and finally, rage.

Chapter Twenty Five

The FBI response team had been in position around Jarrod Connor's house for fifteen minutes, and they waited impatiently for the command. The assault team had been in Atlanta for four days, and all its members were anxious to complete the mission so they could go home.

When the command was given, the team members moved in unison. The first two men moved near the front door of Connor's house. They held the battering ram between them and were ready to pummel the front door when the explosion rocked the house with frightening violence. The force of the detonation flung agents near the house in the air. Terrifying sounds of flying glass, debris, and a fast moving fire echoed through the trees.

Jarrod Connor and the others were waiting near the edge of the woods, watching the assault. When Connor looked through the binoculars, he saw the premature explosion and cursed loudly. The underground tunnel through which they had escaped saved them from capture but they wanted a body count to send a message to the FBI. Jarrod had discovered the tunnel when he first looked at the house and it was the determining factor in the purchase.

Only a few of the agents were close to the house and Jarrod doubted that any of them had been killed. Dr Jekyll's goal had been to blow up the entire team so the news reports would be inundated with coverage of bodies of FBI agents being dragged from the rubble. Then Dr. Jekyll planned to announce their strike against the establishment.

Jarrod was the ultimate willing recruit, searching for a cause for the first thirty years of his life. Dr. Jekyll's passionate nature was more compelling than his cause, but Jarrod was a follower who didn't care to analyze the cause.

Jarrod cursed as he looked through the glasses and realized he would have to report his failure. Dr. Jekyll would develop an alternate plan, and this time, Jarrod would make sure it didn't fail. Jarrod gave the order for them to split up and complete their escape.

A furious wind blew through the bedroom in Garrett's house as Alex and Jaimie stared at each other, aware Rudy's bug precluded any dialogue. Jaimie marched over to her suitcase and pulled out a pair of hikers. She sat on the bed and put the boots on, listening to the familiar words.

Alex watched her as she completed the change, silently cursing fate for Jaimie's discovery. There were no words Alex could think of that would justify his actions adequately to Jaimie. Her furious expression was set, and he knew explanations were useless. The anger continued to roll across her face as she made her way to the door.

Alex closed the door softly behind them. They had only walked ten feet down the deserted hall when Jaimie turned around and delivered a stinging slap to Alex's face.

"How could you do that?" Jaimie asked.

"It's not what you think," Alex said desperately. "I meant everything I said to you last night."

"You should stay with the FBI, Alex," Jaimie whispered viciously. "You never let a little thing like feelings get in the way of your job."

"We don't have time for this, Jaimie," Alex said.

"Fine," Jaimie said. "Let's finish it. When it's over, I never want to see you again."

The gathering clouds rolled and boiled but seemed to back off before the storm could strike. Rudy Fletcher and Wendel Garrett were racing the Jeep toward the boat dock, watching the furious sky, and hoping they could make it before the sky opened.

Garrett turned the receiver on so they could listen to the activity in Alex and Jaimie's room. Jaimie's breathless moans filled the Jeep as Wendel laughed heartily. Eventually, Rudy had a hard time keeping the vehicle on the road. The sounds of Alex and Jaimie making love became so intense Fletcher finally turned the receiver off.

"I can't stand it anymore," Rudy said. "It's making me horny."

"I guess we don't have to worry about them," Wendel said. "They're too busy fucking their brains out to worry about anything else."

"That doesn't mean he's not an FBI agent," Rudy said.

"I'm not convinced we should kill them," Wendel said.

"You're not bailing out now, Garrett," Rudy said nastily.

"Let's get this over with then," Garrett said as Fletcher pulled the Jeep into a parking spot near Garrett's boat.

The wind picked up, providing a distraction from the emotional turmoil that surrounded Alex and Jaimie. Despite the blasts of wind and the impending storm, they made good time as they walked to the maintenance building. The gusts of wind became one loud howl as dark clouds swirled around them with increasingly fierce intentions. When they reached the edge of the woods, Alex opened the briefcase, turned on the navigational device, and phoned Jack.

"Jack, do you have a lock on our location?" Alex shouted as Jaimie stared at him.

"Yes, we do," Jack answered. "Jody suggested you wear the earphones so she can guide you right to the house."

"The woods are really thick," Alex said. "We'll see if we can find a path."

"We can't see anything on the satellite but the storm," Jack said. "It's almost right on top of you, Alex. Good luck."

They walked through the dense, thick woods tentatively, unsure which way to move. Jack issued commands regarding the direction they were to take, and they complied within the limits the thick woods allowed.

Alex finally reached a path, and Jack's instructions seemed to be totally in sync with following that path. Several minutes later as the wind continued to stalk them, they spotted the guesthouse.

Moss and ivy grew wild over the exposed surfaces; the building looked like it had been deserted for years. All the windows had been boarded up and the front porch seemed to be in disrepair. Alex approached the house, searching for trip wires and alarms.

Alex walked around the entire house but couldn't see a door on the back or sides that looked like a viable exit. The intensity of the storm increased, but Alex didn't want to rush their entrance in case the house was booby-trapped.

When he approached the front door, Alex thought it seemed old until he looked closely, and then he could tell it had been artificially weathered. Alex moved the moss that covered the new deadbolt and searched for possible alarms.

Dr. Jekyll sat by the computer, nervously entering commands while the storm increased in intensity. Jekyll copied all his data onto a disc. That task completed, he entered the command for the virus to wipe out everything on the hard drive in ten minutes.

Jekyll was furious at the loss of his retreat. Though he believed they didn't know his identity, he could feel them closing in on him. Alex and Jaimie were not what they appeared to be, and he suspected they were FBI agents.

Jekyll wasn't watching the inconspicuous surveillance cameras around the outside of the house or he would have spotted Alex and Jaimie approaching the front door. At the moment, Jekyll was completely occupied with the tasks of carefully removing the pathogens from the incubator and packing them for transport. The guest house had been transformed into a self contained lab for the secret work Dr. Jekyll had been conducting for the last two years.

The security alarm sounded as a shocked Jekyll turned to look at the camera and spotted Alex and Jaimie standing on his porch. Jekyll felt fear, anger, and finally rage as he cursed viciously while he continued packing his creations.

Jekyll looked at the camera one more time and realized he only had seconds left in which to escape. He picked up the backpack and made his way to the exit, praying the virus could destroy the data on the computer in time.

The water was very choppy, tossing the boat from side to side without interruption. Garrett watched the sky intently until Rudy finally appeared on the deck, wiping his hands on a towel.

"Are you finished?" Garrett asked.

"Yes," Fletcher said. "When we get far enough away from the island, I'll flip the switch and the engine will die. I'll pretend to be trying to restart it and get the drop on Alex. Then we'll take care of them."

"I'll be glad when this is over," Garrett said.

"We're not going to get out of here before the storm hits," Rudy said as the wind, rain, and hail began bombarding the boat.

Rudy and Wendel retreated to the cabin where they waited out the rampage. They couldn't see anything clearly when they looked out the small windows. The strong wind blew the rain sideways against the craft until it was replaced by the torrent of hail that landed on the deck. Wendel's stomach began to lurch as the boat swayed back and forth. The boat struck the dock ominously as thoughts of tornadoes and wind shear flashed through their minds. The barrage only lasted ten minutes but they were both frightened by the time the wind abated.

They walked up the narrow stairs, unsure what they would see when they reached the deck. Layers of hail made the deck a treacherous obstacle course. Parts of other boats were scattered around the docks; seat cushions and other small objects had become airborne and were now residents of other vessels in the harbor.

They secured Garrett's boat, one of the lucky ones to survive the storm as many other damaged boats had not. Debris littered the hood of the Jeep, and they had to clean it off before they could head back to Garrett's house.

Alex worked feverishly to pick the lock, convinced his activity had probably sounded an alarm. He spotted the camera as the wind and rain hindered his progress. Jaimie cowered near the wall of the house, trying to escape the worst of the elements. Alex realized that anyone inside could have already spotted them, so he worried about the reception that might be waiting.

They stood to the side of the door as Alex swung it open and peeked inside. His gun drawn, Alex entered tentatively with Jaimie following close behind. All they saw when they moved inside the house was one large, dimly lit main room that looked like a laboratory.

Alex searched the room carefully and finally spotted the window where Dr. Jekyll had escaped. Convinced they were alone, Alex put his weapon away as the howling of the wind increased and finally blew the wooden hatch totally away from the frame of the window. Several loose boards on the outside of the house flapped back and forth, striking the side of the house repeatedly.

Jaimie walked through the fully equipped lab, evaluating all the equipment until she finally stopped in front of the empty incubator. The door was open but the inside was still warm as if the incubator had been recently occupied. Jaimie's mind could barely conceive what other horrors Jekyll had developed.

"I think he took some things from in here," Jaimie said as she looked inside the incubator and then at Alex, who walked over to her.

"God knows what he's been developing," Alex said.

"This is a fully equipped lab," Jaimie said. "He could do anything in here."

"Do you think this is where he grew the strep-A?" Alex asked.

"That would be my guess," Jaimie said.

"He can't be very far ahead of us," Alex said. "We should try to follow him."

"OK," Jaimie said.

When she walked by the computer, she stopped suddenly. "We should see what's on the computer before we go."

Jaimie typed her commands into the computer. When she pulled up the main menu, the initial introduction on the screen identified the owner of the software as Luke Harper.

"Luke Harper," Alex said. "He's the one who told me there probably wasn't anything back here."

"He certainly has the expertise to pull this off," Jaimie said as she entered additional commands.

"Oh, no," Jaimie said as she read the next screen where a small box was slowly filling in with red.

"What's wrong?" Alex asked.

"He's entered a command for a virus to destroy everything," Jaimie said. "We've only got a couple of minutes to copy everything. We've got to back it up onto a floppy before the virus destroys it."

The storm was reaching a crescendo and it began to sound like a train was approaching. Alex opened drawers in search of a disc, found one, and handed it to Jaimie, who immediately inserted it into the port on the side of the computer. She entered a series of commands as another small screen appeared, indicating the information was being copied.

"Now it's a race to see if we can copy it before the virus destroys it," Jaimie said as they stared at the screen.

The house creaked and groaned as if it might come apart at any second, but they watched intently as the box on the computer screen indicated the information was being transferred to the disc. Jaimie entered another command as the computer spit out the disc. Alex grabbed it and put it in his pocket as the power went out.

Part of the roof groaned as if it were being peeled off as Alex pushed Jaimie under the heavy desk to shield her from debris. They huddled together in terror as the roof finally surrendered and flew past them.

Alex held Jaimie as the deluge of rain, wind, hail, and rubble attacked them. Jaimie couldn't identify most of the objects that flew past their hiding place. They clutched each other, alarmed the shards of glass or other objects might cut them. The huge incubator landed on top the desk, ending their awareness.

Chapter Twenty Six

Luke Harper clutched the backpack while he fought the wind and sheets of rain to make his escape through the dense woods. The tall trees swayed back and forth against the mighty gusts but they also provided some protection from the vicious onslaught.

The weather monster held Luke in a vise grip. At times, the wind was so strong, his progress could only be measured in two or three small steps. He thought the brunt of the storm had passed until he heard the next phase approach. Then Luke understood he desperately needed to find a place to hide.

The ancient tree he spotted had obviously fallen in some previous rampage and fallen limbs surrounded its huge trunk. Luke crawled inside the massive trunk, whose internal organs had rotted away enough to provide a small haven. The hail pelting him seemed like an added insult to Harper, who clung to the interior of the moss covered trunk. His only consolation was the knowledge that no one could follow him through a storm this severe.

The sun peaked through the exposed roof of the guesthouse, the rays glistening off the wet surfaces in the room. Debris littered every square inch of the floor but nothing stirred under the rubble.

Finally, there was movement from under what was left of the desk and the incubator. Slowly, with ever-increasing pressure, the panels of steel and wood were shoved aside from within. The tunnel widened until they could see sunlight streaming through the hole they had made. Alex climbed out first and held out his hand for Jaimie, who looked around the room. The briefcase was the next item to be rescued as they began to walk through the devastation.

The computer they had accessed was lying at an odd angle near the wall, its screen broken and guts spilled out into the room. Alex and Jaimie walked through the ruins carefully, searching for exposed power lines or jagged edges sticking up that might represent a danger.

For all the rain and hail that had fallen, they were almost dry as they walked through the rest of what was left of the guesthouse. The hail was several inches thick, and Alex couldn't resist picking up one of the larger stones.

They picked their way through the rest of the rubble until they reached an open area away from the house. Alex opened the briefcase and placed a call to Jack while they continued to stare at the destruction.

"Jack, this is Alex," he said.

"Are you OK?" Jack asked nervously. "We watched the storm hit. It really looked ominous from here."

"We made it to the guest house," Alex said. "The storm blew the roof off. We're lucky to be alive."

"Was anyone there?" Jack asked.

"We just missed Dr. Jekyll," Alex said. "We were able to access the computer and identify him."

"Who is it?" Jack asked.

"It's Luke Harper," Alex said. "I think he left right before we got here."

"Do you think the storm got him?" Jack asked.

"It's possible, but we can't count on that," Alex said. "He could be far enough ahead of us to get away."

"I'll put an APB out on him," Jack said. "He'll leave the island by boat. He can go anywhere up or down the coast from the island. I've got a chopper on stand by in Atlanta. I don't think the weather's going to clear soon enough to get it there. I'll have the agents I sent to Brunswick search the docks when they arrive."

"We'll go back to Harper's house and see if he's there," Alex said.

"OK," Jack said. "Do you have any idea where Garrett and Fletcher went?"

"No, I don't," Alex said.

"I don't want them to get away," Jack said.

"We'll go back on Garrett's boat," Alex said.

"That works," Jack said. "You can arrest them when you get back to Brunswick. I'll have agents waiting for you at the dock."

The storm had spared Garrett's main house but the power was out and debris from trees and damaged buildings littered the whole area. The rest of the day's activities had been canceled. Margo Garrett walked down the hall toward Wendel's study to tell him most of the members of the Maxicillin team were already en route to the dock. By now, some of them would be on boats headed for Brunswick.

As she approached her husband's study, Margo listened to the last part of Wendel and Rudy's conversation. Margo heard enough to understand they were planning to hurt Alex and Jaimie. Instead of proceeding into the study, she turned around and went to find Carol.

Carol had just completed packing her suitcase when she heard the knock at her door. Before Carol could answer, Margo opened the door and peeked in the room.

"Something's going on," Margo said as she walked in.

"What are you talking about?" Carol asked.

"I only heard part of the conversation, but I think Wendel and Rudy are planning to hurt Alex and Jaimie."

"Why would they want to hurt them?" Carol asked.

"I don't know," Margo admitted. "Wendel was very anxious for me to leave with the other members of the team. I think he's taking Jaimie and Alex back on our boat."

"Rudy told me the same thing," Carol said. "I have a feeling they're involved in something illegal."

"We can't let them hurt Alex and Jaimie," Margo said.

"Let's go to the dock," Carol said. "Instead of leaving with the others, we'll hide on your boat."

In a clearing near the maintenance building, Alex and Jaimie saw the double rings of color from the rainbow. The building had suffered the same total destruction as the guesthouse; the fate of the rest of the island unknown.

When Jaimie and Alex reached Luke Harper's house and lab, they could tell the buildings were only partially destroyed, but the damage was extensive and they found no sign of Harper. After a brief search, Alex and Jaimie returned to the main house. When they reached the crest of the last hill, they could see that Garrett's house had been spared major damage. By the time they reached the front porch, Wendel Garrett had spotted them and was walking toward them.

"I was worried about you," Garrett said.

"We decided to check out the damage after the storm," Alex said.

"Parts of the island were destroyed," Garrett said. "The power is out and all the rest of the guests have already left. Rudy and I are about ready to leave so you can go back with us."

"Do you have any idea what happened to Luke Harper?" Alex asked.

"He left about half an hour ago," Garrett said. "I got a call from the captain of a boat I chartered. Harper demanded the captain let him take the boat out alone. Luke wouldn't take no for an answer so I finally agreed. Why don't you get packed and we can head for the dock?"

Carol and Margo paced around the cabin of the boat, waiting for the other passengers. Several minutes later, when they heard footsteps above, they huddled together in a corner. When Wendel came below deck, he was shocked when he realized they were there.

"What the hell are you doing here?" he asked as Rudy followed him down the narrow stairs.

"We missed our boat," Margo said as she stared defiantly at Wendel. "All the rest of the boats have already left."

"This is the last thing we need," Rudy said viciously as he walked toward them.

"It's OK, Rudy," Wendel said. "Why don't you ladies go up on deck and talk to Jaimie and Alex while we get the boat ready?"

"That sounds good," Margo said as Carol nodded and followed Margo up the stairs.

"This changes everything," Wendel whispered to Rudy after their wives were gone.

"It doesn't change one fucking thing," Rudy hissed. "They've gone along with everything else we've done. Margo knows you've fucked any woman you could get your hands on and she hasn't left you. Carol knows what will happen to her if she crosses me. If they won't go along with the program, this unfortunate accident will just claim a few more victims."

When Luke Harper pulled away from Jekyll Island for the last time, he liked the feel of the sleek craft. The captain had been difficult about Luke taking the boat out alone, and Harper would have killed him if it hadn't been for the other people standing on the dock.

There was a small, secluded cove all the boats would have to pass on their way back to Brunswick, and that was where Harper waited. He looked through the binoculars frequently, checking the inhabitants of any vessel that went by.

The bug Luke had planted in Garrett's study had provided lots of useful information over the last two years. Luke liked Garrett's basic plan to get rid of Jaimie and Alex but felt it required one additional, crucial element. Luke figured since all the people he despised would be on Garrett's boat, it would be appropriate for all of them to perish in the accident.

Luke poured gasoline into the bottles and stuffed rags into the tops of each one. Fury and rage consumed Harper, and he could barely contain himself while he waited for Garrett's boat.

The atmosphere was thick with excitement, fear, and a certain amount of apprehension as Garrett's boat left the dock. Alex watched Garrett and Fletcher carefully, uncomfortable with the tension he felt. He looked at Jaimie frequently but she avoided eye contact with him entirely. The emotions he felt collided until he wasn't sure whether he was picking up vibes from the others or just feeling his own inner turmoil.

Alex wasn't sure Jaimie would forgive him for this latest indiscretion, and he felt regret with a sense of longing. He wanted to grab Jaimie, shake her, and tell her how much he loved her, but he realized this was the wrong place and the wrong time. Instead, he watched Garrett and Fletcher, his hand near his weapon, waiting for any miscue they might attempt.

Rudy Fletcher also felt the tension as he watched the others. Carol had defied him by hiding on this boat. He would be forced to correct her mistake just as he had in the past.

Carol just couldn't seem to avoid doing things to piss him off. Rudy didn't understand why she kept making these mistakes, and he told himself he didn't really like administering the required corrections. Rudy could feel his irritation begin, grow, and finally explode in the torrent of blows he delivered. Rudy felt a brief period of remorse but understood the relationship needed the cleansing effects the beatings seemed to provide.

Rudy looked at Carol and Margo again. Suddenly, he realized he didn't like the idea they would be witnesses to the murders. Though he didn't believe they represented a real threat, there was no reason to leave two witnesses alive. Wendel could be blackmailed into submission, but the wives would have to dealt with today. His decision was instantaneous but irrevocable, and Rudy smiled when he thought about killing them.

The docks on Jekyll Island were small, distant objects when the engine on Garrett's boat coughed, sputtered and died as it came to a standstill in the calm waters. Wendel looked perplexed as he tried to restart the engine without success. Rudy went to his side and pretended to reach in the toolbox to retrieve a tool.

Alex watched them carefully, suspicious the episode was only a ruse. He drew his weapon but Margo was in his line of fire, so he decided to jump Rudy before he could turn around. Alex and Rudy struggled for the gun in Rudy's hand while the others watched.

Rudy delivered a vicious blow to the side of Alex's face, but Alex countered with a blow of his own and was able to knock the gun out of Rudy's hand. Locked in combat, they both fell to the deck. Wendel started to reach for the weapon but Carol grabbed it and stood up, pointing the gun at Wendel and Rudy.

Alex and Rudy stopped struggling and stared at Carol. The impasse continued as Rudy looked at his wife and began to walk toward her.

"Give me the gun, Carol," Rudy said.

"No, Rudy," Carol said.

"I don't want to have to correct this problem, Carol," Rudy said. "You've gone along with everything in the past. Just keep going along with the program."

"I won't let you hurt them, Rudy," Carol said.

"Don't do this, Carol," Rudy said. "You'll be sorry."

"I'm only sorry I didn't do something sooner," Carol said.

"I never liked hurting you, Carol," Rudy said. "You made me do it."

"I don't believe that anymore, Rudy," Carol said. "You enjoyed hurting me, but I won't let you do it anymore."

"Just give me the fucking gun," Rudy said nastily.

"I won't let you do this," Carol said.

"I don't fucking believe you," Rudy said as he moved toward his wife.

The gun exploded as Rudy stopped his forward progress, stared at Carol with a confused expression, clutched his chest, and finally fell to his knees. By the time his body crumpled to the deck, his lifeless eyes were open.

Wendel moved forward to try to get the gun but Carol raised the barrel to stop his progress.

"Don't do it, Wendel," Carol said. "In some ways, Rudy was hard to shoot, but I won't have a problem blowing your sorry ass away."

Luke Harper was energized when he saw Garrett's boat pull away from the dock. He used the glasses to confirm the identity of the passengers. He hadn't expected Wendel or Rudy to bring their wives but he couldn't worry about that. They would just be additional names on the list. If his team in Atlanta had succeeded, there would be dead FBI agents to add to the body count.

When Garrett's boat approached, Luke pulled out of the cove and began following Garrett's boat. On cue, the engine on Garrett's boat died and stopped dead in the water. Luke cut the power on his boat but continued moving slowly toward them, watching the struggle that was taking place on the deck.

Alex moved toward Carol to relieve her of the weapon, but he was distracted by the sound of the other boat. He looked over just as the boat drifted by and the fiery object flew in their direction.

Alex was confused until he realized the object was a molotov cocktail that could ignite their boat instantaneously. The small glow looked like an ominous ball of fire by the time it reached their position. Alex screamed for everyone to get down as the bottle barely missed landing on the deck. Instead, it landed harmlessly in the water just off the port side. Alex looked up and saw Luke Harper turn his boat for another pass.

"Garrett, you've got to start the engine," Alex screamed as he pushed Wendel near the controls.

"No problem," Wendel said nervously as he flipped the switch and started the engine.

"Get us the hell out of here," Alex yelled as Wendel pushed the throttle.

When he saw Garrett's boat begin to move away, Luke increased his speed. Harper had a distinct advantage. He was already alongside Garrett's boat and he was moving at a faster rate of speed.

Alex watched as Luke lit another bottle of flammable liquid and raised it in the air. When Harper's boat was within striking distance, Alex jumped onto Harper's boat and lunged for him. Their collision caused the bottle to drop on the deck of Harper's boat, spilling its contents.

The fire spread rapidly while Alex and Luke punched and kicked each other. Alex's next blow struck the bridge of Harper's nose, the dull thud of cartilage caving in causing Harper's scream. Harper retaliated with a blow to Alex's mid section as the struggle continued and the fire moved across the deck.

Alex saw the hatred and wrath on Harper's face, but when he looked at the fire, he realized it was about to reach the engine. The murderous look on Harper's face was the last thing Alex saw as he broke free and jumped over the side.

The explosion rocked the boat as Alex rose to the surface. The top half of Harper's body was engulfed in flames and he began screaming as he was hurled into the water. Alex swam over and grabbed him, holding him from behind so he wouldn't drown. Harper continued screaming though the water had extinguished the flames.

Alex spotted the chopper and realized it must have approached during their struggle. The craft hovered while Alex held Luke and treaded water, trying to dodge the fiery remnants of the boat.

The disc that had been in Alex's pocket popped to the surface and slowly floated away, joining the rest of debris. Alex didn't notice. He was entirely focused on watching the pilot of the chopper, waiting for him to drop the rescue line. When the cable reached them, Alex grabbed the line and attached it to Harper's waist. Harper's body rose out of the water, and the sight of the charred flesh on the remaining horror of his face terrified Alex.

EPILOGUE

Nathan Carr had been an orderly on the burn unit at St. Francis Hospital for years. Carr's buzz cut was so close to his scalp it was impossible to determine whether his hair was gray or blond. His small, beady brown eyes were deeply set into his huge head.

Carr's body shape made him appear heavy in all the wrong places. And he exercised only when he performed the lifting required in the burn unit. Off duty, the heaviest item Nathan Carr lifted was whatever long neck contained the brew he favored at the moment.

The FBI agent stationed at the entrance to the unit merely waved Nathan through without searching him. When Luke Harper was admitted, a frenzied urgency characterized the agents' activities. Now that they had been on the unit for three weeks, a relaxed resignation lulled the three-man FBI teams who guarded Harper.

Harper was something of an enigma, at least to Nathan Carr. Nathan considered what manner of man could be under the thick, bulky dressings covering Harper's face, arms, and trunk. Those areas were burned so severely Harper hovered near death for the first two weeks. Now that

Harper had periods of lucidity, Nathan could sense naked, powerful emotions when he entered Harper's room.

Nathan was no stranger to the intense emotions experienced by patients who sustain catastrophic injuries. Sometimes, the hungers that lived in Harper's room were so strong Nathan was afraid to look, convinced he would be able to see them huddled in the corners. Nathan decided they didn't pay him enough to deal with those issues so he tried his best to ignore them.

The third degree burns on Harper's face would establish him firmly in the monster category. That was Nathan's personal expectation concerning the outcome Harper could expect. The plastic surgeons would come with their charts, pictures, and assurances, but they wouldn't be able to put Luke Harper's face back together again. In a world where an extra ten pounds caused most people to panic, Harper would be considered a freak.

Though Harper refused to speak, Nathan felt the depression and despair as he cared for the wounded patient. All that changed the morning Nathan brought the tape recorder into Harper's room, placed the earphones in Harper's ears, and played the tape.

The first stack of twenty dollar bills Nathan had found in his car were accompanied by a vague note asking for help. Nathan greedily spent that money and prayed another batch would be delivered. A second cache arrived and several men approached him in the alley behind his favorite bar. Nathan was assured he would be paid handsomely for his role as messenger. Convinced nothing more would be required, Nathan began carrying the tapes back and forth.

Rage and determination replaced the more tolerable emotions, and they were so powerful that Nathan was afraid to be alone in Harper's room. But he was alone with Harper for ten long minutes each day. The routine remained the same. They were left by themselves solely because the agent assigned to Harper's room refused to watch Nathan wash Harper's genitals.

Nothing altered the ritual this morning. When the agent left the room, Nathan pulled the small tape recorder from under the towels and placed the earphones in Harper's ears so he could hear the message. Nathan continued bathing Harper until Harper signaled he wanted to dictate a response. While Harper whispered his instructions, Nathan finished Harper's care.

It was only when he placed the tape recorder between the towels again that Nathan breathed normally. The agent returned while Nathan was standing by the sink, emptying the basin of bath water. After he straightened up the room, Nathan took the towels and turned to leave. He was almost out the door when he ran into the tall man with dark hair who suddenly appeared in the doorway.

The collision caused Nathan to drop everything in his hands. When Nathan scrambled to pick up the towels so he could keep the recorder hidden, the man looked at him curiously.

"I'm sorry," Nathan said nervously as he stood up.

"That's OK," Alex Tanner said. "Actually, I think I ran into you."

Nathan Carr left the room but couldn't resist the urge to turn around and look at the tall man one more time. He would precipitate the explosion Nathan knew was coming. Nathan had been bombarded by another horde of intense feelings when he picked up the towels and looked at the man, so he knew the vehement outburst about to take place was inevitable.

"What the fuck do you want, Tanner?" Harper asked.

"Is that any way to talk to the man who saved your life?" Alex asked.

"You expect me to thank you for making me a freak?" Harper asked.

"Hate works too," Tanner said. "We need to talk."

"Why should I say anything to you?" Luke asked.

"Come on, Harper," Alex said. "I'm sure there are things you'd like to share. Don't you want me to know how smart you are?"

"OK, let's play," Harper said.

"Did you kill Jaimie's father?" Alex asked.

"Of course," Luke said. "I wanted to see if she was smart enough to figure it out."

"Why did you contaminate the tests?" Alex asked.

"I'm only going to tell you what I want you to know," Harper said. "I don't want you to know that."

"Did you really think killing babies would change anything?" Alex asked.

"It already has," Luke said.

"How do you figure that?" Alex asked.

"I killed Ted Drew's son," Luke said. "When his son died, Drew withdrew from the election he would certainly have won. I already changed history and there'll be more to come."

"Like what?" Alex asked.

"I know my comrades in Atlanta escaped," Harper said.

"How did you find out?" Alex asked.

"I have my sources," Harper said. "I'm going to make you wish you had let me die. There are other plans in the works. The first contamination was just a test to see if it would work. The next time, it will be worse."

"So you're planning to kill more babies?" Alex asked.

"It's so easy," Luke said.

"Tell me how you're going to do it?" Alex asked angrily.

"I won't tell you that," Harper said. "I want you to worry about where the next strike will be. Maybe it's already in the works. There's that production facility in Guatemala. What if the pregnancy tests produced there were contaminated and there's another group of newly infected, doomed mothers out there right now?"

"They check those tests for strep-A," Alex said.

"What if they aren't contaminated with strep-A?" Harper asked. "You don't really believe strep-A was the only bug I created, do you?"

"Tell me, dammit," Alex screamed as he pushed on Harper's arm.

A doctor walked in the room and seemed upset when he saw what Alex was doing. On cue, Harper screamed, moaning about his rights, abuse, and the cruelty of FBI agents.

"Mr. Tanner, I'm going to have to ask you to leave," the doctor said angrily. "Mr. Harper is my patient, and I can't allow you to hurt him."

"I'll be back, Harper," Alex said. "Just remember, Doctor, your patient is a monster and kills babies."

Jamie began her walk with no intention of visiting Aunt Sam, but stopping at the cedar house seemed like an irresistible impulse. As she stood in Aunt Sam's studio, Jaimie looked at the expanse of water while she waited for Sam to return with their drinks.

San Diego had seemed like the perfect place to escape after the events on Jekyll Island, but Jaimie was troubled by complex, unfamiliar emotions. Her daily walks were like therapy, a way to try to make some sense of all the things that haunted her.

Aunt Sam came in the room and handed Jaimie a glass of lemonade.

"OK, I've been patient," Jaimie said. "Now I want to see the painting."

"You're not going to like it," Sam said. "I really think it's better if you don't look."

"Come on, Sam," Jaimie said as she lifted the cover off the canvas.

"I told you I have to paint what I feel," Sam said apologetically. "This is what I felt. I know you told me you and Alex were only doing a job, but that's not what I felt when I saw you together."

The beauty and detail of the painting took Jaimie's breath away. Sam had captured the ocean with new depth, and Jaimie could almost feel the swirling mass of color and water leap off the canvas. Jaimie was impressed until she spotted the characters.

Alex was walking along the beach with Jaimie, but Sam had added a small child with curly, auburn hair. Jaimie gasped, dropped her glass, and ran out of the studio. Jaimie was vaguely aware Sam had followed her and was begging her to stay. Escape was her only objective, so she stumbled down the steps and began to walk quickly along the beach.

Troubled thoughts accompanied Jaimie while she concentrated on putting some distance between her and the rest of her life. She realized her panic in Sam's studio was caused by the reality of her situation. Sam's perceptions and intuitions were so accurate they terrified Jaimie. Unfortunately, Sam's premonitions didn't conform to the true facts of the situation. Her marriage to Alex was a sham, and he was not part of her life.

It took another mile of rapid paced walking before Jaimie slowed down and considered the results of her pregnancy test. Jaimie's scientific mind totally rejected the fact the results were positive. The birth control they had used boasted a one percent failure rate, so Jaimie couldn't comprehend how the test could be positive given those kind of odds.

The tears flowed as Jaimie thought about Alex and the child she carried. She could allow it to become a reality, but what kind of future she could offer this child? Statistics about unplanned pregnancies and images of the horror of strep-A rolled through Jaimie's mind while she tried to think of a solution. Along with those thoughts, Jaimie remembered how beautiful and happy the little girl with curly hair had looked in Sam's painting.

Jaimie ran into the man wearing the conservative suit who suddenly blocked her path. He grabbed her and held her in his arms.

"We have to talk, Jaimie," Alex said.

"I don't have anything to say to you," Jaimie said as she tried to pull away from him.

"There's a lot I have to say to you," Alex said as he stared into her eyes.

"OK, let's talk," Jaimie said. "When will our marriage be annulled?"

"I asked Jack to wait," Alex said.

"Why?" Jaimie asked.

"I told him I wanted to stay married to you," Alex said.

"You've got to be kidding," Jaimie said. "There's no way I'd stay married to you, Alex Tanner."

"I saw Sam's painting," Alex said. "That could be us Jaimie. That will be us if you'll just let it."

"I don't know how to trust you, Alex," Jaimie said as she looked into his eyes.

"I know and I don't blame you," Alex said as he reached for her hands. "Don't give up on me. Just give our marriage and me a little more time. I love you, Jaimie." The End.

9 780595 095254